Regr

A Novel

Timothy Allen Smith

Published by

Twenty/20 Productions
1108 Elmwood Avenue

Sharon Hill, Pennsylvania 19079

Originally published by Twenty/20 Productions in
2014 Printed in the United States of America.

For:

Tai Juliette Wright-

You are a much better daughter than I am a father. As with everything I do, this is dedicated to you.

M.G. -

While I cannot definitively say Regret wouldn't have been as good without your input, I can say with absolute certainty Regret never gets written without your inspiration. Thank You.

REGRET

Prologue

In a weird way, I always knew it would come down to this. Unfortunately, knowing didn't make it any easier.

My entire world had just come crashing down around me and I knew, instinctively, I didn't have the strength to rebuild it. Not again. Not after everything I had been through and sacrificed and missed out on. I couldn't go through that again. I wouldn't.

The fighter in me wanted to lash out. Only there was nothing or no one left for me to lash out at. Everything I had worked for, all the dreams and desires I sold my soul to achieve now amounted to nothing and the only thing I would be left with was a legacy of lies, betrayal, and murder.

None of that matters anymore...

NOTHING matters anymore...

Not after tonight...

I barely recognized the disheveled mess staring back at me in the mirror. I tried to look away but suddenly felt light-headed and, before I knew what was happening, felt my body crashing down hard onto the marble floor.

My brain barely registered the pain as I lay there for what seemed like an eternity, trying to compose myself and come up with some sort of plan. I had nothing. In fact, the longer and harder I thought about it, the more clear it became. Even with all of my money and a newly formed contact list filled with some of the most influential people in the world, I was powerless to stop what was about to happen.

I looked around blankly until my eyes settled on a small object in the corner. The room was dark, save for the ominous glow of a full moon protruding through the floor-to-ceiling windows. That was more than enough light to see the object in the corner was my purse.

Salvation...

I clumsily dragged myself across the floor to the four thousand dollar Burberry tote I'd purchased a few hours earlier. I pulled out a small, sterling silver case which, even in my somewhat altered state, I was able to open and access its contents without so much as a stumble.

This was the easy part...

Propping myself up against the tub, I calmly got to work, placing two, tic-tac sized chunks onto the small spoon.

My customized rig included two syringes, one empty and the other pre-loaded with water which I carefully squirted into the spoon. Tossing the water syringe aside, I picked up the cigarette lighter and proceeded to heat the spoon from the bottom, dissolving my 'candy.'

With the steady hands of a surgeon, I set down the lighter, picked up a piece of cotton, and rolled it between my fingers until it was small enough to fit onto the spoon.

Almost there...

I dropped my makeshift cotton ball onto the spoon and watched as it puffed up like a sponge, soaking in the newly dissolved solution. I then picked up the second syringe, pushed it into the center of the cotton and pulled the plunger slowly until all of the liquid was sucked in.

Finally...

Setting down my spoon, I placed the needle of the syringe flat against the skin at the bend of my left arm and inserted it down the length of the vein, carefully pulling the plunger to allow the blood to flow in. When I was sure there was little to no air, I put my head back, closed my eyes and smoothly pushed the plunger, re-filling my veins with the only relief I needed or wanted at the moment.

"What the fuck are you doing?!"

Chapter One
(1 year earlier)

"Can I have a vanilla latte?"

"Size?"

"Medium."

"Milk?"

"Two percent."

"That'll be four dollars and ninety-nine cents."

In truth, I needed a five dollar cup of coffee about as much as I needed a hole in the head. My heart was already racing and, even though five bucks probably wasn't a big deal to the hipsters seated in and around the Bristol Cafe at 6pm on a Thursday evening, in my house that meant a dozen eggs, apple juice and a loaf of bread. In other words, breakfast for the week.

I found a table for two close to the entrance and settled in with my latte and the iPhone I could no longer afford but had somehow lost the ability to live without. Choosing the seat facing the entrance ensured I would be able to see Paul when he arrived. I nervously checked the time.

6:15 PM

Exactly fifteen minutes early, as planned. Plenty of time to relax, log onto eHarmony and reacquaint myself with my date before he got there.

There was a little bell attached to the front door which, while annoying on a busy night, made it easier for me to peruse Paul's profile without missing his arrival.

Flipping through his pics, I was reminded how attractive he was. A forty-one year old attorney with greying hair, kind eyes and a nice smile, his profile said he had three teenage kids from a previous relationship and wasn't looking to have any more.

6:20 PM

It also said he was tall, about six foot two, worked out regularly and lived in Springfield, which was about ten to fifteen minutes north of Bristol. Close enough to be convenient yet far enough away to avoid many awkward path crossings should things not work out. He was perfect.

6:25 PM

I took a sip of my latte, logged off and put away my phone so I could focus on the entrance. My heart was racing again as I knew Paul would be there any minute. I started fidgeting around in my seat, trying to make myself *look* comfortable while also presenting the most flattering angle possible. This would have been easier had I kept up with my morning runs, unfortunately the new job came with a new schedule and so I didn't have the time. At least that's what I told myself. Whatever. Even in my heyday I was never gonna be a fashion model but still, while I certainly *felt* my age in a room filled with half naked twenty somethings, I held it together pretty damn good for a broke, thirty-eight year old, single mom.

6:35 PM

Staring awkwardly out the window, I began to feel a wave of despair that had become all too familiar in my life recently. What if Paul wasn't coming? Or worse, what if he had already been there? What if he saw me, realized I was his date, and ran back down the street before I saw him? What if...

"*No.*" I stopped myself mid thought. First of all, there is no way he could have walked through the door without me seeing him. Secondly, after everything I had been through these past eighteen months, I was certainly due a bit of good luck.

6:41 PM

Paul was probably just running late and since we hadn't yet exchanged phone numbers, he had no way of letting me know. That was it. I was worrying myself over nothing. I simply had to relax, enjoy my latte and think positive thoughts. This first date was going to be the start of a whole new chapter in the life story of Julie Sharpe. Today was the day to say goodbye to all the negativity and drama of the past few years. Today was finally my chance to breathe again. To say hello to...

"Hi."

"Excuse me?" I wasn't trying to be rude, but had been so caught up in my own head I didn't notice someone standing right in front of me.

"Julie?"

I quickly tried to place the face. He was an older guy, I'd guess mid to late fifties, with blotchy skin, thick glasses and balding grey hair. Short and on the pudgy side, he seemed harmless enough though he was obviously nervous as evidenced by the beads of sweat running down his forehead.

"I'm sorry," I replied with a gentle smile, "do you work at Kaiser?" We had only lived in Bristol for a few months and I didn't know anyone outside of a few moms at my daughters school. This must be someone from my new job.

"Julie, it's me," he announced awkwardly, "Paul."

Ever have one of those moments where you try to speak, but nothing comes out? The next two seconds literally felt like an hour as I sat there, mouth open, staring helplessly at a short, fat, sweaty old man who looked about as much like the Paul in the pictures as my thirteen year old daughter Ashley.

"Dammit," he said, breaking the silence and snapping me out of my daze, "I knew you wouldn't like me."

"No no no," I responded hastily, trying to salvage some sort of decorum "it's just that, well I um, I was waiting, and you, you were running late and so I —"

"Can I at least sit down?"

"Of course," I answered, thankful he interrupted my incoherent stammering, "you find the place ok?"

"Oh yeah!" he beamed, "I've been here a bunch of times."

"Isn't this out of the way for you?"

"Heck no, I live right down the street."

My eyes widened. "I thought your profile said you lived in Springfield?"

"Oh no, I moved to Bristol two years ago. Guess I outta update that profile thing huh?"

The next few seconds required an impressive amount of restraint on my part. I managed a polite smile and immediately began searching my brain for an appropriate end to this disaster.

"You new to the neighborhood right?" he asked, before I could think of anything, "want me to show you around? There's a fro-yo place up the —"

"A what?"

"Frozen yogurt. Best in the city. C'mon."

Before I could respond he was standing by the door, looking back at me expectantly. Not knowing what else to do, I dutifully gathered my things and made my way to the entrance where I noticed he and I were roughly the same height.

Six foot two my ass...

It was unseasonably warm for September and, Bristol being a college town, there were plenty of young people out and about. This wouldn't have been a problem if not for the fact that my date, who was not particularly light on his feet, was determined to walk directly beside me. We could

14

barely take three consecutive steps without one, or both of us having to pause and shift to the right or left to avoid smashing into some undergrad whose head was invariably buried in a smartphone. I felt like I was running a three legged race through an obstacle course with an overweight, sweaty uncle tied to my side. And just as I had become sure things could not possibly get worse, I felt my sweaty uncle reaching for my hand!

Wanna go from simple frustration to abject misery? Try holding the disgustingly sweaty hand of a balding middle aged man while navigating a minefield of texting millennials. Fortunately for me, one of those oblivious twenty-somethings walked between us as we arrived at the entrance of the yogurt shop, sparing me an extended finger lock with my uncle's clammy palm.

I have to get out of this...

"You know what time it is?" I asked, subtly wiping my hand on the side of my jeans.

"About ten to seven," he noted cautiously, as if he knew what was coming next, "why?"

"Well actually," I answered evenly, "I have kind of an early day tomorrow and —"

"If you don't like me," he interrupted, "just say so."

I was determined to end this torture and figured, at that point, honesty was the fastest, best way to do so. I pulled my uncle away from the entrance and softened my tone as much as I could.

"Paul, you seem like a really nice guy and I've had a great time meeting you. But I don't think there's any kind of connection for us."

"You never even gave me a chance."

"I just don't think we have anything in common."

"You don't know anything about me."

"Paul I'm just not interested, ok?"

"Ok whatever," he pouted, "come on, lemme walk you to your car."

"That's ok, I'm good from here."

"Are you kidding me?" he hissed, becoming agitated, "I'm not good enough to walk you to your car? Am I that disgusting?"

My uncle was starting to freak me out and, in truth, I didn't want him knowing *anything* about me, much less what kind of car I drove or my license plate number. There was no way in hell this nut was walking me anywhere near my car. The problem was I had a feeling he was about to cause a scene.

Think fast Julie...

"Listen," I said through a forced smile, "I'm sorry things didn't work out the way you wanted but you do seem like a nice guy. I would like to be friends if that's something you're interested in."

He paused for a moment and considered my proposal before answering. "Well, I would still like to get to know you better."

"Great," I smiled, "you still up for some yogurt?"

"Seriously?"

"You said it was the best in the city right?"

"Oh doll, you have no idea."

Did he just call me Doll??

"Awesome," I said cheerfully, "why don't you go get in line and I'll grab us a table."

"Sounds good babe."

Babe????

"Does Vanilla work for you?" he asked, making his way into the line, which was now extended beyond the front entrance.

"You pick," I suggested, "you are the expert after all."

I found an empty table at the far end of the outdoor seating area and pulled out my phone to check my messages. The place was crowded but, thankfully, the line appeared to be moving quickly. I put away my phone and smiled at my uncle, who was waiting patiently for the best yogurt in the city, seemingly content with the way things had turned out. I shifted in my seat to make sure he stayed within my line of sight and as soon as his spot in line made it's way through the entrance, I stood up and took off running down the street.

The old lady sprint to the car was the highlight of my evening and not just because I managed to outwit my uncle, the sweaty palmed, stalker/serial killer. I made it about a block away from the yogurt shop before twisting my ankle, reducing my sprint to a fast limp with intermittent glances over the shoulder. I was pretty sure I looked like a crazy person but if I had any doubt at all, the horrified looks of the college kids hanging out in the city sealed it in my mind. Fortunately for me, I was way beyond caring what anyone thought at that point. I just wanted to get home, take a bath and forget this night ever happened.

By the time I made it back to my car, whatever adrenaline I had fueling me was gone and I felt reality sneaking its way back into the forefront of my mind. My adventure in internet dating, which by any objective measure had to be considered an unmitigated disaster, was now officially done. It was an abysmal comedy of errors from the five dollar cup of coffee to the half mile jog, in heels, back to my car. And yet I found myself feeling sad it was over.

For the past three years, almost every day of my life ended the exact same way. We would begin with homework, move on to dinner and then wind everything down with some reality TV before going to bed. Don't get me wrong, I love my daughter. I treasure every moment I get to spend with her and after everything she'd been through, most of it my doing, I felt like I owed her the kind of stability I could only provide by putting all of my needs aside and focusing solely on hers. I didn't look at it so much as a sacrifice as I did a debt for everything I'd put her through.

The problem is the human body doesn't come with an off switch. Telling myself I didn't miss adult conversation or physical affection didn't make it true. I'd become isolated and depressed and, the truth is, being alone for so long made me miserable to the point of desperation. As evidenced by my decision to join eHarmony.

It is a proven fact that the need to be touched, caressed, and cuddled is as essential in humans as our need for food. Study after study has validated this form of human interaction as playing a vital role in the maintenance of both physical and emotional well-being. And yet here I was, going on three years without so much as a kiss on the cheek.

It took me a second to realize I was crying, not that I was surprised. There was a time in my life when any show of emotion was so rare my co-workers accused me of being heartless. Now? Tears were as much a part of my daily routine as Ashley's homework.

My life wasn't supposed to turn out like this! How long was I supposed to suffer for my mistakes?! There are murderers and thieves walking the streets, more than a few of whom I helped put there, and yet what I did was so awful I'm supposed to spend the rest of my life alone?!

I was about half way home, sitting at a stoplight, when everything overwhelmed me and I found myself banging the back of my head against the headrest in frustration. I finally decided to try and do something about my pathetic situation and this is how it ends up?! Going out was not a small step for me and I'm not only talking about dating. I'm talking about embracing, for the first time in years, the idea of moving on with my life and maybe meeting someone. That's it! I wasn't looking for fireworks and I didn't need the earth to move. I just wanted to meet someone I like who would, hopefully, like me back. Maybe my expectations were too low but I had given up on the idea of a fairytale a long time ago. That night wasn't about that.

That night was about a lonely single mom who loved her daughter more than anything in the world but who, quite frankly, didn't wanna be alone anymore.

Chapter Two

"Hey Miss S. You ok?"

"I'm fine." I closed the door behind me and dropped a stack of mail onto the coffee table. "Everything ok around here?"

"Yep. Homework done and in bed by 8:30 just like you said."

"Great," I smiled, handing her the twenty-five dollars I owed her, "thanks Kristen."

"It's twenty remember?"

"I think you've earned a five dollar tip sweetie. Thanks again."

"Anytime," she offered cheerfully.

I made my way over to the sofa and started opening the mail as my sixteen year old babysitter gathered her things.

"Were you limping?"

"Yeah, I somehow managed to twist my ankle."

"That sucks. I'm free if you need somebody to take your shift tomorrow."

"Oh I'll be fine by then."

The look on her face told me she knew I was lying. What she couldn't have known was that manning the front desk at the studio was the only way I could afford to give her Twenty-five dollars.

"Ok," she shrugged, opening the front door, "if you change your mind —"

"I will let you know. Get home safe." I went over to the door and watched as she got safely into her car and drove off. Once she was gone, I limped back over to the sofa where sifting through a months worth of bills I had no way of paying was actually a welcome distraction for me. I made it about half way through the pile when I finally came across a piece of welcome correspondence, my paycheck.

I'd never bothered setting up a direct deposit with my new employer, so twice a month I still received a physical check in the mail. Psychologically I think submitting those forms would've signified accepting that job as something long-term or, god forbid, permanent. And as down as I might've been I still wasn't ready to admit that particular defeat.

Besides, having an actual paycheck was kinda cool. It made me feel retro and rebellious, like I was thumbing my nose at the digitization of human interaction. I had honestly gotten used to the idea of having something tangible in my hand after putting in my eighty hours of work. I only wished there were a few more zeroes attached to it. Oh well, at least there'd be enough to pay the rent and Ashley's tuition, which was already a month behind.

Thankfully, the two hundred dollars I still had left over from my last check would buy us enough groceries and gas to make it to my next one. If everything went according to plan, by then I would be able to get current with the tuition and start chipping away at the pile of past due drama now covering my coffee table. It was a humbling way to live but we had a roof over our heads and Ashley was thriving in a great school she loved. Those were the important things, I reminded myself. The rest would just have to be figured out later.

I set aside my prize and continued sorting the mail. When I got to the last few items, I saw something that looked out of place so I took a closer look. The envelope was addressed correctly. It had my name on it. It wasn't until I noticed the return address that my heart sunk into the pit of my stomach. It was a letter from the IRS.

I'm not a religious person and nobody who knew me for more than five minutes would ever mistake me for one. But as I sat there, staring at that envelope, I prayed as hard as I possibly could to Jesus, Mary, Joseph, The Holy Spirit, Allah, Buddha, Mohammed and any other god I could think of. Hypocritical? Absolutely. But if this letter was what I thought it was, and I was pretty damn sure it would be, then my little girl would, once again, be the one suffering. If there was a god and if he or she had any compassion, they wouldn't do that. They couldn't. Not to my baby girl who had done nothing wrong. Nothing except having me for a mother.

I took a deep breath, opened the letter and, immediately, my heart fell through my stomach to the floor. It was a surreal moment for me. I literally couldn't move and was having trouble breathing as tears flowed freely down the sides of my face and fell onto the fate sealing piece of paper now attached to my fingers. It didn't matter that my tears were smearing the ink because I had no intention of reading it. I didn't have to. I focused solely on one word. The only fucking word, in the entire fucking thing, that fucking mattered.

GARNISHMENT

I dropped the 'official notice' onto the table and reached frantically for my paycheck. I don't know what I was expecting to see, or what miracle I was hoping for, but I was on auto-pilot at that point. I guess maybe I thought there might be some slim chance the garnishment hadn't kicked in yet? The point is I, for some reason, still had hope.

My hands were shaking like a leaf as I nervously opened the envelope and turned my head to the side so I could only see out of the corner of my eye. It didn't matter. Even with one eye half closed and blurred from crying, it was painfully easy to see what was written in the lower right corner

Net Pay: $110.80

There was a story on the news a few months back about how some kids had their school lunches taken away from them because their parents had past due balances on their accounts. As a mother, I felt sick to my stomach at the image of my baby girls lunch being snatched from her as she was eating. The thought of Ashley sitting somewhere hungry because I didn't do what I was supposed to was unimaginable and yet, because of me, she was about to miss a whole lot more than just a meal.

There was no sugar coating it anymore. After everything I'd put her through, from breaking up our family to taking her from the only home she had ever known, it was obvious I was incapable of taking care of my daughter. Ashley was the only thing in my life that meant anything, and I was now face to face with a reality so painful and humiliating I could barely stand to look at myself. I had failed as a mother.

And with that harsh moment of clarity, something strange happened. I calmed down. My breathing felt steady and my heart, while still racing, seemed to begin pumping adrenaline through my veins. I even managed to stand up on my bum ankle and start pacing back and forth in the living room, willing my mind to get to work.

Because, that's the thing about being a mommy. You don't get to submit a letter of resignation from this position. Every child gets one, and even though I'm sure I was the worst on the planet, I also knew I was the only mommy Ashley Watson would ever have.

And in that moment I made a decision that changed the trajectory of our lives forever. I decided that it didn't matter what I had to do or where I had to go, I would literally DIE before allowing my little girl to suffer one more day because of my bullshit.

I can't necessarily say I had been through worse but I had been through enough, and experience taught me there was a solution to be had. There always was. The key was to stay in the game long enough to find it. So the first thing I needed to do was buy some time. Once I realized that, it was obvious what I needed to do next.

Chapter Three

"Hey mom."

Sometimes it was striking how much Ashley looked like Brian. Sure, she looked enough like me for everyone to know she was mine, and she definitely had my personality. But any time she stood next her father, there was no denying whose genes were dominant.

"Good morning sleepyhead, you hungry?"

"Can I just have some —" she stopped herself mid-sentence and looked around disapprovingly, "what happened in here?"

I hadn't even noticed the complete disaster that was my living room.

"I was doing some work late last night. I'll clean it up later."

"But why is the mail all over the floor?"

She was good at pressing the issue when things didn't make sense. Like I said, my personality.

"Why don't you leave this all to me and you worry about your breakfast?"

"Ok," she yawned and made her way into the kitchen, "can I have some cereal?"

"I don't know. *Can* you?"

"Mom," she whined, "can you please just answer the question?"

"I don't know Ashley, *Can* I?"

"Oh god, whatever," she pouted, "mom, may I please have some cereal?"

"Your command of language matters Ashley, I've told you that many times. Being able to choose the right word for the right situation gives you confidence. Confidence gives you power and power is the key to success in business and in life. Understand?"

She just gave me a blank look.

"Cereal?"

"Go ahead," I let it go and started to pick up the living room, "but hurry, I don't want you to —"

"Weren't you wearing that yesterday?"

"Excuse me?" I chided, not appreciating the interruption by my thirteen year old daughter

"You were wearing those same clothes yesterday when you went out."

That's another thing nobody tells you before you have kids. They notice EVERYTHING.

"Well *mom*," I quipped, "I told you I was up late working and I guess time got away from me. Is that okay with you?"

"Fine by me," she shrugged, "I was just thinking you need to get changed for work."

Shit

"Eat your cereal," I offered lamely as I ran into my room to get changed.

• • •

The rest of our morning was uneventful and, despite my late start, we made it into the car right on schedule. Ashley's school, The Bristol Academy, was about a five minute drive from our house and exactly half way between home and the office for me. Dropping her off was never a problem. In fact, most days I was able to get her to school on time and still make it to work early. That would've been the case that day as well, except I wasn't just dropping her off that morning.

"Um, mom," Ashley hesitated, looking out the window as if she was trying to avoid making eye contact, "is everything ok?"

"Yes baby," I reassured her, "why?"

"Well, you remember Mrs. Blocker needs to see you this morning right?"

Bristol did an excellent job of shielding the students from things like this but everyone knew Mrs. Blocker was the administrator who dealt with the finances and when she wanted to see you, that meant there was a problem with your account. My daughter is a lot of things but stupid isn't one of them, so when she was told that Mrs. Blocker needed to see her mom, she knew exactly what that meant.

"Yes honey I know Mrs. Blocker asked to see me, and I know why, and Ashley?" I put my hand on her shoulder to get her attention.

"Yes?" she turned to look at me. As soon as I saw her face I could see in her eyes that she was afraid.

"Everything is going to be fine baby." I said it with as much confidence as I could.

"Thanks mommy," she smiled, seeming to believe I had everything under control, "I love you more than anything."

It wasn't so much what she said as the way she said it. I could tell my baby was counting on me and if I had any doubt, her words sealed it. I was gonna do what I had to do.

To be honest, I decided on my course of action the night before and nothing occurred to me in the morning that changed my mind. I tried for hours to find different options, determined to use my Ivy League education to come up with a real solution.

Eventually, after sitting up all night wracking my brain, I realized I was kidding myself.

I didn't like what I was about to do but that was beside the point. When you find yourself boxed in like that, whatever decision you make is gonna come with some negatives. I understood that. But I also understood I didn't have any other options.

"I love you too sweetie."

I hope one day you realize how much...

• • •

The wait outside Mrs. Blocker's office was longer than I deemed respectful of my time and, under normal circumstances, I would have let her know it. However, considering the reason for my visit, and what I was about to do, I figured that might not be the best time to assert myself.

Patricia Blocker was an impressive, if somewhat intimidating, Jamaican lady who spoke with what I thought to be the most elegant accent I'd ever heard. The perfect blend of exotic and articulate, I could have listened to that woman read the phone book. Strikingly tall at just over six feet, she had dark skin, shoulder length black hair, was always impeccably put together and, for a woman in her mid fifties, seemed to have an endless amount of energy.

Most impressive though, she was smart. Extremely so, having graduated cum laude from Vassar college in less than thirty months. She earned her PhD in Organizational Psychology from Princeton and had been at Bristol Academy for seven years.

That last bit of info was found courtesy of Google. Once I decided how to approach my situation, I wanted to get a better feel for who I would be dealing with and, by all accounts, Patricia Blocker would not be easily fooled.

"Morning Ms. Sharpe," she said pleasantly as she motioned for me to come into her office and have a seat at her desk, "hope you haven't been waiting too long?"

"No," I smiled half heartedly, "just long enough."

She took my sarcasm in stride, sat down and got right to the point. "I think you know why we're here."

Showtime

"Yes," I interrupted gently, "and before you go any further I want to apologize for taking up your time like this." I reached into my purse and handed her an envelope. "There are two checks in there. The first is for this months tuition plus all late fees. The second, is post-dated for two weeks from today and should cover the prior months tuition, bringing our account current." I smiled confidently before going on. "And again, I apologize for the inconvenience."

"The only problem Ms. Sharpe is I waived all the penalties on your account."

"Oh wow," I said sheepishly, "no I didn't know that."

"Did you not get the notice I sent home with Ashley?"

"She gave it to me but, to be honest, I didn't read it. I glanced at it but figured I knew what it said and since I was planning to come in today anyway...my god Mrs. Blocker I am so sorry."

"It's no problem Ms. Gall —"

"Please," I interrupted, "call me Julie."

She smiled warmly and handed me back my envelope. "I'm sorry but we cannot accept overpayments. Just have Ashley drop off two new checks tomorrow morning and we'll be all set."

"Well, the post-dated check should be good as-is, right?"

"You want me to just hold onto that one?"

"Sure, Ashley will drop off a check for this months tuition in the morning."

She stood up, smiled and extended her hand.

"Looks like we have a plan then."

"That we do," I affirmed, standing up and taking her hand, "and Mrs. Blocker, thank you. Seriously, I appreciate your help more than you can know."

"Please, call me Patrice," she smiled in return, "and I cannot allow you to leave without telling you that your daughter is an absolute joy. I want you to know how much we love having Ashley here."

What I didn't want *her* to know was that I had thoroughly researched every payment policy currently in place at Bristol. Not only that, I could have recited, from memory, every single codification, addendum, update and revision to The Bristol Academy's payment policies since 1997. The point is, I knew good and damn well she wouldn't be able to accept that first check. And the whole charade of giving her a second one was just to give me some credibility, which worked because it was my suggestion. They say you do best what you do most, and lying had become like a second language to me.

• • •

Walking to the car, my nerves were completely shot. It was so bad I couldn't stop my hands from shaking when I reached into my purse for my keys. The entire conversation with Mrs. Blocker took less than five minutes and went exactly as I planned, but knowing that didn't calm me down. Not even a little. My life was already a virtual house of cards and now, here I was building layers of complication on top of it with no clear idea how to come out the other side. *"I was doing what I had to do,"* I tried reminding myself but that didn't help either. I was a nervous wreck.

And I wish I could say there was more to my master plan than a couple of bad checks. The thing is, there wasn't. The rest would come to me eventually, at least that's what I kept telling myself. For the moment though, I was in full-on crisis mode and, as unsophisticated as it was, my plan was classic crisis management, all the way through.

The biggest mistake you can make in a crisis is to indulge the perfectly natural human impulse to try and fix the entire problem right away. Anyone with any level of skill or training knows, the first thing you do in any crisis is assess your time. Which is a fancy way of saying you determine how much time you have before the shit hits the fan and then, immediately start trying to move the finish line. The theory is simple and makes perfect sense both in the classroom and in real life application. The longer you can delay disaster, the more opportunity you have to come up with a suitable solution.

I now had a few days to figure something out. That may not seem like much but the night before, I had twelve hours until Ashley would be kicked out of school and my landlord would begin eviction proceedings. Now, instead of a few *hours*, I had three to five business days. I'll take it.

The problem for me was that still left me with less than a week to prevent my life from completely imploding, and not even one *bad* idea how to do it.

Chapter Four

"Ashley Watson!" Theo screamed from the back of studio A, "what are you doing?!"

"My bad, I thought —"

"No," he scolded, "thinking is what you wasn't doin boo boo. That's why you're the only one on the wrong foot!"

"Sorry."

"Sorry don't cut it baby girl, you need to get it together."

"I know," she apologized, "I will."

"Alright then," he commanded, still irritated but ready to move on, "let's run it again so Miss Watson can figure things out."

Theo Iseman was a brilliant choreographer however, as with many artist types, he was also notoriously insecure. He would throw full on temper tantrums if each movement in a dance wasn't executed precisely to his liking and had been known to extend rehearsals for hours, pushing his dancers past the point of exhaustion until he was satisfied with every single element of a performance. Everyone who'd ever worked with the man talked about his maniacal eye for detail and now his wrath was directed squarely at my daughter.

I heard the entire thing from the adjacent studio, where I was locking up after the Ballet II class had just ended. Cassandra, the studio owner, brought Theo in to choreograph a piece for her advanced girls to perform in the winter recital. Of all the students at the studio, only a select few were chosen to be in the advanced group and I had never seen my baby girl so happy as the day we told her she was in.

Of course, as with all things child related, there was an additional cost associated with this honor. Fortunately, since I worked at the studio part time and generally helped Cassandra as much as I could, Ashley got to join for free. Even if that hadn't been the case, I would have found a way to cover it. There was simply no way I could have let her miss out on something she had worked so hard for.

Getting selected was great, and I couldn't have been happier for her, but the thing that made me proud was the fact that she legitimately earned it. Ashley always enjoyed dance, ever since her first ballet lesson, but she was never the most physically gifted dancer in any of her classes. Then, when Brian and I split up and we had to move and it seemed like her entire life was crumbling around her, dance became her escape. Instead of falling apart and lashing out emotionally, which she had every right to do, she threw herself into dance with a passion and her hard work was paying off.

Just as importantly, Cassandra's studio had become like her second home. It was where she spent most of her free time and it was where she felt safest. So being chosen as one of the advanced girls was like having the place she loved the most actually loving her back. For Ashley, after everything she'd lost, that was huge. Dancing at this studio was the one piece of our new life that felt connected, in a good way, to our old one. It was also the one piece of her life I hadn't managed to destroy, yet.

I peaked around the corner to get a look at what the girls were working on and my eyes, of course, went straight to my daughter. Thank god she was only thirteen because it was easy to see boys were going to like her. Tall, with long, dark hair and deep blue eyes, I could foresee a challenging few years once she discovered the opposite sex. Fortunately for me, she was a late bloomer in that regard. For now, she still had a genuine innocence about her that even the most seasoned mean girls would find disarming. Ashley was a difficult young lady not to like, though judging by the look on Theo's face at the moment, he was beginning to find it a little less than 'impossible.'

"Miss Watson you need to do better than this," he shook his head in disgust, "all y'all do! And I hope nobody got no plans on goin home no time soon, cause what I'm seein right now is unacceptable!"

There was an audible gasp from the girls, most of whom were supposed to be home over an hour ago. In his defense, I think Cassandra forgot to tell this lunatic he would be working with twelve to fourteen year old kids, but I'm not sure that would've mattered. They would all be made to stay until everyone got it right. That's just the way Theo Iseman worked.

The last thing Cassandra or her studio needed was a gang of pissed off parents pulling their daughters and threatening to sue because of some idiot choreographer with a Napoleon complex. Only Cassandra had already gone home for the evening, leaving yours truly as the last sane adult on the premises. I guess it was up to me to do something.

"Places dammit!" he demanded impatiently, not happy they were taking their time, "I aint got all —"

"Theo, I think the girls need to take five?"

He didn't even look in my direction, not willing to acknowledge the poor excuse for a human that had the nerve to interrupt HIS rehearsal.

"Ma'am," he said slowly, not trying to mask the disgust in his voice, "do we have a problem?"

He didn't scare me. In fact, it was all I could do to keep from laughing. "No problem," I replied calmly, "but what we do have is a room full of teenage girls who probably have to pee."

To be honest, it was more of a snicker than an actual laugh. Either way, the sight and sound of HIS dancers laughing at HIS expense was more than Theo was willing to put up with.

"See what you did?" he asked, before looking around the room dramatically, "y'all look a hot, raggedy, ghetto-ass mess before the biggest show of your lives and this shit is funny?!"

"Seriously?" I interrupted sternly, "it never occurred to you to watch your language in a room full of teenage girls? That thought never crossed your mind?"

He just glared at me.

"Girls," I decided I had to take control of the situation, "go ahead and take a bio break."

"Who ARE you???" he muttered loudly, the frustration building in his voice. Apparently no one had spoken to Mr. Iseman like this in quite some time. I was just getting started.

"Who I am doesn't matter," I answered evenly, "what I know however, that most definitely matters."

"Listen, I don't know who —"

"Exactly," I interrupted loudly enough to stop him but still maintained a smile on my face. Poor kid had no idea this is what I do. "So now, since we both agree you don't know certain things, why don't you let me educate you —"

"Ma'am, I'm sorry but —"

"Oh no sweetie," I interrupted as gently as I could, "I think you misunderstood. See, that was a rhetorical question. No need to answer because this is the part where I talk and you listen, ok? Now the two things I know are that, number one, you have been contracted to do a job and that you will find a way to do said job without using improper language. If you cannot find a way to control what comes out of your mouth, I will have you brought up on charges of indecency. Charges that absolutely won't stick, but that will be public enough to ensure you are never contracted to work in this state with anyone under the age of thirty ever again. Do we understand each other? A

43

simple yes or no will suffice." He nodded, I continued. "And as for number two? Well I know for absolutely certain, beyond any shadow of any doubt, that you will never, under any circumstance, ever raise your voice at me again."

I turned and walked away before he had a chance to respond, not that there was much he could say. For a brief second I almost felt bad for him. I once reduced the CEO of a fortune 500 company to tears in open court, so smacking down an obnoxious choreographer was hardly worth celebrating.

For me, the best part about the whole episode was the proud look on Ashley's face. I imagine its the feeling a man might have when his son sees him hit a home run or dunk a basketball. I only wish she had gotten a chance to see me do the real thing. Too bad those days were long gone.

"Daddy!"

I was jolted out of my own head and back into reality as my daughter bolted across the studio and into her father's arms as if he had just returned home from war. He hadn't. In fact, they texted every day, spoke every night on the phone and had just spent a weekend together two weeks ago.

That was all a part of the court mandated custody agreement, which I made a point of following to the letter. It's just that, with everything going on, I had completely forgot this was the weekend Ashley goes and stays with Brian.

None of that is to suggest Ashley's excitement wasn't genuine. It most definitely was. The two of them had always been close, like a lot of fathers and daughters, but ever since the divorce they had developed a special bond. It's kind of hard to describe in words but if you ever saw them together, you would pick up on it. I know I did.

Not that I had a problem with it. To the contrary, Brian was a good man and a great father and neither of them deserved any of what I had put them through. I was genuinely happy for them that they had each other.

As close as the two of them had remained through the breaking up of our family, the same could not be said for Brian and me. He hadn't spoken two words to me, that didn't have something to do with Ashley, since the day the divorce was finalized. And even when it did have to do with our daughter, he literally looked constipated every time he had to say so much as hello to me. Still, we were in public and there was no way to walk out of the studio without passing within a foot of the man, so —

"Hi Brian."

"Hey," he scoffed dryly, mostly for Ashley's benefit as she was still standing next to him. Even though he technically spoke, he made a point of not looking at me.

"Baby, I'm gonna go read in the car," he turned to leave, still ignoring my presence, even though I was now practically standing on top him, "I'll be outside in the parking lot so just text me when you're done ok?"

"You might as well wait daddy. We're wrapping up now."

"I thought you said you were gonna be really late?"

She looked at me with a huge smile. "Mom took care of that."

She gave her father a kiss on the cheek and ran back to join the rest of the girls for one last run-through before calling it a night.

"I'll be outside," he said with disgust, "have her call me when she's ready."

He walked out the door, but I followed him out into the hall. "Brian, wait. There's something I —"

"What is it Julie?" he interrupted harshly.

"It's about Ashley's tuition."

"You mean the tuition for the school you enrolled her in without consulting me? The school I specifically said I didn't think was right for her? That school??"

"Brian she's thriving at Bristol. Her grades are excellent and every report —"

"Julie what do you WANT?!" he spat out venomously, cutting me off mid-sentence, "and please tell me you're not about to ask me to help pay for a school I don't think she should be going to."

I just shook my head. "Brian this isn't about me or you. It's about our daughter's education."

"Bullshit Julie. This is about you doing whatever the hell you want and then asking me to bail your sorry ass out when things don't go your way. Well, those days are over. I've read the divorce decree and it clearly states I don't have to give you one dime more than I'm giving you now."

He was seething. I knew it would be a long shot but I had to try and, even though it led to nothing, I wasn't sorry I did. At that point however, I knew there was no water coming from that particular rock, so I just stood back and let him vent.

"Hell, you're the big-time lawyer," he continued sarcastically, "at least you were until you decided to choose your psycho client over your own daughter."

"That's not true."

"Really?"

"Brian, stop. I would never choose anyone over our daughter and you know it."

"Oh, so you lied under oath and lost your license to protect Ashley? Give me a break."

"Never mind," I sighed, "just forget it."

"Trust me," he grunted as he walked out the door into the parking lot, "I've been trying to do exactly that for three years."

That last jab struck a chord with me. It had been three years since we split up and, it was easy to see, he wasn't close to getting over it.

I wasn't surprised. If there was one thing I always knew about Brian Watson, it was that he loved me. He truly did. From our second date to the day he proposed; through our wedding day and the day Ashley was born; through everything, he worshipped the ground I walked on. And as much as I know he'd rather die than admit it, it was obvious he still had some of those same feelings. I took no pride in that realization, if anything, it made me sad.

One of the things that comes with divorce and single parenthood, is way too much alone time. Add the fact that I lost my career and all of my friends at the same time I was losing my family, and what I was left with was a lot of opportunity for honest self-reflection.

And in those many moments of pure honesty, when there was no one in the room but myself and the woman in the mirror, I had to face some harsh realities. One of the most painful was the fact that, as much as I knew Brian loved me, I had to admit I was never truly in love with him.

I know it sounds cliché, but clichés are clichés for a reason. Looking back at everything that had happened, it was as obvious as it was ugly. I appreciated and respected and liked my ex-husband, but he was never the man of my dreams. I never felt butterflies in my stomach when he walked in a room or felt like a piece of me went with him when he left. Sure, I'd miss him when he was away but it wasn't as if something was missing from my life while he was gone.

He was a good man who happened into my life at a time when it made sense for me to settle down. He was kind and supportive and he treated me well, so I just kinda went with it. He was a good choice. He was a smart and safe choice. But when I was being honest with myself, I had to admit that's all he was. He was my husband and he was my friend, but he was never truly my man.

I felt disgusting, and it wasn't the kind of dirt that could be washed away with soap and water. Had I really devastated a man's life because I wanted to play house? Was I really that person?

"Bye mom."

Ashley's voice ended my journey down guilt trip lane.

"Ok honey." I gave her a big hug and kiss. "You have everything?"

"Yep, oh wait, weren't you supposed to give me something for Mrs. Blocker?"

"I already put it in your backpack." I reached in and pulled out a small envelope. "Now make sure you give this to her at the end of the day on Monday."

"Why not in the morning?"

"Because she and I talked about it and agreed you would be dropping it off after your last class."

"But mom," she pressed, "what if she's not in her office after class? I can't be late for rehearsal so I won't be able to wait for —"

"Ashley," I said calmly, trying to be patient, "If she's not in her office after school, just leave it in the in-box on her admin's desk. You understand?"

She looked at me, confused, but decided to let it go. "Whatever mom." She shook her head and turned for the exit. "I'll see you Sunday."

And with that, Ashley and my worthless check were both out the door, taking my one woman pity party with them.

Now was no time for honest reflection, I admonished myself. Sure, I had bought some time, but the pitiful attempt at reaching out to my ex went about as far as expected, which means nowhere. And that's exactly where I found myself, nowhere.

I had less than a week to figure something out and was no closer to a real solution than I was the night before. My situation at 9pm, was almost exactly the same as it was at 9am, when I was shaking so bad I could barely drive. Almost.

There was one key difference.

I was now twelve hours closer to running out of time.

Chapter Five

Who ever said time flies when you're having fun must have never dreaded a hard deadline. You wanna see time fly? Try staring down a locomotive.

The weekend was gone in a blink and we were back into our daily routine without much excitement. For Ashley, that meant school, homework and dance rehearsal. For me, that meant work, worry, work at the studio, and worry some more.

Monday night classes were always the most popular, but with the extra rehearsals for our winter recital, the place looked like the opening scene from Grease on steroids. Cassandra was in her late sixties and, while certainly spry for her age, wasn't getting around well enough to manage the influx of pre-pubescent bodies, with post-pubescent attitudes, filling her hallways. She could have used two or three extra people just to help direct traffic, but the studio was barely making ends meet as it was. So she had me.

"Alright ladies listen up." Everyone froze in place as I stepped into the long, narrow hallway outside of Cassandra's office. "Ballet II will be taught by Kristen in Studio A, Intermediate Hip Hop has been moved to Studio B and Theo and Preston are with the advanced girls in the big room."

On cue, the hallway erupted into a chaotic medley of voices and movement. "Please take ALL of your belongings with you!" I reminded them as they dispersed, "I promise if you leave anything in the hall it will either be confiscated or stolen. Either way, you will never see it again."

I helped point a couple of confused, late arriving stragglers in the right direction before making my way back to the office, where Cassandra was sitting, looking impressed.

"They listen to you," she smiled.

"Eh," I shrugged and flopped down in the seat across from her desk, "they're still young enough to be more scared of me than I am of them."

She shook her head, laughed and smiled at me again. We couldn't have been more different that way. The woman always had a smile on her face, always. And yet she wasn't one of those annoying, new age, pain in the ass, power of positive thought types. She had a genuine warmth about her that was intoxicating, which is probably why we became such close friends, that and the fact that she doted on my daughter as if she was a part of our family.

Cassandra Chavez was the most welcoming person I had ever met. In the entire time I'd known her, I don't think she ever had a single negative thing to say about anybody, which is why I just about fell out of my chair when she said "I hear Theo is a pretty big asshole."

"Listen to you!" I managed to say before bursting out laughing, "I think I'm rubbing off on you."

"Hey," she shrugged, "I don't mind callin em like I see em. Especially if the shoe fits right?"

"Well that one," I quipped, "fits like a damn glove."

She smiled, "I heard you handled the situation thoroughly though."

"No big deal."

"Well, the girls are still talking about it. Sylvia's calling you el abogado."

"It wasn't that serious Cassandra. Theo just needed to be reminded he wasn't god, not unlike most of the men I know."

She laughed loudly. "Well you made quite the impression on the girls, and apparently put the fear of god into him. He brought backup."

"I was gonna ask you about that. Who is Preston?"

"I don't know him, but according to the girls, his job is to protect Theo from el abogado."

I laughed at how ridiculous that sounded. "Mr. Iseman will be fine," I assured her, "his ego? Maybe not so much."

"Thank you for stepping in like that Julie. Seriously, sometimes I don't know how this place would run without you."

"Well, hopefully you won't have to find out any time soon."

With everything well under control, I suggested Cassandra take off for the evening. Her granddaughter was visiting from Texas with her new husband so I told her she should go be with her 'real' family and I would take care of things at the studio. I had to wait for Ashley anyway, and there was no sense in both of us sitting around doing nothing.

She relented, but not before reminding me that Ashley and I *were* her real family and how she never again wanted to hear me suggest otherwise.

The rest of the night was uneventful and, as things wound down, I was looking forward to going home, climbing in bed, and entering the magical land of denial. My brain hurt from thinking and it wasn't like I was making any progress. The clock was still ticking and I still had nothing remotely resembling a solution.

Of course, the only group left in the building was Theo and the advanced girls. They were twenty minutes over and, as such, the only thing standing between me and the one thing of value I got to keep from the divorce, my three hundred thread count, Egyptian cotton bed sheets.

I double checked the time and decided he had ten minutes to wrap things up before I would step in and do...

"Hi."

I was so caught up in my own head I hadn't noticed the tall kid with dark hair standing in the doorway. He looked to be in his early twenties and was fairly good looking, if somewhat uninteresting. With a chiseled face and dancers body, he was right out of central casting for a twenty something white male. If that wasn't enough of a give away, his pants were hanging down around his ass. This kid was a walking cliche.

"Disculpeme, estoy buscando para el abogado?"
Was he serious?

"Si su nombre es Preston, en lugar de tratar de ser gracioso, le sugiero que decirle a su amigo que tiene diez minutos para terminar antes de cumplir el defensor apaga las luces. Entender?"

He just stood there with a dumb look on his face.

That's what I thought.

I stood up and started gathering my things. "Tell Theo he has ten minutes."

"I'm sorry," he smirked, "your daughter made me promise to do that."

"My daughter is thirteen, she didn't *make* you do anything."

"She can be persuasive."

Something about the way he said it got my attention. I stopped what I was doing and looked him square in the eye. "You did hear me say she was thirteen right?"

He threw up his hands. "Whoa, wait a minute. I didn't mean anything like that."

"Good."

"Wow, she warned me you would be mean."

"What I am, is bored with this conversation and thoroughly unimpressed with the participant." I grabbed the last of my things and approached the door. "Now if you will just run along and let your friend know he needs to be wrapping —"

"That's what I'm here trying to tell you. We're finished."

"Good. Then so are we."

I pushed him into the hall so I could close the door. As I turned to lock it I could feel him still behind me. "Preston, is there something else I can do for you or are you just staring at my ass?"

"You do get right to it don't you?"

I finished locking the door and turned around. "I don't have time for games and even if I did, I prefer not to play with children."

"Well, for the record, I wasn't staring at anything. Theo just wanted to ask if he could add a rehearsal on Friday. He says they need the work."

"Let me check with Cassandra and get back to you."

I walked away knowing I was being a bitch but not having the time or energy to concern myself with his feelings. All I wanted to do was go find my daughter, finish locking up and head home to my bed because, quite frankly, if I didn't think of something soon, we weren't gonna have a home to go to.

Chapter Six

The next two days were pretty much carbon copies of Monday, except for the increased pressure to make something happen as each day passed.

Not surprisingly, the physical toll of all the stress was starting to show. My skin was an odd combination of pasty and blotchy, the bags under my eyes seemed to be growing by the hour and I had to have lost ten pounds since this all started. My hair? Don't even get me started on my hair. It was a matted, disgusting mess. I put it up on Friday, after my little run-in with Brian, and barely touched it since. There was a time in my life when I wouldn't have been seen outside of my bedroom looking like this, much less parading around in public. But my life was different now. I was different.

Beyond looking like a drug addicted street walker, I was absolutely exhausted. I had been way too nervous to eat anything, and sleep, while a great escape in theory, only came to me in short, fitful, bouts of thirty minutes or less.

The one bit of relief I found was my time at the studio, not that a building filled with energetic teenage girls did anything to ease my foul mood. It's just that the place was so busy I didn't have time to obsess over my situation.

Of course even there, in those rare moments when everyone was where they were supposed to be and doing what they were supposed to do, reality would find me again. In those moments, there was no place to hide from what was about to happen.

Any day now, two checks totaling three thousand nine hundred and seventy-five dollars would hit my checking account, where there was a current balance of one hundred twenty-three dollars and sixty-seven cents. That discrepancy, whenever it was found, was going to trigger a chain of events that, almost certainly, would lead to Brian seeking full custody of Ashley. And this time, in every single realistic scenario I could think of, he would win.

My heart ached at the thought but there was no sense denying it any longer. The reality was as clear and unavoidable as a full moon in a cloudless sky. I was about to lose my baby girl.

A part of me died with that realization even though I knew, as much as he hated me, Brian would never keep me from seeing our daughter. He was a better man than that and, if nothing else, he would never do that to Ashley.

I knew all of that in my head but in the place that mattered, in my heart, I knew something different. I was a mommy, and mommy is supposed to always be there. Always. Mommy is supposed to be there for every bad dream and to wake you up on every birthday. Mommy should be the first person a child sees every morning and mommy's should be the last face they see every night. Daddy may be big and strong, but mommy is the one to make you feel safe when you're scared. She is the one you believe when she says everything is gonna be ok and she is the one you turn to when you have nowhere else to go. Every child needs their mommy and, of everything I had failed at in my life, I would regret most, failing to give my baby girl the kind of mommy she deserved.

Cassandra walked in from outside and stopped cold in the doorway to her office.

"Julie, are you crying?"

I honestly hadn't noticed. "No no, I'm fine," I said, quickly trying to get myself together, "just have a little bit of a headache."

"You ok?"

"Yeah, I'll live. I thought you were going to the bank?"

"Forgot my keys," she lied, looking at me closely, "you sure it's just a headache?"

"Yes," I smiled unconvincingly, "but ok, maybe it's not so little."

"Want a painkiller?"

"Actually, yes."

She laughed. "You were supposed to say no thank you."

"Excuse me?"

"I don't have any. I'm allergic to the over the counter stuff and I know better than to keep the prescription stuff around the studio."

"Excuse me?"

"Prescription pills and a building overrun with teenage girls is not a recipe for anything good."

"I see your point. Well don't worry about it," I smiled weakly, "I'll just go to CVS on the way home."

"Go now."

"I can wait Cassandra. It's not —"

"Stop it," she commanded, "you ok to drive?"

I could see she wasn't going to take no for an answer and besides, I needed the fresh air. "Yes, I can drive fine."

"Ok, you go. I'll mind the store til you get back."

"Thank you," I said and started putting on my coat before stopping myself, "but wait, don't you have to get to the bank?"

"That can wait."

"No, Cassandra it can't. There's not enough money in the account to cover the rent, which is already ten days past due, and the vendors for the recital have to be paid this week."

"This is what I get for letting you look at my books. Here," she handed me one of her two deposit bags, "This is the cash deposit. You do this one and I'll deposit the checks tomorrow. There's enough there to cover everything."

She took a seat behind her desk and looked up to see me just standing there, not moving.

"You should hurry up and go before the bank closes," she smiled, "otherwise, according to you, we'll be out of business next week."

Chapter Seven

I left the studio at exactly 5:27 and went straight to the bank, which was less than two miles away. So why was I still sitting in the parking lot at 5:51? Because Antonio Olivares, my favorite law professor at Princeton, used to always scream at me to 'make the damn case.'

"Stop limiting your argument based on what you believe to be right!" he would shout in frustration as he obliterated another one of my briefs, "You have to trust the system Miss Watson. If you want to be focused on things like the truth and what's right or wrong, go join the FBI! If you want to be a lawyer, you have to accept that your role in our system is to make the best case you can and leave right or wrong where it belongs, in the hands of a jury!"

So thats what I was doing as I was sitting there in the parking lot. I was making the case, to myself, for an unthinkable betrayal. But, as Professor Olivares would say, it wasn't my job to choose between right or wrong. It was my job to make the best argument for the situation, period. And when I looked at my situation, I was quickly disavowed of the illusion I had any 'right' choice left to make.

If I had any other option, even a bad one, I wouldn't have been sitting there seriously considering stealing from the only friend I had left in the world. And that is exactly what it would be, stealing. In less than eight minutes I had to make a classic Sophie's choice. Either accept the title of failed mother and everything that came along with that, or upgrade that title to thief. There was no in between.

The penalty for the first would be yet another disappointment and change of address for Ashley, and a shattered heart for me. The other title offered only another three to five day extension on my current situation but carried with it all the penalties of the first, with the additional bonus of prison time.

It didn't add up. There simply wasn't enough upside to justify the risk, and yet I was still sitting there, frozen in place as if I was awaiting some sort of divine intervention.

The bible says to be still in times of trouble so that you may hear the whispered voice of the lord. I always thought that sounded like a bunch of horse shit but maybe, just maybe, if I sat there in silence long enough, god would speak to me. Maybe, if I was patient, the king of kings would take pity on me and guide me down the path to absolution.

So I waited.

And I waited some more.

And nothing happened.

It was over.

There was no salvation coming, not for someone like me. I could cry, pray and beg as much as I wanted but there was no denying the fact that everything happening to me was of my own doing. No one forced me to make the decisions I'd made, and no one could have saved me from suffering the consequences. It was time to suck it up and accept my fate.

"Hi. How may I help you?"

"Hello, I'd like to make a deposit."

"Checking or Savings?"

"Checking, please."

"Name on the account?"

"Julie Sharpe."

• • •

They say an attorney who represents herself has a fool for a client. Some would say that's just an old, outdated cliche. I say cliches are cliches for a reason.

Professor Olivares would have been proud. I objectively laid out the argument, with no predetermined bias, and the facts clearly argued against doing what I had just done. Too much risk for too little gain, it was that simple.

The problem is I was also the client and what was at stake for me was worth any risk. And don't talk to me about perspective or objectivity when it comes to my child! All I had to do was visualize the look of disappointment on Ashley's face when I would have to tell her she couldn't go to Bristol anymore. Or I could envision the day, not long after, when she would be leaving to go live with her father. I was the only person Ashley had seen every single day of her life and now I was supposed to be ok waking up without my baby in the house with me?! Put any of those images in my head and perspective went right out the window. I wouldn't survive that. Any of it. Literally.

Fuck it. I had already lost too much. Yes, I made mistakes but dammit so had everyone else. I wasn't about to just sit by and continue taking it up the ass as if I was the only one on earth who had ever done anything wrong.

I had been a strong, accomplished woman my entire adult life. I had an ivy league education, graduated magna cum laude from a top tier law school and had argued two cases before the Illinois state supreme court.

This was a joke. A bad fucking joke. I was a few thousand dollars short and suddenly, even the piece of shit life I had managed to salvage for Ashley and me was going to be taken away?! For a few thousand dollars?! I used to have a closet full of two thousand dollar suits and a collection of designer shoes that would have paid Ashley's tuition for life, five times over! I built all of that from nothing and so there was no way I couldn't figure my way out of this. I just needed more time and if borrowing money from Cassandra's studio was the only way for me to get the time I needed, then fuck it, that's just what I was gonna have to do.

Something changed in me that night. It was as if, in that moment, I suddenly stopped living in my past. Call it denial or belligerence or whatever you want, but for the first time in three years I didn't feel like a helpless victim of my circumstances. Something needed to be done and sitting around waiting for the other shoe to drop wasn't gonna cut it, not for me. I went out and I made something happen because that's what I do. That's who I am.

It was time I accepted certain realities about myself. Yes, I had just broken the law but it wasn't my first time. Far from it. I had also violated the trust of someone who had been nothing but good to me. Again, not my first time.

The pattern was clear. I just had to open my eyes and free myself of the charade of any kind of ethical dilemma. Those ethics were tied to a past version of myself that, if I'm totally honest, probably never really existed.

I was a liar and a thief and a user. That's who I was and that's who I'd always been. I'd proven that time and again in my life, so there was no sense denying it. And I didn't feel bad about it anymore either. In fact, acknowledging the truth made me feel powerful, as if I had taken back control over my destiny.

Until recently, I had excelled at everything I'd attempted in my life, and saw no reason this should be any different. If lying and using and stealing were in my DNA, then I had it in me to refine those skills to an art form.

I had no career, no friends, and no social life to speak of. All I had was my little girl and my only job was to protect her. If the only way I could get that done was to indulge the unsavory parts of my personality, then that's just what had to happen.

In hindsight I can see I was taking the first steps down a dark and dangerous path, but I honestly don't think I would have done anything differently. My old life was gone, never to return. It was time I stopped crying over it and started living the one I still had. It was time for Julie Sharpe to start playing by a whole new set of rules.

Chapter Eight

"Feeling better?"

"Yes, thank you so much Cassandra." I took off my coat and hung it on the back of the door. "I think the fresh air was as good for me as the pills."

"Probably better." She stood to leave. "Julie are you sure everything's ok? You seem troubled."

"It's nothing serious. Things have just been a little weird at home lately."

"Todo esta bien con mi chica?"

The level of concern in her voice when she asked if everything was ok with my daughter would have felt strange coming from anyone else, but Cassandra was more than a friend. She considered us family and had proven herself to be exactly that on many occasions.

If I was ever working late while Ashley was at the studio, Cassandra would make sure she got something decent to eat and let her use the office to do her homework. She even allowed us to keep a spare key to our house in her desk. A part of me wanted to believe she cared so much about Ashley she might even understand what I did, not that it mattered. What was done was done and there was no going back.

"Ashley is doing fine," I explained with a smile, "her father, not so much."

"Ah, problems with the ex," she nodded emphatically, as if that explained everything.

"They never make things easy do they?" I complained, going with her assumption

"If they did, they wouldn't be exes."

"You have a point," I laughed, "how did you get to be so smart?"

"I got old," she smiled, "you'll get there one day."

"We'll see about that."

"It happens to us all my dear." She put on her coat. "You make it to the bank in time?"

"Yep, but their computers were down. They took the deposit but it won't show up online until they get the system back up. Probably some time tomorrow afternoon."

She looked concerned. "Is the money in the account?"

"Oh yes yes, absolutely," I reassured her, "it's just that you won't be able to see it online until the system is back up."

"Oh please," she waved her hand and smiled, "as long as the money is in the account, that's all that matters. I don't know how to check anything on that dumb computer anyway."

"Why don't you get going, I can take it from here. And Cassandra?"

"Yes?"

"Thank you. For everything."

"Tu eres mi familia Julie Sharpe. Please never forget that."

"I won't," I assured her and gave her as big and genuine a hug as I was capable of giving.

My heart felt sick with guilt. I was perfectly willing to live with what I did because I had convinced myself I did it for Ashley. But I now had to acknowledge there was a part of me, a big part, that would forever regret what I had done TO Cassandra.

In that moment I realized whatever feeling of confidence or illusion of control I had gained by accepting the reality of the person I had become, I lost something equally important, maybe even more important, my self respect.

"Excuse me."

We looked up to see the ever so annoying Preston Richards standing in the doorway.

"What is it Mr. Richards?" Cassandra asked.

"I'm sorry to interrupt," he smiled, "but I need to speak with El Abogado."

"My cue to go," she laughed, "you kids play nice."

"My name is Julie Sharpe," I said, once Cassandra was gone.

"Ok well, Ms. Sharpe, I wanted to remind you about Friday."

I suddenly felt exhausted, almost to the point of being light-headed. I went and sat behind Cassandra's desk to settle myself.

"Hello?"

I had forgotten, for a second, that Preston was still standing there. "What do you want?"

"I asked you about Friday?"

"Friday?" My exhaustion was quickly turning into agitation.

"Yeah, Theo wants to add an extra rehearsal and you were going to get back to us, remember?"

"Shit, you're right. I'll let you know tomorrow."

He just smiled.

"What?"

"You really need to learn to watch your language."

"And you really need to get the fuck out of my office."

Out of nowhere my slight agitation had turned into full blown anger and, to be honest, it had nothing to do with anything Preston had done or said, just that his presence was making my skin crawl.

"Whoa," he protested loudly, "where the hell did that come from?!"

"You just need to leave, ok?"

"Bullshit, you have no reason to be pissed off at me! All I did was ask a simple question!"

Imagine eating a large pizza right before having to stand naked in front of your ex, who'd just left you for an underwear model. That's exactly how I felt, inadequate and weak and disgusting, and completely exposed. The thought of someone's, anyone's, eyes on me at that moment tied my stomach up in knots and made me feel like throwing up. Unfortunately, Preston 'pain-in-the-ass' Richards wasn't getting that. "Look," I said harshly, "what part of 'leave' are you too stupid to understand?!"

"Don't fucking call me stupid!"

"Then don't act like you don't understand what I'm saying when I tell you to get the fuck out of my office!"

My heart felt like it was going to jump out of my chest. I would have seriously sacrificed a body part to get him to leave at that point, but he wasn't having it.

"Why do you act like such an evil bitch all the time?"

"Did you seriously just call me a bitch?"

"Did you seriously just call me stupid?"

It was all I could do to keep from completely meting down right then and there. "What do I have to do to get you to leave?!"

"Lady, I wouldn't even be here bothering you right now if you had done what you said you would! So maybe you should be apologizing instead of trying to act like such a hard ass?!"

My chest felt heavy. I was having trouble breathing and my skin felt like there were millions of tiny little bugs crawling out of my pores. I had never experienced a panic attack but I can imagine this is what it might feel like. "Close the door," I said, trying desperately to hold it together.

"Why? So you can bitch me out in —"

Before he could finish, I stood up, stumbled over to the door and managed to close it myself. He just looked at me as if he didn't know what to think.

"Um, are you ok?"

I leaned my forehead into the door to compose myself and kept my back to him to hide that I was crying. Before he could say anything else, I turned around, walked into his chest, and kissed him as deeply as I had ever kissed anyone in my life.

• • •

Looking back, it would be easy to say I didn't know what I was thinking.

It would be more accurate to say I wasn't thinking at all.

We fell back into Cassandra's desk and, amazingly, I felt my pulse begin to settle down and I began to breathe easier. It was as if the distraction of physical contact allowed my mind to ease slowly away from the brink of its complete collapse and, even though my reality hadn't changed, I was able to start relaxing into a different space.

I purposely kept my mouth on his to give the illusion of uncertainty as to what I wanted to happen next. Any break would risk eye contact, and continuing beyond that would mean I'd made some sort of conscious decision.

I didn't want that. I didn't want to face the reality of what I was doing. I was tired of reality. I was exhausted from it. I needed to silence my mind and I needed to lose myself. I needed to forget.

Thankfully, Preston's lips were soft and full and worthy of my complete attention. I put my hands on either side of his face and explored his mouth with the patience of a nurse and the precision of a surgeon.

I playfully parted his lips with my own so that I could gently nibble on the tip of his tongue. I ran my fingers lightly across the moistness of his bottom lip while tracing my tongue across the top. I put the tips of my fingers into his mouth, allowing him to taste me. My kisses were soft, yet purposeful. The tip of my tongue lightly painted his lips as I slowly, meticulously, savored every inch and crevice of his mouth from one corner to the other. And then, when I couldn't take it anymore, I thrust my tongue hungrily into his mouth as if my life depended on it.

The sensations were exquisite in their complexity. I would get chills through my entire body every time our tongues touched, followed by an incredible sense of warmth whenever I pulled his body closer into mine. I was in complete control, selfishly leading this dance and taking what I needed, when I needed with no thought of anyone or anything but me.

He sat on the edge of the desk, leaned back onto his elbows and allowed me to climb on top of him. I pulled my dress up, placed my knees on either side of his waist and continued devouring his mouth as he undid his pants. Then, as my hands started to clumsily pull on his shirt, young Preston, keeping his upper body perfectly in place, reached around and grabbed me by the waist.

Announcing his presence so forcefully sent me into another gear. I started grinding into him hungrily, desperately needing to feel as much of him as I could. It was as if my entire body was alive with pure, primal lust. My skin tingled. My heart raced.

I was ready

Every cell in my body was alive and literally ached for what I knew was coming. As if he read my mind, the impressively strong young Preston lifted me up by my waist, ripped my panties off and thrust himself into me, all in what seemed like a single motion.

There was nothing subtle or sexy about the guttural sound I made as he entered me. My entire body convulsed as I took every inch of him, placing my hands on his chest and pausing for just a second with my eyes shut and mouth slightly open. I felt my tongue slowly tracing back and forth over my teeth as instinct replaced conscious thought. I spread my knees apart and relaxed, allowing my body to adjust to his size, before starting to slowly grind into him.

He was deep…

Oh my god, soooo deep…

We moved well together from the start. There was no awkwardness, no lack of chemistry. He filled me completely and, with each movement, touched a different part of my body. There was literally no part of me he couldn't reach and the more he gave me the more I wanted.

Oh my god...baby

I wrapped my arms around him and kissed him with a hunger and passion that exceeded anything I had done earlier. It was as if I was trying to breath him into me. As if, no matter what I did, I couldn't get close enough to him.

MMMM...

I continued grinding into him, savoring every movement, until it seemed like my hips started to take on a mind of their own. Again, there was nothing seductive or sexy about the way I was moving at this point. But I didn't care. My mind and body were working together as one, toward a single purpose. Toward the only thing that mattered right now. I could feel it within reach.

YES...

It was like I felt a second heartbeat, deep inside my core. It was subtle at first, emanating small, rhythmic waves of electricity throughout the rest of my body. Those waves continued to grow in intensity with each movement and so my hips kept moving, grinding, working, until the waves were building to an explosion

I'm gonna cum...

What began as slow, rhythmic grinding was now a frantic, almost spastic thrusting of the hips back and forth as that last, intense, exquisite explosion of electricity shot through my entire body.

Baby I'm cumming...

My toes curled, hips convulsed involuntarily and my eyes rolled into the top of my head. I didn't try and control it. I just rode the waves of electricity until my body had never felt so completely drained. Then, without saying a word, Preston thrust his hips upward, causing me to fall forward onto his chest. He wrapped his arms around me, holding me in place, and began thrusting himself into me with purpose.

Oh fuck...

He was in complete control now and I was so spent I couldn't have fought it if I wanted to. I didn't want to. It was as if my body instinctively knew what he needed. Without thinking, I arched my back, giving him all the access I could.

Get it baby...

I felt his body begin to tense as he drove into me with an animalistic passion. I spread my knees as far apart as I could on the desk to completely give myself to him. I closed my eyes and moaned

81

loudly as I felt his warm, wet load spill into me. Filling me with his release allowed me to lose myself in his ecstasy, keeping me lost in the moment for a few more precious seconds until the seeds of my reality began to sprout back to life.

Chapter Nine

We lay there still for what seemed like an eternity. In reality, it was more like two minutes. Which was still long enough that our bodies, though still physically connected, could no longer prevent our minds from making the awkward but inevitable journey from orgasm intoxication back to harsh, unforgiving reality.

In the movies, there would have been some other room to escape to. At the very least, I would have been given a commercial break to collect my thoughts and some sort of oversized bed sheet to cover myself with. I had nothing. And to make matters worse, I'd seen walk-in closets with more room to run and hide than Cassandra's so-called office.

So with no other options, I did the only thing I could think of. I kept my face buried in Preston's neck and had no intention of moving until I came up with an exit plan that didn't involve me actually speaking to the young man I had just sexually assaulted.

That's when it hit me and I received yet another jolt of electricity through my body. Only this time there was nothing pleasurable about it.

"How old are you?"

"You ask me that now?" he laughed and stood up. He moved effortlessly, even with my full body weight still draped all over him. The shift in position officially ended our coupling, so I detangled my legs from around his waist and allowed my feet to find the floor.

To say things were awkward would have been like comparing an aircraft carrier to a Taiwanese fishing boat. There's awkward and then there are moments in life that defy description. This was definitely the latter.

"Shit."

"What's the matter?" I asked, still making a concerted effort to avoid looking at him.

"It's all fun and games til somebody gets jizz running down their legs."

I reached into Cassandra's desk, tossed him a role of paper towels and flopped down in her chair. It was a perfectly inelegant way to end another perfectly fucked up day. If I had any doubt before, his adolescent attempt at humor sealed it in my mind. Not only was I a bonafide thief, but I now got to add statutory rape to my growing list of crimes.

"You can relax," he said.

"I am relaxed," I scoffed defensively.

"Good," he smiled, "because I'm legal. You're not going to jail."

"At least not for rape." The words just sort of slipped out before I could stop myself.

Get it together Julie...

"You plan on robbing a bank?"

"What?"

"Well, if you're not going to jail because of me, what kind of crime spree you have in mind?"

"Are you trying to be funny Preston?"

"Depends on your answer," he smiled, "maybe I'll want in?"

I tuned him out, threw my head back and stared at the ceiling, still not quite able to wrap my mind around what just happened.

"Is it working?" he asked.

"Is what working?"

"Am I being funny?"

"What?" I was officially annoyed, "you know what? Forget it. Look, Preston," I leaned forward and looked directly at him for the first time since we started kissing, "are you ok with what just happened?"

"Yeah," he smiled, "I think I'll survive."

"Good," I leaned back in the chair and pretended to start doing work, "because I'm ok too. Now you better get back into your rehearsal before Theo wonders where you went."

"But wait," he protested, "don't we need to, like, talk about, you know, like, everything?"

"We just did," I smiled weakly and continued shuffling meaningless folders around Cassandra's desk, "have a good night Mr. Richards."

It didn't feel right being so dismissive but I seriously needed some alone time.

"Alright," he said, standing up to leave, "let us know about Friday?"

"I will."

"And you're sure you're ok with everything?"

"Preston," I looked up from the desk and smiled. He was showing genuine concern and I felt like I should at least try and reassure him, "I appreciate your concern, I really do. And for the record, I apologize for the way I acted earlier. I had no business speaking to you the way I did." I paused for a second to make sure he knew I was being sincere.

"Now as for everything else," I continued with a smile, "I'm fine. I really am. And the last thing I want to do is be rude but I have a lot of work to do and I don't want to be here all night."

"Alright," he replied, apparently feeling better about the situation, "as long as you're sure."

"I am."

And with that, he picked up his cell phone and walked out the door.

I waited a few beats to make sure he wasn't coming back. When I was sure the coast was clear, I leaned as far back in the chair as I could, stared up at the ceiling and told myself I wasn't allowed to move until I figured out what the hell had just happened.

"Why are you sitting like that?"

There's nothing quite like the disapproving tone of a teenager to make you feel worse about yourself, even when you don't think that's possible.

"I was trying to remember something," I lied, quickly sitting up and trying to pull myself together.

"Well don't sit like that. You look like a weirdo."

"Thank you for the advice."

"Daddy wants to know if he can switch weekends from next week to this week."

"Why?"

"Aunt Kim's birthday."

Brian's sister had never been my favorite person, far from it, but Ashley adored her so I tried to keep my feelings to myself.

"That's fine," I said, gritting my teeth.

"What's with you two anyway?"

"Me and your aunt?"

"Yeah, it's obvious you guys hate each other."

I guess I should have tried a little harder...

"Hate is a strong word baby. We're just different people that's all."

"There's more to it than that."

"Not really, it just is what it is."

"You guys can't even be in the same room together."

"Ok, that's enough about me and your aunt. Tell your dad it's fine if he wants to switch weekends. Now are you ready?"

"Wait," she objected, ignoring my question, "what were you trying to remember?"

"Excuse me?"

"You said you were trying to remember something?"

For the daughter of a once prominent defense attorney, Ashley certainly had the memory and natural instincts of a prosecutor.

"If you're done with your interrogation counselor," I deflected, "you think we can get a move on? You still need to do your homework."

"Already done."

"Really?"

"Yep," she smiled proudly, "I only had Spanish and Cassie helped me before rehearsal."

"You mean Cassandra?"

"Mom, she told me I could call her Cassie."

"Ashley, the woman is almost seventy years old. Does she look like a Cassie to you?"

"She says it reminds her of Victor. He used to call her that."

Victor Manuelle Chavez was Cassandra's husband. They met as teenagers, got married before her twenty-first birthday and were married for forty-one years before he died eight years ago. In her own words, she had no idea what it would be like to live without Victor and wasn't interested in finding out.

A combination of family and faith helped her make it through that difficult time. But even after the shock and depression had faded enough for her to want to move on, she realized she didn't know what 'moving on' meant. She had no clue what to do with herself. That's when she decided to open the studio and even named it after him.

They raised four kids together, all of them girls, who danced all the way through high school. In that entire time, Victor never missed a single performance. Cassandra described him as a typical latin man in so many ways, full of machismo with more than a hint of chauvinism. Despite that, he absolutely loved watching their girls dance. It was his 'great joy' as she put it and so opening a dance studio in his name seemed like the perfect way for his family to honor his memory.

Victor's Academy of Dance was born of love and a father's lifelong commitment to his family.

Just when I thought I couldn't possibly feel any worse...

I had Ashley do a walk-through to make sure all of the studio doors were locked while I set the alarm. When we were done, I turned out the lights, locked the door and we walked out into the parking lot. Finally, it was time to go home, take a shower and put an end to this wretched day.

"Preston?!"

I looked up to see Ashley running over to greet my young lover, who was casually leaning on the hood of his car.

"Whoa," she said, as she reached his spot, "nice car!"

"It's my sisters," he volunteered casually.

"Mom, come check out Preston's car!"

"It's my sisters'," he repeated as I walked over to where they were standing.

"Ashley honey, time to say goodnight."

"What are you still doing here?" she asked, flexing her selective teenage hearing skills.

"I just need to talk to your mom real quick."

"Here," I handed Ashley my keys, "go wait in the car, I'll be right there." This time she decided she would hear what I said, did some kind of fist bump, jazz hand thing with Preston and ran off. When she was a safe distance away, I looked at him like he had grown two heads.

"Seriously?" I said sharply.

"Before you say any —"

"Look, I don't know what kind of milf, cougar, Mrs. Robinson fantasy you have playing in your head but come on Preston," I pleaded, "please don't be that guy."

He reached into his pocket and handed me an iPhone. "I took yours by accident."

"Oh."

"Mine was in my gym bag the whole time. I didn't even have it with me when —"

"Ok," I stopped him, "I get it."

"You're welcome," he smiled and went to get into his car.

"By the way," he said as I started walking, "I entered my number for you."

Before I could respond, he sped off.

Chapter Ten

If I knew switching weekends would mean me dropping Ashley off instead of Brian picking her up, I might have reconsidered. Don't get me wrong, it certainly wasn't out of bounds for him to ask. Aldan, where he lived, was only a fifteen minute drive and since he normally did both the picking up and dropping off, asking me to step up on this one occasion shouldn't have been a problem. And it wouldn't have been, if not for who would be waiting on the other end when we got there.

I had never been a fan favorite with Brian's family, even when things were good. They were these ultra conservative, religious types who honestly believed there was a 'real America' that existed in the fly-over states. It was no surprise they had trouble relating to an outspoken, liberal, agnostic from South Jersey. If that wasn't bad enough, by the time Brian and I started dating, I was a prominent criminal defense attorney who, when I wasn't freeing murderers and rapists from prison, was busy championing things like immigration reform and a woman's right to choose. Looking back, I'm surprised they didn't spontaneously combust when we told them we were getting married.

For the most part though, everyone was always cordial and treated me with respect. Everyone that is, except for my ex sister-in-law. While the rest of Brian's family was falling all over themselves to show how gracious and tolerant they could be in my presence, Kim made it clear she couldn't stand me and never felt a need to hide it. In a weird way, I always respected her for that.

Now let me be clear about something. To this day, I would love to see that nosy, self-righteous cunt get hit by a bus, even better if I could be the one doing the driving. But never let it be said that she was a phony. She was far from it. I knew exactly where I stood with Kim from the day we met. I had to give her that much.

"Did you call your father and tell him to meet us outside?"

"I texted him but he never texted me back."

"Did you try calling?"

"What's the difference?"

"Ashley please just call him."

The difference was that the last thing I wanted to do was get out of my car and have to deal with any of Brian's family, especially the guest of honor.

"No answer."

"Leave a message."

"Mom," she whined, "What's the big deal?"

I shot her a look, which she correctly interpreted as the signal to keep any additional commentary to herself.

"Hi daddy, mom wants you to meet us outside. I don't know why so don't ask me. I'm just doing what I'm told," she hung up.

"Ashley, I'm starting to have a little bit of a problem with your attitude."

"What?!" she exclaimed dramatically, "You told me to leave a message so I did! What is your problem?!"

"First of all young lady, you need to watch your tone. Secondly, when I ask you to do something, you need to do it, sans attitude. Understand?"

"Who are you," she muttered under her breath, "The Taliban?"

I slammed on the breaks hard enough to throw her forward in her seat. "Who I am Miss Mouth is your mother! Who I am is the person that pays the tuition for the school you love going to! I'm the one who puts food in your stomach, iPhones in your pocket and a fucking roof over your head! That's who I am! Who I'm NOT is someone you will disrespect, ever!"

Tears welled up in her eyes but she managed to keep it together, nod and look away. Satisfied I had made my point, I started driving again.

Ashley is a good kid but, like I said before, she had inherited my attitude. Genetics being what they are, that was pretty much unavoidable. What I could do for her, however, was make sure she knew how to keep her mouth in check before it got her into any real trouble.

It wasn't that big of a deal. Every child subconsciously seeks their boundaries, and this was just my opportunity to establish how far I was willing to tolerate my daughters increasingly smart-ass mouth. She needed to be reminded that, in spite of everything, I was still the mother and she was still my child. She also needed to be reminded that she wasn't in charge, at least not yet. Knowing that could one day save her life.

We made the rest of the drive in silence and arrived at the security gate without having heard back from Brian.

"Julie Sharpe and Ashley Watson here to see Brian Watson," I said as we pulled up to the guard.

"Hey Sam," Ashley smiled from the passenger seat.

95

"Well hey there Miss Ashley!" he smiled broadly, "how's the dancing coming?"

"Awesome, we rehearsed for an extra two hours tonight!"

"Well, you make sure I get a video of your show ok?"

"Ok, I will."

"Alright, ma'am." He stood up stepped aside. "You're all set. You know where to go?"

"I got it Sam," Ashley chimed in before I could say anything.

"Alright then, you folks enjoy the party." Sam opened the gate and we were on our way.

This was my third time driving to Brian's house but it still made me extremely uncomfortable. It was like traveling through time to a place that looked like my old life but, at the same time, felt completely foreign.

Aldan was one of the wealthiest communities in the nation that you've probably never heard of. It had always been that way and, over the last few years, the stock market had been exceptionally good to many of its old money inhabitants. Aldan was the kind of place hedge fund managers in New York or Los Angeles would speak of only in hushed tones, lest they risk being overheard and have to share an address with some nouveau riche Hollywood or professional athlete type. This was where the next generation of billionaire, republican, power brokers was being groomed for world dominance. God forbid their talent pool be diluted with the evil ghetto spawn of some reality star or professional football player.

Over the years, the city had become subdivided into a collection of over-the-top gated communities, each giving its own take on what it meant to own a piece of this prestigious zip code. Make no mistake though, regardless of which version of opulence you chose, if you lived in Aldan you were a member of the elite.

Brian chose Drexel Hill Commons, a newer subdivision situated around the Drexel Hill Golf and Country Club. It was the kind of place where I regularly negotiated plea deals back in my days as a high priced attorney. I always thought it was amazing what you could get a young ADA to agree to after eighteen holes, lunch and a few beers.

The houses were oversized with circular driveways and each lawn was more beautifully manicured than the next. Aside from the elaborate landscaping, Drexel Hill Commons was known for tree lined streets fitted with jogging paths AND bike lanes to keep the locals healthy and moving. If that wasn't enough, every home came with its own golf cart as a welcome to the community gift. Yep, this was the real America alright.

We pulled up to Brian's place and, of course, his driveway was packed with cars.

"You can just drop me off here if you want."

For a half second, I considered it. In the end, my inherent paranoia wouldn't allow me to leave without seeing her all the way into the house.

"Come on."

I parked my used toyota in front and walked Ashley past the impressive collection of luxury imports lining her fathers' driveway. Apparently Kim's birthday party was in full swing so, hopefully, she would be too busy to come to the door.

"Aunt Kimmy!"

No such luck...

"Oh my god girl, look at you! You're beautiful!"

"Happy Birthday!"

Ashley gave her aunt a big hug. They had always been close and hadn't seen each other in a while, so I faked a smile and patiently waited out their greeting

"Thank you sweetie." Kim said, "Now come on in and say hi to your grandma."

"Bye mom!"

Ashley excitedly ran into the house to be with her family, leaving me standing there with the one person on earth I hated more than myself.

"Kim," I said coldly, "here's Ashley's stuff —"

"I hear you got a new job?" she interrupted.

"And?"

"Answering phones or something?"

"Why do you care?"

She shook her head and smirked and all I could think about was smacking that crooked smile off her face and shoving it up her ass. Par for the course considering the last time I was this close to Kim Watson we got into a fist fight.

"Whatever I do or don't do is none of your business Kim. It never was."

"Oh, how the mighty have fallen," she cooed gleefully.

I am seriously about to kill this bitch...

"Where's your brother?" I asked impatiently, trying desperately not to lose my temper.

"I'm not sure," she smiled and took Ashley's bag, "I think he's taking out the trash, oh wait, he already did."

She slammed the door in my face and left me standing there seriously contemplating the merits of barging into my ex-husbands house and beating his kid sisters' ass in front of her whole family. As far as I'm concerned she had it coming, and not just for tonight.

I was long past the point of assigning blame to anyone other than myself for the things that happened to me and my family. But if I was the one who built the bomb that blew up my life, that cocky little stuck up bitch was the one who lit the fuse. And I would never forgive her for that.

To be honest, I don't know what I would've done if Ashley hadn't been there. Fortunately for me, and for Kim, she was. So I took a deep breath, regained what little composure I had left and walked to my car.

The drive home didn't do a damn thing to calm my nerves. At each stoplight I literally had to close my eyes, take another breath and resist the temptation to go back to Brian's house and commit felony assault.

When I got home, I went straight to the refrigerator, grabbed a bottle of wine and made a beeline for the bath tub. I figured the best way to avoid spending my night in a holding cell was to fully purge my brain and body of Kim's annoying voice and disgusting stench. And what better way to do that than to submerge myself in steaming hot water, surround myself with scented candles and down a glass or two of merlot? The way I saw it, nothing bad could come from any of those things. Besides, if it didn't work, I could always just go back and kill the bitch in her sleep.

Luckily the bath seemed to be doing the trick. For a few brief moments I was able to close my eyes and forget about, almost, everything. I guess warm water is only good for so much mental purging by itself. It was time for phase two.

I poured myself a glass of wine, took a small sip, followed by a bigger one and could literally feel the stressful thoughts fading from my consciousness.

I finished off that first glass and poured myself another, downing half of it in one shot. I closed my eyes, shifted my lower body forward and sank even deeper into blissful, quiet serenity. My world felt pretty damn close to perfect at that moment, as I surrendered myself into the comforting arms of my hot bath. My purge was just about complete.

Out of nowhere I felt a sudden rush of giddiness. I don't know if it was the wine, or the wine combined with the hot bath, or the fact that I hadn't eaten anything since breakfast. More than likely, it was a combination of all of the above. Whatever the cause, I didn't try to fight it.

An involuntary smile pursed my lips as the wave of euphoria seemed to settle in and take hold. I took another, longer, slower sip of wine and then sat my glass on the tile floor. I rested my head against the back of the tub and let the soothing warmth of the bath water take me even further away from the thoughts and worries that had been haunting me for the past week. Slowly, almost instinctively, I arched my back and allowed the subtly pulsating waves to caress my body. I slowly moved one hand around in the water to keep it moving rhythmically over my torso, while my other hand reached outside the tub for my glass. Desperately wanting to keep my eyes closed, for fear of breaking whatever spell had taken over my body, I fumbled gingerly around in darkness in search of my magic potion. What I found instead was my phone.

If I felt any hesitation at all, it was fleeting and not noticeable. After all of the selfish, and illegal, things I had done, this was as close to a victimless crime as I was gonna get.

"Hello?"

"How old are you?"

"Miss Sharpe?"

"I think maybe you can call me Julie at this point. Now answer my question."

"You think maybe you should start with hello?"

"Preston," I said as I finished off my glass, "do you wanna be a smartass or do you wanna get laid?"

"I'm twenty."

102

"You have a girlfriend?"

"What's with all the questions?"

"I don't need some pissed off coed showing up at my house. Now answer my question or I'm hanging up."

"No, I don't have a girlfriend."

"How close are you to 533 Clifton ave?"

"I can be there in twenty minutes."

"Make it fifteen or you're not getting in." I dropped the phone on the floor and poured myself another glass.

Chapter Eleven

I somehow managed to extract myself from bathtub bliss and made it into my bathrobe by the time there was a knock on the door.

I was also a glass and a half into my second bottle, but who's counting....

"Come in. Lock it behind you."

"Nice view," he commented, as I turned and walked into the living room.

My robe was short and I had given zero thought to putting anything on underneath it, so I was fully aware of the view to which he was referring.

"Have a seat."

I walked past the sofa, toward the kitchen to retrieve my glass. Another sip or two and I would have my way with...

Before I could finish the thought, his hands were around my waist.

Nicely done Preston...

I stopped in place and leaned back into him as he undid the belt of my robe and let it fall open. Having my naked body exposed to him like that made me feel vulnerable. Feeling his hands exploring me in ways he didn't get to the other night, made me want him to take me. That thought sent violent chills through my entire body. He started kissing my neck as I continued slowly, rhythmically grinding my ass into him. I wanted him to have more of me so I let my arms fall to my sides, dropping the robe to the floor.

On queue, he pushed me forward so that I was leaning on the counter.

Yes...take it...

His powerful hands gripped my waist firmly, holding me in place exactly where he wanted me.

I'm ready baby...

My legs were quivering in anticipation of the feeling of fullness that was only milliseconds away. I moaned softly, arched my back and made myself fully available to him. I was beyond hungry. I was ravenous. I felt as if every fiber of my being craved his penetration. I wanted to feel him reaching deep inside me. I wanted, no I needed him to take it. I felt myself trembling at the thought. My hands gripped the counter so tight my fingers started to feel numb. That's when it happened.

As I stood there, vulnerable and exposed, desperate to receive him, he gave himself to me in a way that defies description.

I felt his hands slowly moving down the front of my legs until, out of nowhere, he kneeled down, grabbed my legs and lifted my ankles up onto his shoulders. It happened so fast I didn't have a chance to physically respond, and just as I was about to look back and ask what the hell he was doing, I felt the most exquisite combination of warmth and wetness I had ever experienced.

I had been sexually active for more than twenty years. As an attorney, I had seen death row executions and, as a mother, I had experienced child birth. I can honestly say I had never made or heard sounds like the ones that came out of me the moment he put his mouth on me.

I screamed in what I can best describe as a combination of ecstasy and agony. His mouth, that amazing, beautiful, sexy as hell mouth, had just launched my entire body into simultaneous sensory overload. Every part of me came alive, all at once. It was all I could do to keep from passing out.

I wiggled and I squirmed and I reached back to pull him further into me as he continued patiently devouring my essence, awakening pleasure centers in places where I didn't know they existed.

From the rush of blood through my cheeks to a persistent tingling sensation that started behind my ears and traveled down through the tips of my toes. There wasn't a single part of me that wasn't on fire. Not one single cell.

Yesssss...

I felt him all over and in and through me. His hands massaging my ass while his mouth and tongue were working magic I didn't know was possible. It was like he was everywhere, doing everything, all at the same time.

The rush of sexual euphoria, mixed with four and a half glasses of red wine, made me feel sublime, unlike anything I'd experienced before. And while that first touch of his tongue was slightly overwhelming, he proceeded after that with a patience and restraint that made me feel I could trust him to take care of me.

Lick it baby...

I found his rhythm and started working my hips in concert with his tongue. He kept kissing and licking and sucking me until it felt like I was going to climb out of my skin. I shifted forward, not because I wanted him to stop, I just needed a moment. The physical sensation was unimaginable, but there was an intensity to our sex that I wasn't prepared for. I needed a second to gather myself. Preston wasn't having any of it.

He moved forward with me, until my knees were on his shoulders and went back to work. Then, to make sure I couldn't escape again, he stood up. *uuuuhhhhhhh...*

This sent me over the top. I tried to maintain some sense of control but the feeling was just too intense. I started squirming and wiggling and gyrating like I was possessed.

OOOOHHHHHH...

He held me in place as if I weighed nothing. His mouth and tongue, now focused on the perfect spot, began working me over with purpose. He knew what he wanted and he was going for it. Oh my god, he was doing it. He was taking me.

Oh god, Oh god, Oh god...

I had never felt so completely, so deliciously, out of control. It was like I had no say in what was being done to me OR in how I was reacting to it. My mind wasn't spinning out of control anymore. He was in full control of it.

Goddamn it!!

I closed my eyes tight, made a fist and pounded it on the counter as hard as I could. I then rested my head on my forearm and surrendered. Biting into my arm and arching my back, giving in, giving him what he wanted.

You want me to cum???

This wasn't like before. These weren't tingly little waves of electricity emanating from my core. These were full tidal waves of soul shaking ecstasy taking over my whole body.

Oooohh Fuck...

I tried to consciously ride the waves but I wasn't in control of my body any more than I was in control of my mind at that point. I literally started crying as the intensity of what I was feeling physically overwhelmed me emotionally.

Oh Oh OOOOOh...

My legs shot straight up in the air and started shaking violently. My hips went crazy, grinding into his face uncontrollably. But he wasn't fazed. He was strong. He was so damn strong.

uuuuhhhhhhh...

My clenched fist involuntarily shot open, as if three years of pent-up sexual energy were escaping my body through my fingertips. My mouth dropped open and my eyes rolled into the top of my head.

Hoooollllllyyyyyy fuuuuck...

The entire sequence repeated itself several times and I rode every amazing wave until the violent earthquakes gradually turned into the kind of convulsions I was more familiar with. I kept grinding myself into his face until there was nothing left for me to give. Nothing except the tears.

I tried to stop myself from crying. I really did. But it was useless and once I realized there was nothing I could do, the flood gates were opened en masse. I felt the weight of everything, Cassandra, Ashley, Brian, Kim, The Studio, everything. All of it came crashing down on me at once and I couldn't stop it. I didn't want to be this out of control. Not with him. Not like this. But it was too late to fight it. I just let it go.

I collapsed to the floor as my body went about the business of purging itself of despair. I didn't even have the strength to fight it when he bent down to pick me up. I just buried my face in his chest and let him carry me into my bedroom.

• • •

That's weird...

Like any mom whose child spent the night away from home, I made it a point to check for missed calls or texts the moment I woke up whenever Ashley stayed at Brian's. Only this time, when I reached for my phone, it wasn't in its normal spot.

I felt around under the covers to see if I had fallen asleep with it next to me or something. No luck.

Hmmm...

Like a lot of people, I had a pretty set bed time routine that included plugging my phone into its charger and setting it on the nightstand next to my bed. I especially made a point of this on those nights when Ashley was at her dads, so it was definitely out of character for me to forget, much less to have no idea where it was.

I gingerly dragged myself out of bed and checked the floor around the nightstand. No luck.

I tried to think, a process that would have been a lot easier if I hadn't made the brilliant decision to down a bottle of red wine the night before. Oh well, I could berate myself later. Right now, throbbing headache aside, I needed to focus on finding my phone because, like most people in the digital age, I was lost without it.

My iPhone was also my alarm clock, my radio, my morning newspaper and, generally speaking, my connection to the outside world. Without it, I had no idea what time it was, how my daughter was doing, or if world war three had started while I was passed out drunk. Most importantly right now, I didn't have Siri to tell me the most effective remedy for a merlot induced hangover.

I staggered into the bathroom, where a brief glance in the mirror verified I looked every bit as much the train wreck as I felt. I did, however, happen to

111

see my phone sitting on the floor next to tub and an empty wine bottle. I picked up the phone and checked my messages. I had one text.

Call me P.

I stood there frozen as the memory of everything that happened the night before started playing on a loop in my brain. Every mortifying minute.

I sat down on the side of the tub and debated everything from leaving town to running down to the Verizon store and changing my number. Eventually I decided the best thing to do was deal with the situation head on.

I brushed my teeth, cleaned myself up as much as I could and flopped down on the sofa to make my call of shame. I was just about to press 'send' when I looked over and noticed my robe on the floor beside the kitchen counter. Despite myself, I couldn't stop from smiling at one more, extremely vivid memory from the night before.

Talk about getting something behind me...

I shook off the distraction and went to make the call but, for some reason, found myself hesitating.

I thought for a second and realized, I had no idea what I was going to say.

"What's up dude? Thanks for the incredible sex but I don't think we should see each other anymore. Peace out."

Some, hopefully more mature, version of that might actually work, save for the fact that I wasn't entirely sure we were technically seeing each other.

I couldn't help but laugh at the ridiculousness of my situation. Not only did I drunk dial my daughters twenty year old dance teacher for a booty call, but the kid turns out to be some kind of sex ninja. Most twenty somethings are lucky if they know which hole to put it in, but this guy shows up and gives me the most mind blowing orgasm I'd ever experienced.

MMMMM...

Even the thought of it sent small chills through my body. I lied back on the sofa and closed my eyes, wanting to briefly indulge my mind as it travelled back in time to just the right...

My thoughts were interrupted by my phone. It was Preston.

"Hello." I noticed my mouth felt dry.

Bitch are you nervous?

"Hey," he responded, "you doing ok over there?"

"I'm fine." I sat up on the sofa and tried to relax. "I was just about to call you."

"Grab a coffee with me?"

"Preston I don't know if that's such a good idea."

"Why not?"

"Well, I kinda think we need to talk about last night."

"And we can't do that over a latte or whatever caffeinated beverage you prefer? Besides," he laughed, "I'm pretty sure a cup of coffee might do you some good right about now. And maybe some aspirin?"

"I'm glad my agony is a source of amusement for you."

"Hey, that's just the cost of doing business. So we on or not?"

"Fine," I relented, "Bristol Cafe in a half hour."

I hung up, tossed the phone aside and stared at the ceiling.

WTF are you doing Julie??

I could have easily recited ten reasons meeting Preston Richards for a cup of coffee this morning was a horrible idea. The problem was none of those could explain the huge smile on my face.

Chapter Twelve

I chose the Bristol because it was so close and because I knew it wouldn't be terribly crowded on a Saturday morning. Confidence is key in any sensitive discussion or negotiation and rule number one for establishing confidence is to control the real estate. I should've been able to throw something on and easily make it to our meeting place before Preston did. Arriving first would allow me to choose where we sat and set myself up comfortably by the time he walked in the front door. That was the plan anyway.

But that was before I suffered through three humiliating wardrobe changes and an extra fifteen minutes trying to undo as much of the damage from the previous night as possible. I had no idea why I was treating this like a date when it so clearly wasn't one. I was there to quietly, respectfully, put an end to this thing with young

Preston before it got out of hand. That's it. It shouldn't matter what I was wearing or what my face looked like. At least that's what I told myself as I checked my makeup in the mirror of my car after arriving at the Bristol fifteen minutes late.

"I'm surprised you're not still in bed," he said with a smile, as he saw me enter.

I thought I was having some kind of weird deja vous moment until I realized he was sitting in the exact seat I was sitting in when I met my sweaty uncle. Hopefully this date would turn out better than that one.

This is not a date Julie...

"I got you a black coffee."

"How did you know?"

"You don't seem like the macchiato type."

"I'll take that as a compliment."

"That's what it is."

Focus Julie. And stop smiling...

"Listen," I said sitting down across from him, "I'm really sorry about —"

"Don't apologize," he interrupted, "We've all been there."

"So you've had an emotional breakdown during sex?"

"Ok," he laughed, "you've got me there. But I have been pretty wasted once or twice."

"I wasn't that drunk." I smiled sheepishly, even I couldn't pull of that lie.

Before he could respond, his phone started buzzing.

"You need to get that?"

"Nah, it's just my sister. I'll call her back."

He reached over and silenced his phone.

Whoa...

"Nice watch."

"Thanks, now where were —"

"Can you grab me a couple sugars?" I asked before he could finish.

"Sure," he smiled eagerly, "How many?"

"Two should be good."

He stood up and walked over to where the sugar packets were, allowing me to get a good look at his jeans.

Shit...

He came back to the table and handed me my sugar packets. As he sat down his phone started buzzing.

"Your sister again?"

"Probably yeah," he mumbled as he shut it off.

"Maybe she needs her car?"

"What?"

"I saw her car parked out front. The same one you were driving the other night. It's hers right?"

"Oh, yeah. No, she doesn't need the car right now."

"So," I said evenly, "what does your sister do?"

"She's a hairdresser."

I had done this enough times in my past life that I could clearly see he was uncomfortable with this particular line of questioning

"You guys close?"

"Ok," he said, "you're starting to freak me out. Why the sudden interest in my sister?"

I just shook my head in disgust, stood up and grabbed my purse.

"Goodbye Mr. Richards."

I walked out the door without giving him a chance to respond. I don't know what pissed me off more, the fact that he lied or that I was too stupid to see it before.

"What the fuck?!"

I looked back to see him running after me.

"Let it go Preston," I said without breaking my stride, "I don't have time for this."

"What the hell are you talking about?" he asked as he caught up.

I kept walking as I answered.

"Those jeans you're wearing are APO's. They retail starting at about a thousand dollars for the economy version, and you're not wearing the economy version."

"Ok wait," he said as he continued after me, "at least let me explain."

"I don't wanna hear it Preston. That Bvlgari Chronograph you're wearing goes for over fifteen-thousand dollars. I know because I bought one for my ex-husband a few years ago. Oh and by the way, what kind of hairdresser drives an eighty thousand dollar car?"

"Ok," he acknowledged, "but it's not like that. Let me explain."

I stopped walking and turned to him.

"Are your parents rich?"

"No, but —"

"Are you a famous rapper?"

"No."

"Singer? Actor?"

"No, nothing like that but —"

"Goodbye Preston." I started walking again

"Would you hold up a minute?! You don't know the whole story!"

"The only thing I need to know is that I am a single mother of a thirteen year old girl and I can't afford to be associated with whatever kind of drug dealing drama you've got going on in your life."

He caught up and grabbed me by the wrist.

"Is that what you think?"

"I don't think anything! I know you are a full time college student with a part time job teaching hip

119

hop dance classes three nights a week, and you're driving an eighty thousand dollar car that you lied about being your sisters. I don't need the calculator on my phone to tell me that shit doesn't add up."

"Ok, I get what you're saying," he responded, "but it's not like that. It's all legit."

"You're standing in front of me right now wearing almost twenty thousand dollars worth of clothing and you're telling me whatever you're doing to afford it is legitimate?"

"I'm saying I'm not doing anything illegal. At least I don't think I am."

"What?"

"Can we please just go somewhere and not do this out here?"

"Preston, we don't have to do this at all."

"ok, ok," he said before I could turn and start walking again, "It's gonna sound weird I know, but I um, I'm kinda like a bank."

"You're a what?"

"A bank. Listen, I know it sounds crazy but if you just hear me out I promise you'll see it's really nothing like what you're thinking."

"If I hear you out, do you promise to leave me alone and never call me again?"

"If that's what you want, then yes I promise. All I need is fifteen minutes."

"You have ten."

Chapter Thirteen

I let him into my car so we could speak privately.
"Let's hear it."

"Ok, it's um, it's actually kinda funny when you think about it."

I rolled my eyes. There was no way this stammering idiot was the same guy that had rocked my world the night before. I suddenly found myself feeling embarrassed.

"You have nine minutes."

"Alright, ok, just listen. You've heard of Aldan right?"

"The city?"

"Yeah, well I grew up in Prospect Park but I went to Aldan Heights my junior and senior year."

Prospect Park was to Aldan what The Bronx was to the Upper East Side, and Aldan Heights was probably the most exclusive school in the area. None of the schools in Aldan put much emphasis on athletics, so there really was no opportunity for a kid from the wrong zip code to get in at all, much less to transfer in their junior year.

"How'd you manage that?"

"My dad worked for a City Councilman so he knew a few people. Plus, I scored off the charts on some test and —"

"Ok," I cut him off, "I get it, move it along."

"Well anyways, people always think because they're a bunch of trust fund babies that the kids in Aldan don't get into shit. They're wrong."

"Get to the point Preston," I said, losing patience.

"Ok, so one of my best friends was a kid named Ira Benson. Ira used to sell his moms pain meds to his friends at parties —"

"And let me guess," I interjected, "your buddy Ira asked you to help him with distribution?"

"What?! No! Nothing like that at all."

"Then what Preston?! You're running out of time."

"Alright, well obviously selling your moms pain pills is pretty much a cash business right?"

"And?"

"And since Ira had been getting into trouble since before he could walk, his parents kept a real close eye on him."

"Obviously not close enough," I said sarcastically.

"Ok I guess you're right, but the point is Ira didn't want to keep his extra cash in his house because he was afraid his mom or dad might find it."

"So he gave it to you to hold for him?"

"Exactly."

"How much money are we talking about?"

"Well, when it was just me and Ira we're only talking about, at most, a few hundred here or there. No big deal."

"Ok, so how do you go from holding two or three hundred bucks in a sock for your buddy, to wearing a fifteen-thousand dollar watch?"

"First of all it was an envelope, not a sock. And secondly, Ira, being the natural born entrepreneur he was, realized I was an asset he could pimp out to all of his other shady ass friends. I mean, he was just into selling off some of his moms Vicodin for walking around money, you know? But some of his boys? They were into some much more serious shit."

"Like what?"

"That's the beauty of it for me. I have no idea and I don't really give a shit. They do what they do and I hold onto their cash for them. That's the sum total of my involvement. That plus ten percent of whatever they give me to hold."

"But why you?" I asked, my curiosity growing, "I mean, I can see Ira asking you to help him out. He was your friend and we're not talking about all that much money. But why would these other guys trust you?"

"Trust is definitely too strong a word. They don't even know me and have no intention of ever meeting me."

"Because," I interjected, "if the worst ever happened and there was any sort of connection, their money would be at risk."

"Exactly," he smiled, "the whole thing works because I am a complete stranger to them."

I had to admit it was fairly inspired. Every low life throughout history, from the mid-level drug dealer to the high profile mafia don, thought they had figured out the perfect way to hide their ill-begotten gains.

Back in the old days, it was common practice to simply bury it somewhere in a suitcase or plastic bag. If that was too primitive, they would just give it to a trusted relative, like an elderly aunt or distant cousin. Of course, if they were in the really big leagues, they would hire a consultant and hide the cash overseas somewhere.

The point is none of it worked, ever. The feds always, and I do mean always, found every single penny. I had seen it a thousand times in my old line of work. Between the IRS, the Secret Service, and the FBI's forensic accounting units, every crook I ever had the pleasure of doing business with ended up virtually bankrupt if they made it onto the governments radar. All the Feds needed was the flimsiest of connections and your money was as good as theirs.

And that's why what Preston was describing could work, at least in theory. If he truly had no connection to any of the people he was providing this service for, the Feds could look all they wanted. As long as he remained a complete and total stranger to the people he was holding for, he would be virtually invisible to the feds or anybody else trying to find their money trail. All they had to do was make sure they never crossed paths with anyone even remotely connected to Preston Richards and their money would be safe.

"Ok," I said, "I have a few questions."

More than a few...

"Shoot."

"Before we get into that, you do realize you have a flaw in your setup right?"

"What do you mean?"

"Well, your buddy Ira is still sorta your middle man right?"

"If you wanna call him that, yeah."

"Preston, that's what he is, at least the way you described. You might not have to meet or interact with any of his friends, but HE still does. And then he, in turn, interacts with you. You see what I'm getting at?"

"I do, but I haven't seen or spoken directly to Ira since we graduated high school."

"Then how does he get you the cash?"

"He just does. I'd rather not say exactly how."

Young Preston might be smarter than I thought...

"Ok, that's fair, but that doesn't change my point."

"Yeah but remember," he protested, "I only went to Aldan for two years so there was only like an eighteen month window where anybody could even argue that we even knew each other."

"That's all well and good but there's still a connection with not that many degrees of separation. Trust me Preston, somebody looking hard enough will find that connection. You're vulnerable. You may not think so but believe me, you are."

"No I get it," he admitted, "but I'm not really all that worried about it. I mean, it's not like I'm doing anything illegal or anything."

Nope, I was wrong...

"Excuse me?"

"That's the other reason this works, I have to stay vanilla."

"Vanilla?"

"No record, no warrants or anything like that. I have to stay completely out of the system and as far off the grid as possible."

"Ok, but you can't possibly believe what you just said."

"About it being illegal?"

"Yes."

"You're the lawyer, you tell me."

"Well," I paused, "I guess, in a way, you're right."

"So I'm not breaking the law?"

"Technically no, you're not breaking A law, you're breaking at least five that I can think of."

I spent the next fifteen minutes explaining to Preston how he was looking at anywhere from seven years to life in prison if this thing ever blew up on him. The entire time I was talking his phone was buzzing, but I was on a roll and he was hanging on my every word. His sister would just have to wait.

"You see what I'm saying?"

It was a rhetorical question. I could see by the look on his face that he was absolutely scared shitless. His phone started buzzing again.

"Wow," he said softly, "so what should I do?"

"Well, you should probably start by taking a deep breath and answering your phone."

"It's just my sister. I'll call her back."

"She's been calling non-stop for twenty minutes."

"Yeah, but I know what she wants. It can wait."

I just looked at him.

"Seriously, I'm not lying!" he insisted, "she wants to borrow some money."

"And what's the problem?"

"There's no problem. It's just that she wants to use it to open her own salon and I have to be careful with stuff like that."

"Stuff like what?"

"That's the other part of this deal. I can't ever show too much cash."

"And yet you drive an eighty-thousand dollar Mercedes?"

"Our father passed away last year so I could justify the car with the life insurance money. The watch and the jeans are legitimate gifts I got for a music video I choreographed for Wiz Khalifa."

"Wiz what?"

"Never mind," he laughed, "the point is I have to be real careful about flashing too much cash and my sister opening a hair salon could draw the wrong kind of attention."

"Wait, does your sister know what you do?"

"God no," he answered quickly, "as far as she's concerned I get all of my money from doing choreography and teaching classes. You're the only person I've ever told."

Shit...

"Preston, I need to be clear about something and I need you to listen to me carefully."

"Ok."

"I am not an attorney anymore so nothing you say to me is, in any way, privileged. What that means is I could be compelled to testify against you if things ever went bad for you. I need to know you understand that before you tell me anything else."

"Fine, I understand," he said impatiently, "now would you please just tell me what to do?"

"How much money are we talking?"

"I'd rather not say."

"Is it more than ten-thousand."

He just laughed.

"More than a hundred-thousand?"

"Let's just say, it's more than you think."

"Ok, fair enough."

I paused for a minute to gather my thoughts. Young Preston had gotten himself in WAY over his head and now he was sitting in my office, I mean car, desperate for me to give him a way out. I could feel his eyes burning a hole through my brain as he waited for the great Julie Sharpe esq. to hand him his golden parachute. This all felt way too familiar.

Except this time I didn't have the wall of attorney client privilege to hide behind. That would be a problem. The longer I continued this conversation, the more exposed I became. The smart thing to do, the responsible thing, would be to cut this off right here, advise Preston to get a good lawyer and then never speak to him again. That is absolutely what I should have done under the circumstances. Hell, I had Ashley to think about and just knowing what he already told me was enough to make me an accessory after the fact. My daughter needed me and I did not want to be in the business of letting her down ever again. I knew all of that and yet, I also knew I had no intention of walking away.

I could say I liked Preston and wanted to help him and, technically, I would be telling the truth. But that's not what this was about. None of that is why I was so willing to go out on this particular limb. And no it wasn't about the money, although this was clearly a way to dig myself out from the rather large hole I had put myself in. This was about one, undeniable fact. I missed the action.

As I was sitting in my beat up old car, next to my young sex ninja turned wannabe underworld financier, my brain was spinning back to life in a way it hadn't worked in years. I had honestly forgotten what it felt like to be pushed to my intellectual limit with the stakes this high, and believe me, the stakes didn't get much more real than this.

I screw this up, I get arrested, lose my daughter forever and end up in a cell right along with Preston for the better part of twenty years.

But if I do this right, everything would be different. I was never going to get my old life back, I had already accepted that. But this could give me a chance to build a new one, maybe even a better one.

The bottom line is I felt alive in a way I didn't think would ever happen for me again. Like an addict who just had my first line of coke in years, I was overcome by the familiar sensation of adrenaline pumping through me. I was about to risk everything I had, but that was ok, because I would be betting on myself and I always liked those odds.

I remembered this feeling. I liked it. I missed it. There was no way in hell I was going to walk away from it.

"Well?" he said, snapping me out of my trance, "what should I do?"

"What if I told you there was a way to protect yourself and stay in business?"

"I'm listening."

"First, let's take a ride." I started my car. "I want you to see something."

Game on...

Chapter Fourteen

There are some, ex-inmates mostly, who describe prison as a sort of crime school. The theory is, if you spend twenty-four hours a day surrounded by nothing but criminals, you don't get rehabilitated. You become a better criminal.

Having never been to prison, at least as a resident, I couldn't speak to whether or not that was true. What I could say, is that if any intelligent person spent enough time around someone who excelled at something, it would be impossible to not pick up a few things. Given enough time and access, even the most ignorant person in the world would have to learn a little something. I had been a lot of things in my life. Ignorant was never one of them.

Up until a few years ago, I spent most of my days working side by side with some of the most notorious thieves, drug dealers and murderers to ever walk the earth. I'm not talking about gang bangers and shoplifters. I'm talking about some of the smartest, most cunning individuals you could find.

Don't get me wrong, I had to represent my share of low level thugs in the beginning, but once I made a name for myself, I moved up the food chain and into the all boys club of elite defense attorneys who represented the FBI's most wanted. And I stayed there. From that point on, all of my clients had one thing in common. They were all extraordinarily good at what they did.

"Um," Preston said, looking around nervously, "where are you taking me?"

I just smiled.

"Seriously," he said, "w here are we going?"

"Would you calm down. You've never been to Winnfield before?"

"Not on purpose, no."

"Well we're almost there, you can relax."

Not that he didn't have reason to feel tense. Winnfield was a pretty rough place, seemingly immune to the wave of gentrification that was taking hold in so many of the other surrounding cities.

Only fifteen minutes south of the fully gentrified Bristol, Winnfield might as well have been in a different universe. Where Bristol now had tree lined streets, filled with boutiques and cafes,

Winnfield remained a despondent maze of abandoned buildings, burnt out row homes and the occasional Laundromat or liquor store. Where Bristol's streets, cafes and shops were teeming with young coeds excited about their future and middle aged intellectuals determined to solve the problems of today, Winnfield's corners were occupied by tough looking teenagers for whom hope was an urban legend and life or death decisions were a part of the daily routine.

An especially angry looking group of four gave Preston and I an intense stare-down as I turned onto Sharon avenue, arriving at our destination. These local kids could spot an outsider from a mile away, and outsiders weren't exactly welcomed in a place like Winnfield.

"What's this?" he asked nervously, as I stopped the car.

"That," I said, pointing across the street, "is A Touch of Class Hair and Nails."

"I can read the sign thank you. Why'd you bring me to a beauty salon in the hood?"

"I brought you to a drug front."

"A what?"

"That sad little beauty salon, in this miserable, depressed neighborhood, is actually a front for one of the biggest, most notorious drug cartels in all of Mexico."

"How do you know that?"

"Old client of mine."

"So they wholesale drugs out the back or something?

"No, they actually do hair," I answered dryly, "nails too apparently."

"So then why the hell are we here about to get carjacked? What the hell does a hair salon in Winnfield have to do with drugs from Mexico?"

"Not a damn thing."

I just looked at him. It took a few seconds longer than I hoped for his expression to go from agitated to enlightened, but it was still cool to watch. It was like I could literally see the wheels turning in his head.

Maybe there was hope for young Preston after all...

"Oh," he said, turning to look again at the salon, this time with a new appreciation for what he was seeing.

"Exactly," I smiled, "this business exists for one purpose and one purpose only. To take dirty money in off the street and send clean money back out the door."

"And it's owned by drug dealers?"

Calling these guys dealers was like comparing a mountain lion to a house cat, but that was a lesson for another day.

"Technically, yes, but you'd never be able to prove that on paper. That's the point Preston, the guys with the money that opened that salon have no visible connection to it at all."

"And even though that's how they make their money," he interjected, "no drug of any kind will ever come within a mile of this place."

"Not unless somebody wants to lose a limb."

He laughed but I wasn't kidding. The Mexican cartels were infamously violent, and this one was known for decapitating their enemies and chopping off the hands of anyone caught stealing.

"So," he asked, "how does it work?"

"We'll get into the how later. For now I just wanna focus on the 'why'.

"Which is?"

"Preston, in order for this place to serve its intended purpose, the owners can't afford to have it land on anyone's radar."

"So no drugs or anything else illegal goes down here. I get that."

"Forget just illegal. Nothing that is in any way interesting is allowed to take place anywhere near that building. Not so much as a bootleg dvd gets in the door. In other words it has to stay as 'vanilla' as possible."

"Just like my situation."

"The advantage they have is that once the money comes out the other side, it's free and clear."

"So you're saying I should give my sister the money she wants and use her salon for the same thing?"

"Well, yes and no."

"What do you mean?"

"Yes, you could do sort of the same thing but no I wouldn't try and use your sister's place for it."

"Why not?"

"Mostly because you'd have to tell her what you're doing, but also because she would still have to justify where she got the money, and that, like you said, might attract the wrong kind of attention."

"So what are you suggesting?"

I started the car. It was time to show young Preston the how.

• • •

I pulled up in front of the Bristol Cafe and parked behind Preston's Mercedes.

"You know where Citizens National is on 5th and Oak?"

"Yeah."

"There's a Party City in the strip mall across the street. I need you to go and get five thousand dollars in cash and meet me in the costume aisle in twenty minutes."

"Party City?"

"Is that a problem?"

"No, it's just not what I expected."

"It'll make sense when we're done, trust me."

"Ok, but why can't we just go together?"

He had a LOT to learn...

"Because the less I know about the physical specifics of what you're doing, the better it is for both us."

"You already know pretty much everything."

"I don't know where you keep your cash or how much of it there is."

"I see your point."

"Besides," I said and unlocked the doors, "I have to go take care of something before we get back together."

Preston got out of the car and I pulled away.

• • •

Right on schedule, he walked up to me in the costume aisle of Party City. He looked noticeably more relaxed than when I left him twenty minutes earlier, which is good. That meant he was trusting me. I smiled and handed him an envelope.

"Put this in your pocket."

"What is it?" he asked, doing as he was told.

"Here," I ignored his question and handed him a few masks from the shelf in front of us, "hold these."

I picked up a few other items and walked toward the checkout lane.

"What the hell are we doing?" he whispered.

"Just shut up and give me those."

I took the masks from him.

"Now," I said evenly, "let me pay for this stuff and then we'll hit the bank."

"Together?"

"Yep."

"But I thought —"

"Let's try and not do too much of that."

We checked out and walked into the parking lot. I handed him the bag of merchandise from the store and pulled out my keys.

"Let's go in my car," I said.

We got in and drove across the street to the bank where I pulled into a spot off to the side.

"Where's the cash?"

He handed me a plain white envelope.

"Lemme guess," I said, "All hundreds?"

"Yeah, why?"

I rolled my eyes.

"We'll discuss that later. Sit tight, I'll be right back."

I went inside and made the deposit. When I returned, He looked at me expecting some sort of explanation. I ignored him, drove back over to Party City and pulled up beside his car. He was still staring at me.

"What?"

"What just happened?" he asked, starting to sound annoyed.

"Calm down," I laughed, "do you still have the envelope I gave you?"

"Yea."

"Give it to me."

He handed it to over.

"Preston," I started to explain, "what happened at the bank is a five thousand dollar deposit into the account of Victor's Academy of Dance."

"Ok, and?"

"And what you just handed me are three invoices, one for each of the next three months, totaling four-thousand and ninety dollars. Those invoices are for services rendered in relation to our winter recital."

"I'm lost."

I love it when they're new...

"Preston, it's called laundering for a reason. You just handed me five-thousand dollars in dirty money that you had to keep hidden, and the studio is going to pay you four-thousand and ninety dollars in legit, clean funds that you can use however you like."

"Ah," he said as yet another light bulb turned on for him, "bad money in, good money back out."

"Exactly."

"Just that simple?"

"That depends. How much money are we talking?"

"Why does that matter?"

This was the second time I asked him how much money he was dealing with and both times he had gotten nervous, and defensive. My radar was officially up.

"Well," I said, "if this is a one-time thing with five thousand dollars, then yea it's that simple. But I have a feeling there's a bit more involved than that."

"Yeah, a little bit," he smiled sheepishly.

"Why are you being so evasive?"

"I don't know. This is all just moving kinda fast you know?"

"Just ballpark it. I'm not looking for exact numbers."

He paused for a moment before deciding to answer.

"Over a million."

I let the words hang out there for a few seconds to make sure he wasn't joking, and that I wasn't hallucinating.

"What did you just say?"

"All totaled, a little over one million dollars."

"And how much of that is yours?"

"All of it."

"But wait," I said quickly, "I thought you only took ten percent?"

"That is ten percent."

It took a second or five for that to sink in.

"So you're telling me you are holding over ten million dollars in cash?"

"A little less, but close, yeah."

"And it never occurred to you to ask your buddy where any of this money comes from?!"

"Why would it?"

I shook my head in disbelief and started having second, third and fourth thoughts all at the same time. Whatever this kid and his friend were into was a lot more serious than I thought and I started to feel like this was just the tip of the iceberg. The kind of money he was talking about was the kind of money people got killed over.

"Preston, nobody generates that kind of cash selling prescription pills at house parties. You need to know the kind of people you're involved with."

"It's really not that serious."

What?!

"Ten million dollars is not that serious?"

"First of all, it's not all from one person. Second, this is Aldan we're talking about. A half million dollars is a graduation gift for some of those hedge fund babies."

He had a point but I still didn't like what I was hearing. Regardless of who or where it came from, hiding ten million dollars implied a level of sophistication I just couldn't see at that point. Preston seemed like a smart kid, but he was nowhere near sharp enough to pull this off, not without major help. So either he had someone pulling the strings that he didn't want to tell me about, or that he didn't know about. Either way, there was another piece to this puzzle I wasn't seeing and that's what was making me so uncomfortable. I had been around this block enough times to know it was always the things you couldn't see that came back to kick you in the ass.

Fortunately, it wasn't too late to back out and walk away without getting in any deeper. Thanks to young Preston, I had, kinda-sorta, solved my temporary financial problem and, in return, I had given him a beginners guide to money laundering. As of right now this was a win/win for everybody.

"What are you thinking?"

I was so lost in my own thoughts his voice startled me.

"Preston, I'm starting to think this might not be a good idea for me."

"But why not?"

He sounded genuinely disappointed.

"Well, the more I think about it, the more I realize how much I don't know about what I'm about to get involved in. And in my experience that is always a sure recipe for disaster."

"Come on Julie," he pleaded, "what more is there to know?"

"It's not any one thing. Your system makes perfect sense for fifty or sixty grand, maybe a hundred thousand tops. But you're sitting there telling me you have ten million dollars of illegal cash hidden in your bedroom somewhere? Come on."

"Ok," he admitted, "It's a little more involved than I —"

"Exactly," I interrupted, "which means the chances that you or your buddy haven't been as smart or as careful as you think grow exponentially. For all I know, you're already being watched."

"No way."

"See?! That's exactly what I'm talking about! You think you're the first so-called genius I've met who thinks he's running two laps ahead of everybody else, only to realize, too late, that he was running two steps behind the whole time? You're not original Preston, you're a goddamn walking cliche!"

"Then help me! Let's say you're right and I'm as clueless as you say. Then why not help me figure it out?"

Before I could respond my phone rang. It was Kim.

"Kim," I answered, "is Ashley ok?"

"Oh yea, Ashley's fine."

"Then I'm kind of in the middle —"

"I just wanted to know if I could take her shopping."

"What?"

"We want to go shopping and Brian told me to make sure you were ok with it."

The sound of her voice was annoying enough, now she was taking to asking me dumb questions. "Why would I not be?"

"Well," she said smugly, "I know things haven't been easy for you and I just didn't want you to feel undermined. You know, seeing as I'm doing things for your daughter that you can't."

146

You bitch!

"Kim," I said as calmly as I could, "if you would like to take your niece shopping, then feel free. As for what I can or cannot do for MY daughter, that is none of your fucking business."

I hung up.

"Everything ok?"

"Yeah, I'm fine. Look Preston, I have to go so —"

"But wait. What about what we were talking about?"

"What about it?"

"You going to help me or not?"

"I'm sorry, it's just not worth it for me right now."

"Not even for twenty percent?"

"What?"

I was still distracted with thoughts of choking out my ex sister-in-law and was only half paying attention to young Preston and his drama at this point.

"I gave you five grand and you are gonna give me back four."

"And?"

"That's twenty percent. A thousand bucks for fifteen minutes work. You telling me you can't use the money?"

"I'm telling you that thousand dollars was a one-time transaction fee."

"Then how much gets you to do more?"

"Fifty."

"Fifty grand? Hell yeah, that's a done —"

"Fifty Percent."

"What?! Hell no! No way. You can go fuck yourself for fifty percent."

"Ok, have it your way." I unlocked the doors so he could get out. "Good luck staying out of prison." He didn't move.

"There a problem Mr. Richards?"

"Thirty percent."

"Preston, I'm sorry if I gave you the wrong impression, but this is not a negotiation. You will give me what I am asking for or you will get the hell out of my car and try to figure things out on your own."

"Why are you being such a bitch?"

I smiled.

"If that's what you call looking out for my own interests, then I guess that's what I am."

"Fifty percent is a lot of fucking money Julie"

"How much good is any of that money gonna do you if you're locked up in prison getting ass raped for the next twenty years?"

He laughed.

"You think I'm joking? Then you go back out there on your own and see for yourself. I will tell you this much though, it's obvious you have NO fucking idea what you're doing and yet you have

148

this arrogance like you've got it all figured out. Like I said before, you're not all that original Preston. I've seen this movie many times, and it always ends badly."

He sat silently for a moment before responding.

"And what do I get in return for half my money?"

Got em...

"For fifty percent of your illegal cash, you get one hundred percent of your freedom. I'm offering you a way out Preston, and yes that costs. But believe me when I say, it costs a helluva lot less than the alternative."

"Fine, fifty percent it is. Wanna shake on it?"

I smiled.

"I have a better idea."

Chapter Fifteen

I realized something as I sat on the edge of my bed waiting for Preston to remove his shirt. We had been intimate twice in less than a week and I had never once seen his eyes.

"Wait," I said and moved over, "come lie down next to me."

He did as asked and I took a moment to just look into his eyes. I loved the way he just let me take the lead when we were together. I'm sure at least some of that had to do with his being twenty years old. At that age he was probably just happy to be getting some and didn't want to screw it up. Still it was remarkable how he was able to patiently let me take what I needed, with no thought of himself.

His eyes were green, and kind. There was a sincerity to them that couldn't be faked, a sense of vulnerability that made me feel instantly closer to him. I found myself wanting to protect him. I wanted to take care of him.

I pulled him into me and yielded my lips to his. I opened my mouth, allowing his tongue to reach for mine as my hands explored his tight, muscular, twenty year old frame.

Our lips separated just long enough for him to help remove my shirt. We found each other again as I took off my pants and, just like that, we were completely naked together. Another first for us.

I rolled onto my back and pulled him on top of me. The feeling of his body weight pressing down against me felt, in a word, perfect. I felt safe and warm in a way I had forgotten was possible. Somehow our connection had gotten deeper. Where both times before were amazing and intense and passionate, that passion was fueled by my desperate need to escape, to lose myself with him.

This felt different. I didn't need or want to escape anymore. I wanted to be present with him, to fully share myself with him for the first time.

I pushed his face gently away from mine and waited until he looked down at me. I wanted him to know I was exactly where I wanted to be. I needed him to know I was with the only person I wanted to be with.

"I want you inside me."

I reached down with one hand and found him hard and waiting. I spread my legs and watched his face as I guided him into me.

MMMMM...

It was incredibly difficult to keep my focus and not close my eyes, but I needed to be with him this time. And I needed him to be with me.

Our eyes were locked into each other as our bodies moved in unison. It was more of a slow, rhythmic grinding than thrusting. It felt amazing. It felt exquisite. It felt right.

Baby...

I blinked first. I couldn't take it anymore and grabbed his face and forced his mouth down onto mine. I spread my legs further and gyrated my hips underneath him. Taking my cue he started slowly working me with long, deep thrusts.

Yes baby...

I had felt all of him before, but never like this. I spread my legs wider and angled my hips up for him. He was in total and complete ownership of my body, not because he was taking it, because I was giving it to him. And he knew what to do with it. Oh my god did he know what to do.

He slowly pulled himself out until our connection was almost broken, and then he would pause just long enough for me to miss him, before slowly, deliciously giving himself back to me.

Oh my god baby...

I looked down to see him moving in and out of me. His rhythmic thrusting was exquisite. It looked and felt perfect seeing him slide into me. I greedily took all of him, only to find myself yearning for him as he pulled away seconds later.

fuck me baby...

I was mesmerized by the sight of him doing me. He was so hard and glistening from my wetness as he plunged in and out with increasing purpose. I could feel him throbbing inside me. I could feel his muscles tensing. He was almost ready.

Cum for me baby...

He reached down and put his forearms behind my knees, spreading my legs even further.

Oh shit...

"You want it baby?"

Hearing the sound of his voice sent me through the roof.

"Take it Preston," I said breathlessly, excitedly, as he continued stroking me with increasing force, "it's yours baby."

It wasn't so much what I said as the fact that I meant it. It was his.

"Don't stop baby."

He did as told and, amazingly, even though I knew he was close, he never changed his tempo. He pulled out and thrust back into me with more force, but he never went faster. His control was amazing.

It was enough to work me right to the edge, and take me over.

"Preston you're making me cum!"

And he was. I surrendered myself to the tidal waves of ecstasy as they washed over all my body, sending me into a series of involuntary, if increasingly familiar, convulsions.

He had me and he knew it. My body was mush. My body was his.

"Fuck, Julie I'm cumming!"

My still curled toes were now on his shoulders as he drove himself into me one last time. Without pulling back out, he kept grinding himself into me as deeply as he could. He was filling me up and I was taking it. I wanted it.

Slowly, surely he gave me all that he had. When he was fully spent, he collapsed down on top of me and kissed me softly.

And he kept kissing me. Lightly teasing me with his lips and tongue. It was perfect.

He continued kissing me as he pulled out and rolled to the my side. We kept kissing and touching each other softly until we, literally, fell asleep with our lips still touching.

• • •

Forget Ambien. As a life long sufferer of insomnia, I can state definitively that nothing works better as a sleep aid than the good old fashioned orgasm. And it has been my experience that the better the orgasm, the longer and deeper you slept.

When Preston and I fell asleep together, it was no later than 3:00 in the afternoon. I opened my eyes at 11:37pm. This from a woman who hadn't slept more than an hour at a time in two weeks.

Our bodies were still wrapped up together and, if it were up to me, we would have stayed that way forever. Unfortunately real life had a nasty habit of intruding on all of my fantasies, so I decided not to push my luck.

I didn't want to wake him, so I took my time detangling myself and getting up to visit the ladies room. Once there, I put on my robe and did a quick spot check to make sure everything was clean enough for company. When I was sure things were in order, I took a second to look at myself in the mirror. I couldn't help but smile.

It had been a good day. I no longer had to worry about my daughter getting kicked out of her school, the studio going out of business or

Cassandra pressing charges against me for stealing her money. Not only that, but with the deal I just made with Preston, my entire financial outlook was about to be ridiculously improved.

And then there was Preston himself. Even thinking about him made my mind take off in five different directions at once. Because of him, no one would ever again be able to accuse me of not being able to take care of my daughter.

Eat shit Kim...

But I had to admit my feelings for him weren't only about gratitude. Not even close.

Could this be happening? Was I really starting to feel something significant for a twenty year old kid? Was he feeling anything in return? Could he seriously be interested in a woman almost twice his age?

Snap out of it Julie...

I splashed some water on my face and tried to wash away the stupid looking grin that seemed permanently implanted. No luck.

"What are smiling about?"

I turned to see a naked Preston Richards standing in the doorway.

"Don't you knock?"

"Maybe I would if you shut the door."

"Whatever smart ass. Can I do something for you?"

"I need to pee," he smiled.

"Sounds personal."

"But Theo told me you were all about making sure people get proper bathroom breaks."

"Theo is a bully," I asserted, "and an asshole."

"Yeah true, but the kid's a freaking genius."

"That's no excuse to act like a prick."

He laughed.

"Now you go ahead and do what you have to do," I said, walking past him, "then put something on and meet me in the living room. We have to talk."

"That can't be good."

"Just shut up and do as you're told."

"Yes ma'am," he smiled, saluted and shut the door.

Keep it together Julie...

Chapter Sixteen

"**Ok**, it's real simple," I said, as he sat down next to me on the sofa, "I need to know everything."

"Like what?"

"Like everything Preston. I need to know exactly how this whole thing works."

"Ok, I can show you how we keep the money —"

"Wait, how? What do you mean 'how' you keep the money?"

"Well, like you said before, that's too much cash to keep hidden in my apartment."

"So, where is it?"

"I'd rather show you —"

"Ok, fine."

"Other than that, that's pretty much it. You know everything else. Everything I know at least."

"That's what I'm getting at Preston. If you want me to help you, I need to know what you don't know."

"Julie, how the hell can I tell you something I don't know?"

"You can't. But you can connect me with the person who does."

"Ira?"

"Yes."

I studied him closely to gauge his reaction and, as I suspected, me asking to meet his partner made him instantly uncomfortable.

"No way," he said, "you already said yourself it was best we stay away from each other and —"

"That was different."

"That was less than twelve hours ago! How is anything any different now?"

"Because," I said calmly, "that was before I knew how much money was involved. Listen, this is what I do, at least it used to be, and I am good at it. I can protect you, I will protect you, but you have to trust me."

He thought about it for a moment before speaking.

"Ok," he said, standing up, "take me to my car."

I was confused.

"Wait, what?"

"You wanna meet Ira," he shrugged, "I need something outta my car."

"Alright," I said, "let me put something on."

I threw on some clothes and we were on our way. Neither one of us said a word until I stopped behind his car. Even then, he just sat there, so I figured I better try and break the ice.

"Sorry."

"For what?"

"You got a ticket," I smiled, pointing to his car.

"Forget the ticket," he said softly, "I don't like this."

"Tell me why."

"Because Ira and I have been doing this for years and, I swear, we have never had a single problem. Not one. Now all this, and, I dunno, I mean, it kinda feels like I'm fixing something that aint broken."

"Preston, can I ask you a question?"

"Go ahead."

"You've never told me why. I mean, I get how you got started. It was easy and he was your friend. But you could've stopped it at that point. Why didn't you?"

"The money, obviously. When I saw how much money I could make, basically by doing nothing, I couldn't say no to that —"

"Bullshit," I interrupted, "you had the choice to say no at any time."

"Yeah and then what? How many people you know paying their way through college as a dancer? This was a hustle I could do that didn't mean selling drugs or robbing people or anything like that."

"And that is exactly my point. You kept doing it because it was easy. But what you didn't see, what you still don't see, is that it was TOO easy."

"Too easy?"

"Preston, take it from somebody who knows, nothing in life comes without a price, nothing."

He thought for another moment before responding.

"And you're sure there is no other way?"

"There isn't," I said, "because if I am going to protect you, I need to know what I'm protecting you from."

I must have gotten through to him because he stopped fighting me.

"Wait here," he said and got out of the car.

This is the part where my old partner and I used to play a fun little game we called 'guess the show'.

Every time some knucklehead walked into the office with a paper bag full of money, we could tell their TV watching habits by reading the indictment. Inevitably their master plan to avoid arrest was given to them by the plot of some crime drama or gangster movie. All we had to do was read it, and we could guess which show gave them the dumb ass idea that eventually led them into our office.

I watched as Preston reached into his backseat and grabbed a large gym bag. Now if young Preston was a fan of The Wire, there would be an unopened, pre-paid cell phone somewhere in that bag. The Soprano's would mean an address of some physicians office and GoodFella's always led to conducting business in the back office of some noisy restaurant. My money was on The Wire.

"So," I asked as he and his gym bag made their way back into my car, "where is it?"

"Where is what?"

"Isn't this the part where you give me some kind of burner phone to contact your partner?"

"Burner phone?" he laughed, "I think somebody's been watching too much TV."

He reached into his bag and pulled out something that looked like a stack of oversized business cards. He took one out of the pile and gave it to me.

"Here."

"What is this?"

"What's it look like?"

"It says a three day pass to the 24-hour Fitness on Main street."

"That's three consecutive days, starting from your first visit. Don't go before this Tuesday, but whenever you go after that, make sure you go for three consecutive days at around the same time each day."

"Are you screwing with me?"

"You said you needed to meet Ira. This is how you do it."

"But I don't even know what he looks like."

"You don't need to."

"So, what do I do when I get there?"

He was getting frustrated.

"I don't know, you work out, take a class, whatever normal people do when they go to a 24-hour fitness alright?"

"Fine," I said, realizing I wasn't going to get anywhere by arguing, "we'll do this your way."

"Thank you. Now seriously, I'm not talking about this anymore. You said this needed to happen so give me til Tuesday to get in touch with Ira and then go for three straight days after that."

"What part of 'we'll do this your way' don't you understand?"

"Whatever," he laughed, "what do you wanna do now?"

"I really should try and get some work done."

"But it's after midnight."

"And? Keeping you out of prison is going to be full time job."

"So wait," he smiled, "this kinda means you work for me."

I laughed.

"In a manner of speaking, yes I do."

"Then I order you to take the rest of the night off from working."

"And what, Mr. Richards, do you suggest I do instead?"

As if I had to ask, he was twenty after all.

• • •

Now what...

I didn't realize it when I agreed to this ridiculous arrangement, but I had never actually belonged to a gym. I ran track in high school and continued to be a recreational runner through college and law school and well into adult life. Running, outside, had always been my only form of exercise so I hadn't seen the inside of any kind of workout facility since my freshman year in college. I had absolutely no idea how these places worked.

Fortunately, all of the kids that worked at the 24-hour fitness on Main seemed to have a healthy dose of the helpful gene.

"Can I help you with that?" asked a particularly friendly blonde girl named Lyndsey.

"Do I look that lost?"

"No, not at all," she smiled, "half the people who work here have no idea how any of this stuff works."

Lindsey proceeded to spend the next few minutes instructing me how to safely operate the treadmill. She offered to give me a tour and a quick introduction to all of the available equipment, but I politely declined. I had no intention of becoming a regular visitor. In fact, if a certain someone were to show up I would likely never set foot in this, or any other, 24-hour fitness ever again.

Despite myself, I managed to get into a groove on the treadmill and, before I knew it, I was seventeen again, pounding the pavement in Somerdale New jersey to Alanis Morissette's Jagged Little Pill.

Forty-five minutes of sweat drenched, cardio-nostalgia later, me, Alanis and my thirty-eight year old legs were all done. I made my way over to the designated stretching area and started cooling myself down.

All together I had been in the gym for a little over an hour and still no sign of the mysterious Ira. I half expected him to walk up to me while I was on the treadmill though, in hindsight, I'm glad he didn't. I needed the workout and my runners high had me feeling pretty damn good about myself at the moment.

Then I thought maybe he would approach me while I was stretching. Wrong again.

hmmmm...

It was fairly obvious, from the way he and Preston set this system up, that he was an employee. At least that would have been my educated assumption. Only it wouldn't have done me any good to look around for him because I had no idea who to look for. That's when it hit me.

The only way this could possibly work was if he knew who I was. Which means he had to know what I looked like. Which meant he could watch me, without me knowing. He could already be watching me. He could be watching me right now.

The thought gave me a chill and I instinctively sat up and glanced around the gym floor. I saw nothing out of the ordinary but that didn't make me feel any better. I was exposed and I wasn't in control of the real estate and this whole thing suddenly felt extremely uncomfortable.

A voice inside my head started telling me to back out, and I was tempted to listen. I could still walk away, having dodged a major disaster with Ashley's school and Cassandra's studio, without having cost myself a thing. As much as I might have wanted to help Preston, whenever I thought objectively about everything I didn't know about what he was doing and what I was getting myself into, I wanted to head for the hills. As tempting a carrot as a half million dollars in clean cash was for me, I knew nothing in life came without a cost. The problem with this deal was I had no idea what that cost would be or if I would be willing to pay it.

I was playing with house money and I knew it. Every instinct in my body was telling me to cash out. That I had already extracted all of the good I was going to get from this situation. That no good could come from getting in any deeper with this many unknowns. It still wasn't too late. I could still quit while I was ahead and walk away unscathed. Or could I?

It was perfectly reasonable to expect this Ira person to look into me. In fact, I would have been surprised if he didn't. Considering the amount of money involved, he certainly had the motivation and the resources to get a thorough background done on me.

Shit...

That's why Preston told me to wait til after Tuesday. That gave Ira enough time to research who the hell I was and decide if he wanted to meet me or not. Now I had no choice but to assume he already knew things about me, my past, and my current situations that would allow him to, at a minimum, complicate my life should he choose to do so. And I knew exactly nothing about him.

That imbalance was unacceptable and I had no one to blame but myself. The old me would have seen this coming a mile away.

Dammit Julie...

I guess three plus years on the sidelines had dulled my senses. Now, like it or not, I had to stay in this thing until I got a bead on this kid Ira. I needed to know exactly who he was, what he was about and, most importantly, how he needed to be dealt with should it ever come to that.

Chapter Seventeen

"Hey Julie, how's it goin?"

"I'm fine Lyndsey. How are you?"

"I'm doin awesome thanks! Need some help with the elliptical?"

"You're always around to save me," I smiled.

"That's my job!"

Quite frankly, Miss Lyndsey's over the top perkiness was a little much after a full day at work. But I had to admit, she was helpful, so I smiled politely and dealt with it.

Preston told me to go to the gym for three consecutive days, at around the same time each day. Obviously, for me, that meant going after work, while Ashley was still at the studio. What I didn't anticipate was everyone else in the world having the same schedule.

The place was a zoo, with almost every piece of cardio equipment in full use. So instead of running my troubles away to a custom designed cardio-mix of The Gin Blossoms, Sheryl Crow and Jewel, I was stuck with this elipti-thing.

"And if you wanna adjust the resistance, you just use the up and down arrows here."

"Thanks so much Lyndsey, I appreciate your help."

"Oh, it's no problem," she insisted, "has anyone talked to you about your free evaluation yet?"

I so wanted to tell her to go away, but I knew she was just doing her job. It wouldn't kill me to listen to her spiel for a minute.

"No they haven't," I conceded patiently.

"Well, as a new or potential member, you're entitled to a free, thirty minute evaluation with one of our trainers."

"And would that be you?" I asked.

"No, I'm not a trainer, but I could schedule it for you if you like?"

"Thanks Lyndsey, but I don't think I'm interested."

"Are you sure? We have some excellent trainers."

"I'm sure you do. But I have an impossible schedule."

"Ok, well just let me schedule you fifteen minutes with Ira. He's one of our best train —"

"Excuse me," I interrupted, "what did you say his name was?"

"His name is Ira Benson," she smiled, "you know him?"

"Um no, no, I just um, my nephew is named Ira. I always found that to be an unusual name."

"Well, Ira is one of our best trainers and you really should do the eval session with him. What have you got to lose?" she smiled, "It's free."

"Ok, Miss Lyndsey," I smiled in return, "you've talked me into it. Go ahead and schedule the session for tomorrow."

"Oh," she grimaced, "I'm pretty sure he's all booked up for tomorrow. It'll have to be some time later this week."

"But I'm only on a three day pass that ends tomorrow."

"That's ok," she smiled knowingly, "let me talk to you about our membership options."

Thirty minutes later, the 24-hour Fitness on Main Street in Bristol had a new member and I, for the first time in my life, had a gym membership.

I had something else as well, something far more important. An appointment on Friday with my new personal trainer, Ira Benson.

• • •

"Hi, you must be Ms. Sharpe," he extended his hand.

"You can call me Julie," I offered, shaking his hand firmly.

The instant I made eye contact with Ira, I knew he had done his homework. It was clear he knew who I was, and I don't just mean his buddy's girlfriend. He knew enough about me and my background and the things I had done to know I was someone he should take seriously. How did I know this? You can't be a successful attorney and not be good at reading people. It comes with the territory.

Ira wasn't all that different from the type of people I dealt with in my past, though not like a client. His vibe was more that of an opposing council I was facing for the first time.

Any lawyer worth their salt does background on the opposition, that's just part of the job. The problem was, once an opposing attorney knew my reputation, they would go out of their way to let me know they weren't intimidated. And, nine times out of ten, they'd make an ass of themselves in the process. I had seen it a thousand times.

The ridiculous lengths they would go to convince me they were on my level bordered on the insane. I had one guy hire a social media consultant to fake an online profile of himself and then *accidentally* include the link in an email correspondence to my office. Another genius had the nerve to tell me that after he kicked my ass in court, he was going to take me to bed, with his wife, and his girlfriend.

As pathetic as all of that sounds, that kind of thing happened often enough that I learned to pay attention when someone *didn't* feel the need to be impressive. When someone knew all about me and my reputation and didn't give a shit, that's when I knew I needed to be on my toes. That was Ira Benson.

I sized him up much like I would an opposing council and, I have to be honest, I was impressed. He was average height, with dark hair, intense brown eyes and the compact, powerful frame of a professional athlete.

Only I wasn't fooled, or distracted, by any of that. His physical stature, while impressive, was more a facade than anything else. It was a mask he wore to work. He knew he had to look the part of a trainer and so that's what he was doing.

What stood behind that facade was what I found interesting. There, lived an ambitious young man who knew his place in the hierarchy of society and would accept no less. He had an air of subtle arrogance about him that said, '*I know what I want,*

I will get what I want and I will do it in a way that makes you remember my name.' He was confident, but not so much that he was ok with anonymity. Ira Benson was a front man, plain and simple. This was not a young man who would be comfortable existing in the shadows.

Gotcha...

I instantly felt better. I now knew how to deal with young Ira should he ever start to get out of line.

"So," he smiled as we walked together toward the designated stretching area, "you're the avocado."

"I don't think we're here to tell jokes are we Mr. Benson?"

"Call me Ira."

"Ira, is there somewhere we can go to talk?"

"We can talk here."

"Right here in the open?"

"Look around," he gestured toward the main floor, "everybody in here has headphones on. Plus, the music playing in the club keeps people from getting too nosy even if they wanted to."

Sopranos...

I sat down on the mat and he handed me some sort of foam roller thing. He grabbed one of his own and demonstrated the proper way to use it.

"Wanna give it a try?"

"Sure," I said and proceeded to place the roller under my left leg.

"Good," he said, in full-on trainer mode, "now slowly roll forward and back."

"Ouch!"

"That's it," he laughed, "find those knots and roll em out. When you're ready you can switch legs."

I quickly moved the foam roller underneath my right leg and started the process over again.

"I have some questions for you."

"Not now," he replied quickly, "I want to offer you a deal."

"Excuse me?"

"Ok good," he said, standing up, "you feel that?"

"Uh, yeah I think so."

"Excellent, let's go over here."

He put our foam rollers back on the rack, helped me to my feet and led me over to what looked to be a massage table.

"Lemme walk you through some assisted stretches."

He put a towel down and had me lie on my back. He then put my left leg on his right shoulder and slowly walked forward.

Hello hamstring...

"You interested?"

"In what?"

"Making a deal."

"Ira," I said as he walked around the table to stretch my right leg, "I think you misunderstood the reason I wanted to meet with you."

He laughed.

I didn't like how this was going. He was in control of the agenda, the real estate and, right now, my body. I was way too far out of my comfort zone

"Did I say something funny?" I asked, as he went back for another crack at my left leg.

"Julie, I didn't misunderstand anything. My boy said you were helping him out with some stuff and wanted to meet me."

"To get information."

"I know who you are," he smiled, as he switched back to the right side, "and the only reason I'm here is to make you a proposition."

He gently let my leg down, grabbed a small towel and draped it over my right foot. He then placed my foot against his midsection and slow guided my right leg out, away from my left, pausing when they were at almost a forty-five degree angle.

"Now I want you to tell me if this starts to feel too uncomfortable."

He walked forward some more. My ego wouldn't allow me to tell him to stop, but I instinctively tapped my hand on the table when I felt as if he was going to rip me in half.

"Breathe," he coached as he backed off slightly and settled into the stretch, "Preston tells me you can help free up his cash."

"Preston talks too much," I said as switched over to my left leg.

"Well then I'm sure you already know his is just a tiny piece of the pie."

"What's your point?"

"If you can do what he says you can, I want in and I wanna talk expansion."

Finished with my left leg, he stood at the end of the table and placed both of my feet on his chest. He grabbed my wrists to keep my arms in place and leaned forward until my knees were touching my chest.

"So," he said, "you interested?"

The phrasing of his question was a little awkward considering our body position at the moment.

Focus Julie...

"Define expansion."

"What Preston's holding are crumbs compared to what I could do if I had your expertise."

"Be more specific," I said evenly.

"Sit up," he ordered as he let my legs down, "lock your fingers behind your head."

He got up on the table behind me, grabbed my elbows.

"Tell me if this hurts," he said as he began to gently pull back.

"I'm good, so you were saying?"

"Think order of magnitude."

"Ok, so are we talking double, triple?"

"Think bigger."

"Five times?"

"Try ten, annual."

He hopped down off the table before I could respond.

"So," he said, "Lyndsey tells me you're a runner?"

"A little bit."

"Let's head over to the treadmills and see what you got."

He led me over to the cardio area, giving me a chance to process what I'd just heard. If what he was saying was true, and I had no reason to believe it wasn't, Ira had just offered to partner with me in building a money laundering operation that could accommodate upwards of a hundred million dollars a year.

Think Julie...

It was decision time and I had less than thirty-seconds to determine how I wanted to live the rest of my life. I could follow Ira over to the treadmills and continue the conversation, thus getting myself in deeper. Or I could tell Mr. Benson to screw himself, run out the door and never look back.

Twenty Seconds...

Could I really do this? After having lived the best, most successful years of my life as an officer of the court, was I truly ready to be on the other side?

Ten Seconds...

And it wasn't just about me. With each step I took toward that treadmill, the deeper Ashley was pulled into this drama as well. Could I do that to her? Would I still be able to protect her from the other side? Could I still provide for her and be everything she needed?

Five seconds...

And then there was Preston, my delicious, twenty year old, sex ninja. Even the thought of him made me smile like a teenager and, I had to admit, it wasn't just about sex anymore. The most amazing and surprising thing about him was the way he made me laugh. He had this wonderful, sarcastic sense of humor that was a perfect match for me. There was a lightness, an easiness, to our conversations that made them seem comfortable and familiar. I had absolutely no idea where things were going but it was obvious Preston had become an important part of my life and he was trusting me to take care of this for him. If I walked away now, I felt like I would be letting him down. I didn't want to let him down.

Decision time...

"So," Ira said as he fired up the treadmill for me, "what do you think?"

"I think you need to rethink your plan," I countered and started running, "what I agreed to do for Preston is a one time thing for him and his family, and I can do it specifically because the numbers involved aren't too big. What you're talking about is a permanent infrastructure for on-going operations in the tens of millions. Do you have any idea how involved that is?"

"No, I have no clue. That's why I'm talking to you."

"And that's another thing, why me? Do you really think it's a good idea to start something this big with somebody who'll be learning on the job?"

"Well, let's be honest," he replied, as he increased the incline on my treadmill, "I can't exactly put an add on craigslist. Besides, from what I can see you're perfect for the job."

"Based on what?" I asked before turning up the speed myself, "I'm a lawyer not a —"

"You used to be a lawyer," he corrected, and hopped onto the treadmill next to mine, "listen, you and I both know I've done my homework on you. So I know you've been barred from practicing law."

He increased his incline and speed to match mine.

"Now let's see if you can keep up," he smiled and increased his speed.

I followed suit and smiled to let him know I wasn't remotely uncomfortable.

"Well," I said, "if you know that much then you're aware this is not exactly my field of expertise."

"What I also know about you is that you completed your undergrad at Princeton in two years, you were the youngest person to pass the bar exam in state history and you were the youngest attorney to ever make partner at Governalli and Stern, the biggest law firm in New Jersey."

I noticed he was breathing a little heavy as he finished that last sentence. I winked at him and increased the speed on my treadmill. He followed suit.

At least he's not a wimp...

"I know my resume, thank you. What's your point?"

"My point," he said slowly, trying to catch his breath, "is that, you've pretty much never failed at anything, and I'm willing to bet a lot of money you're not gonna start now."

He admitted defeat by slowing his treadmill to a walk. I smiled and increased my speed a little more.

"I appreciate your confidence but what you're asking is a lot."

"And what I'm offering is even more. Look, I don't know what kind of deal you made with Preston, but it can't be more than fifteen, twenty percent right?"

I smiled, kept running and increased my incline. He looked impressed.

"Well whatever the deal," he said, "the most you walk away with is a couple hundred thousand and then what? You put that in a college fund for your daughter and go back to being a dance mom, working five nights a week, part time, at a dance studio?"

"What's wrong with that?"

"Nothing," he said, getting frustrated, "if you're ok with being a middle class nobody. If that's the case then we're done."

It was obvious he wasn't used to working this hard to get someone to agree with him.

Got em...

"Ira," I said, slowing my treadmill to a walk, "the risk involved with something like this is huge and the likelihood I can pull it off? I don't know."

"Julie I understand the risk, but what I'm offering you is a chance to get back in the game. To be a deal maker again, at the highest levels."

He paused for a moment to see if his words were having an effect. I stopped my treadmill, took a long drink of water from my bottle and leaned against the window.

Come to mommy...

"What would the deal look like?" I asked, after a moment.

"Well, we start with you taking care of everything Preston has right now. You make good on that and we can be off and running."

He leaned back against the window beside and waited for my response.

"What's my piece?"

"Five?"

I laughed out loud and took another sip of water.

"Try again."

"You do realize I'm talking about the whole thing right? Not just Preston's ten percent."

"Five doesn't get this done Ira. There's too much risk for me."

"Seven?"

"Seven and a half is good for me *if* we go forward, but for this initial job I need fifteen."

"What?!"

"This has to be worth the risk for me Ira."

He thought for a moment before speaking.

"How much does it cost to process?"

"No more than five cents on the dollar," I said.

"You're paying that," he insisted, letting me know it wasn't a question.

"Fine, but only for this job. If we go forward after this, my fifteen percent comes off the top of every dollar I touch. All processing fees are paid by the client.

Without looking over at me, he extended his hand across his body. I stood up from the window and shook his hand.

"So," he said as he led me over to the entrance of the women's locker room, "stop by the front desk and tell them you want to buy a package of ten sessions. Tell them you wanna schedule the first one for next week. Sound good?"

"Yeah," I smiled, "I can be ready by then."

"Cool, have a good week. But I'm sure I'll see you around the club before then."

"Thanks again Ira," I smiled, walking into the locker room, "I'll see you soon."

Chapter Eighteen

"**Mom**?"

"Yes baby?"

"Are you ever going to start dating again?"

"What?"

"I think you should try and meet somebody."

"Where is this coming from?"

"I dunno. I mean, it's great that you have a new job and all, but, I dunno, It just seems like you spend all of your time either at work or the studio or hanging out with me."

"Well," I smiled, "what if I like hanging out with you?"

"Mom, I'm being serious."

"Ashley if you want to be successful in life you have to make certain sacrifices, and starting a company takes a lot of time and energy and focus."

"But does it make you happy?"

"It does. I'm actually excited about going to work again."

"ok."

She didn't sound convinced.

"Ok, so why the sudden interest in my social life?"

She didn't respond.

"Ashley?"

"I um, I, I think dad might be dating somebody."

"Oh really?"

"Yeah, but you know what? I'm not even sure it's —"

"Ashley," I cut her off, "it's fine. Really. Your dad and I aren't together anymore but that doesn't mean I don't want him to be happy."

"Well," she noted, "I want you to be happy too."

"Come here."

I gave her a hug and kiss.

"What was that for?"

"For being the most thoughtful daughter in the entire world."

"Does that mean I get to pick the restaurant this time?"

"We'll see about that after class. Now come on, it's about to start."

The news about Brian caught me off guard, even though I absolutely meant what I said about wanting him to be happy. It was just an oddly uncomfortable feeling knowing he might be moving on.

I guess a part of my ego had taken solace in the fact that he wasn't over me, or us, after all this time. It allowed me to indulge the selfish fantasy that what we had together was of such earth shattering importance that he might never be able to get over it.

But in the end, that's all it was, a selfish, hypocritical fantasy. Brian was a good man and a great father and deserved to have someone in his life that loved and appreciated him. Regardless of anything I had accomplished in my past or whatever I might manage to build in the future, the fact that I wasn't able to give Brian the love he needed and the respect he deserved would always be one of the greatest disappointments of my life.

Ashley finished putting on her shoes and we hurried together into something called Cardio-Barre Bootcamp with Jake which, as far as I could tell, was a weird combination of aerobics, ballet and strength training. Not exactly my cup of tea but it was the only class at the gym my daughter agreed to take with me.

Normally we would be at rehearsal right now, but I was having the mirrors replaced in all the studios, so rehearsals and classes were cancelled for tonight.

For the first time in a long time, things were good. Preston had delivered my half of his personal funds and I used part of that to set up and test the network I was building. The sudden influx of cash also allowed me to quit my job, which was cause enough for a grand celebration as far as I was concerned.

How any remotely competent individual functioned in that environment without falling into a massive state of depression was beyond me. My former co-workers referred to it as cubicle hell, and I honestly couldn't imagine a more appropriate name. Helping me escape that soul-sucking hell hole was the best thing Preston had done for me.

Well...one of the best...

"What's wrong with you?"

"What? Nothing why?"

"Why are you smiling like that?"

"I'm just smiling Ashley."

"But why? Nothing even happened."

"Why don't you focus on the instructor instead of me."

"Whatever."

I love my daughter, I love my daughter...

• • •

"You sure you want to eat here?"

"Why not?"

"Because Ashley, the last time we tried sushi you stared at your plate for thirty minutes and we had to stop for a hamburger on the way home."

"Mom I'm fine ok?"

I decided to let it go. I could tell by her tone that nothing good was going to come from pressing the issue.

The waiter came and she ordered something called a spider roll. I was tempted but decided to go with something safe and asked for a basic salmon and rice entree.

"Spider roll huh?"

"Sylvia said it was bomb."

Sylvia Pavani was my daughters latest obsession. They met in ballet class before realizing they were in the same class at school and, from that point on, they were inseparable.

I only knew Sylvia from seeing her around the studio but, as far as I could tell, she seemed like a nice young lady. She carried herself well and was always polite, respectful and pleasant. I was actually happy when she and Ashley started bonding. Spider roll aside, this particular bff relationship had mommy's stamp of approval.

Reminder: get together with Sylvia's mom some time soon.

"You remember I'm going out of town next weekend when you're at your dads right?"

"Where you going again?"

"I have to go to Chicago and then Minnesota."

"For work?"

"Yeah, I have to look into a couple of properties in both cities."

"Will you be back on Sunday?"

"Yeah, I'll be back before noon."

"Awesome, so you can come to Preston's party."

"What party?"

"Preston's birthday is next Saturday and we're throwing him a surprise party at the Studio on Sunday."

"Really? Who's idea was this?"

"Cassies'."

"Ahem."

"I'm sorry, anyway it was *Cassandra's* idea to throw the party but Theo told us Preston won't be around on Saturday, so we decided to get him a cake and a present and give it to him before rehearsal on Sunday."

"Sounds nice."

"By the way, everybody agreed to give twenty dollars."

"Twenty bucks from everybody? That must be one heckuva cake."

"Is that ok?"

"Sure, why wouldn't it be?"

"Just making sure."

"Baby I told you, now that I have a new job, things aren't so tight. We still have to be responsible, but we don't have to count every penny anymore."

God it felt good to say that, and mean it. Don't get me wrong, Ashley never wanted for anything financially, her father pretty much saw to that. But the terms of our custody agreement were such that I was responsible for day-to-day care, and if I ever had to go to Brian for money, he would assume full custody. I know that sounds crazy but when I agreed to those terms, I was pretty much desperate.

Considering the circumstances of our divorce and my emotional state at the time, Brian, had a real good shot at full custody. I couldn't afford to take that chance. I had just lost everything that had ever meant anything to me and I know for a fact I wouldn't have survived losing my daughter too. I was willing to agree to whatever Brian put on the table, if it meant me keeping Ashley with me.

Besides, money wasn't an issue for me at that time. I was still pulling in a six figure salary plus a large bonus and had no reason to suspect that wouldn't continue. When I lost my license and my situation changed, the way our agreement was structured prevented me from going back to court.

So I had no choice but to keep things afloat as best I could, with no help coming from anyone. I did what I could to shield Ashley from the worst of it, but there were too many times when she had a front row seat to my struggles and I hated myself for that. She didn't deserve to have her life uprooted or her family torn apart, and she certainly shouldn't have a part of her childhood stolen from her by having to deal with the money problems of her disgraced mother.

But that was then, I reminded myself. Now, thanks to an insanely fortunate series of coincidences, I was once again in a position to properly take care of my baby girl. No more grimacing when she asked if she could go to a movie or needed money for a field trip. All that was over now. A few weeks ago I was literally down to my last fifty bucks, and now I was on the cusp of setting her up for the rest of her life. Even better, if a few things broke my way, I would be able to give her back a big piece of the life I had taken from her, while she was still young enough to enjoy it. Words cannot describe how good that felt.

"Here you go ladies."

Our waiter delivered our dishes and it was all I could do to stop myself from laughing out loud at the look an Ashley's face when she first got a look at what she ordered.

"Can I get you anything else?"

"No, thank you," I smiled politely, "we're fine."

"Enjoy."

He left us to our meals and I looked at my daughter, who was quite adorably speechless at the sight of her spider roll.

"Baby that looks good. Mind if I try?"

"Um, sure, go ahead."

I tried one piece.

"Wow, that really is good! You wanna try my salmon?"

"Can I?"

"Absolutely, sharing is the whole point of eating sushi."

Thirty-seconds later, we ended any pretense of sharing and had effectively traded entrees.

God I love taking care of this girl...

Was I taking an unthinkable risk getting into business with Ira and Preston? Of course I was. I'm not a fool, but that's the thing about losing everything. If you live through it once, you're not quite as afraid the next time.

In hindsight, fear is a much more useful emotion than I gave it credit for.

Chapter Nineteen

*"**Ladies** and gentlemen, welcome to Chicago's O'hare Airport. Local time is 9:45AM and the temperature is thirty-seven degrees celsius..."*

"Seriously?" I said as the flight attendant finished her statement.

Preston had fallen asleep shortly after takeoff and slept through the entire two hour flight.

"What?" he asked, still half asleep, "what did I do now?"

"Preston, are you seriously going to sit there and not tell me today is your birthday?"

He rubbed his eyes and laughed quietly.

"I thought you knew."

I punched him in the arm.

"Seriously," he laughed, "I just thought you didn't care."

That got him punched again, harder.

"Ow!"

"Oh shut up."

"What are you mad at me for?!"

"Preston, how was I supposed to know today was your birthday if you didn't tell me?"

"I figured Ashley or one of the other girls had to have mentioned it. What did they tell you the party was for?"

"You know about the party?"

"You didn't?"

"Not until last night, no."

"How does that happen? I thought you ran that place."

"Cassandra is the owner, I just help her. But that is beside the point. The point is you should have told me yourself."

"Fine, I'm sorry."

"Don't worry about it," I smiled, "it's your loss."

"What's that supposed to mean?"

"I'm just thinking of all the amazing *things* we could've planned if I had known."

"Like what?"

"No sense thinking about it now."

"Come on babe, don't be like that."

"Babe?"

"Yeah, is it ok I called you that?"

"I prefer my name, thank you."

"Then why you smilin?"

"Whatever," I looked away to hide what felt like the goofiest smile in history, "let's stick with Julie, ok."

"Whatever you say smiley."

"Shut up."

• • •

I didn't like lying to my daughter, but I justified it in my mind by reminding myself that we've all done it. Whether it's by allowing them to believe in flying reindeer or convincing them that some magical fairy turned their tooth into a dollar bill while they were sleeping, every parent has lied to their child at some point in time. This wasn't all that different.

If I had told her the real reason I was going to Chicago, she would have asked more questions. Which would have led to even more lies. And the more lies you put out there, the greater the chance one of them ends up biting you in the ass. I had learned that the hard way.

So it was both smarter and easier to allow my daughter to believe I was in the windy city to look at investment properties, when I was actually there to see an old friend.

"Preston hurry up," I said as I finished my makeup, "the car's downstairs and I don't want to be late."

"I seriously have to wear this?"

"It's a suit Preston. It's not gonna kill you."

"You say so."

He walked out of the bathroom wearing the charcoal grey, Joseph Aboud, three piece suit I bought him specially for this trip.

"How do I look?"

Damn...

"Wow," I smiled, "you should dress like a grown up more often."

"And who knew you could look so hot in a floppy hat? Wanna tell me where we're going?"

"You really want to know?" I asked, grabbing my purse.

"Yes, that would be nice."

"Son," I smiled in my best southern accent and walked past him into the hall, "we are going to praise the lord."

• • •

"Y'all looking good tonight Amen?"

Amen!

"I mean, I'm seeing Designer dresses, Designer suits and Designer shoes. Oh I can see some real nice things in the congregation tonight church."

"Say it Pastor..."

"And I aint here to tell y'all there's anything wrong with having nice things. But I am here to tell you what second Corinthians, chapter five, verse twenty-two says. Can I do that? Y'all got time for that?"

"Take your time reverend...take your time"

"Therefore if any man be in Christ, he is a new creature: old things are passed away; behold, all things are become new, behold all things are become new."

"MMM HMM"

"That's alright pastor...that's all RIGHT!"

"Church, I remember a time when I didn't have nice clothes or shoes and how I had prayed for God to change those things and somehow make them new. But you know what? My God didn't change my shoes; My God changed me!"

"You better PREACH!"

"Amen, Amen, Amen!!!"

"So church my testimony is this: I gave Christ my sins and my heart and He gives me His righteousness; Every day; ALL DAY! Because God is GOOD!"

"ALL THE TIME!"

"Church, I said my God is GOOD!"

"ALL THE TIME!"

"Who else is ready to kick off their ugly shoes and be transformed?!"

"Hallelujah!!"

"Thank ya JESUS!!!"

"Who else is ready to take off the ugly shoes of selfishness?!"

"Say it Pastor!!"

"SAY IT!!"

"Who else in here is ready to take off those ugly shoes of guilt and put on God's Glory."

"YESSAH!!"

"HALLELUJAH!! HALLELUJAH!!

"Who else in here is ready to take off those ugly shoes of foolishness and put on God's forgiveness?!"

"TELL IT PASTOR!"

"Who in here is ready to take off those ugly shoes of pride and put on God's purity."

"PREACH MY BROTHER!!"

"THANK YA FATHER!!"

"THANK YA, THANK YA, THANK YA!!!"

"Who in here is ready to take off those ugly shoes of weakness and put on God's strength?!"

"AMEN AMEN AMEN!!!"

"Is anybody in here is ready to get rid of those ugly shoes? Because God is waiting."

After the sermon, tradition was that the congregation formed a sort of receiving line, giving everyone exiting the church the chance to be greeted by the preacher or one of his deacons. The preacher, in this case, was one Doctor Drake Strong, lead pastor of The First African Baptist Church of Chicago.

Drake was a stunningly attractive, dark skinned black man in his mid forties. He played college basketball for the University of Illinois and still had the long, lean physique of a division one athlete all these years later.

He stood about six feet, five inches tall, had a shaved head and piercing, dark brown eyes, but the most impressive thing about him was his voice. He had this deep, booming voice that could be equal parts intimidating and seductive, depending on his mood. It was the perfect instrument for his chosen profession.

"Pastor," I smiled as I approached him in line.

He recognized me and immediately got a huge smile on his face.

"Well, would you look at this," he smiled, "look what the doggone cat done dragged in!"

We hugged, giving me the opportunity to whisper something in his ear.

"We need to talk."

He stepped back but kept his hands on my shoulders and still had a huge smile on his face.

"Sister Riley," he said in the direction of a heavy set black woman standing to his right, "could you show this young lady to my office downstairs? Let me finish here Julie and I'll be right down."

Preston and I followed Sister Riley down to Pastor Strong's large, well appointed office. It had been a while since I'd been here but everything looked about the same.

He had an oversized mahogany desk with a twenty-seven inch flat screen monitor, two land lines and a docking station for his lap top. The whole thing looked more like something you'd see on Wall Street than on the lower level of a Baptist Church.

The walls were adorned with various sports memorabilia and a forty-two inch flat screen television so he wouldn't have to miss any of his beloved Bears games on Sundays.

The best thing though, were the chairs. Drake had this thing about chairs. His feeling was the world had a severe shortage of truly comfortable places to sit for anyone over six feet tall, so he had all the chairs in his office ergonomically designed from scratch and then custom upholstered with insanely soft imported leather. You could literally sit in one of those things and forget where you were. It had happened to me on more than one occasion.

"Can I get you folks anything?" Sister Riley asked, "coffee? Water?"

"No, thank you." I declined.

"What about you young man? You hungry or thirsty?"

"No ma'am," Preston mumbled shakily. He was obviously a bit nervous in this environment.

"You sure?"

"Yes ma'am, I'm ok."

"Ok," she smiled, "but don't y'all leave here talking about we aint feed you. Pastor will be down in minute."

Chapter Twenty

"Julie Sharpe, as I live and breath."

I looked up to see Pastor Strong standing in the doorway to his office with the same huge smile plastered to his face.

"How are you Drake?" I smiled warmly in return.

I walked over to where he was standing and gave him a hug. I have to admit, it genuinely felt good to see him. We were more acquaintances than actual friends but Drake and I had hit it off since the day we met. He was one of the few people from my past life I had a genuine respect for, especially after seeing the way he had turned his life around. It was just one of those odd things where we clicked instantly, despite the fact that we met under far from ideal circumstances.

"How long's it been," he asked, shaking his head, "five years?"

"Five years and seven months, but who's counting? Drake," I said to Preston, "was one of my last clients at G and S."

"Before she decided to go solo," Drake smiled.

"That seems like a lifetime ago doesn't it?"

"Well you look as young and beautiful as ever."

"And you lie like a preacher."

"Ha! Now there's the biting, satirical wit I've missed so much," he laughed and walked over to his desk, "where have you been hiding yourself?"

"Here and there," I responded carefully, "your congregation is growing I see."

"We're doing good work," he said proudly.

"That was some sermon," I smiled, and returned to my seat.

"Did any of it take?"

"You mean, am I ready to accept Jesus Christ as my lord and savior?"

"Don't knock it," he smiled, undeterred by my cynicism, "my god is a patient and forgiving god."

"Well, I think he's gonna have to be a little more patient and forgiving for the time being."

"What about you young man?" He turned his attention to Preston. "You ready to take off those shoes of sin and take on God's hand of righteousness?"

"Uh."

"Actually Drake," I jumped in before Preston could respond, "That's kinda why we're here. This young man would like to repent."

"Repent?"

I nodded.

He sat back in his chair and studied me for a long moment. Once he was certain he had heard me correctly, he looked over at Preston.

"What are we repenting for?"

"Drake," I interrupted again before Preston could say anything, "as his representative, I cannot allow him to get into any specifics. Suffice it to say he isn't proud of the things he's done and would like to make some kind of amends."

"What do you have in mind?"

"Well, a sizable donation to your foundation would be a good start."

Silence filled the room but I knew better than to say anything. Drake needed time to process the shift in the conversation.

While the affection we showed upon seeing each other was genuine, this was now business and of all the people I had come to know in my past life, few showed the ability to separate business from friendship more completely, and ruthlessly, than Drake Strong.

"You guys sure about this?"

"Listen," I replied evenly, "I know nothing's gonna undo the past. Whatever my friend did to make his money, he's gonna have to live with that for the rest of his life. I get that. But by doing this, at least there's the possibility that some good can come of it."

After a few more awkward moments of silence, he grabbed a pen and a Post-it pad from his desk drawer and slid them over in my direction. On cue, I picked up the pen, wrote on the top Post-it and slid it back over to Drake.

10

"Give or take," I added softly, as he studied my note.

He nodded, tore off my note from the pad and put it through the desktop shredder in the corner of his desk.

He then wrote a note of his own, picked it up and showed it to me.

I nodded, he shredded his note and handed the pad back to me. I took it and answered his question.

30 & <5

"That soon?" he asked as he shredded my last note, "why the fire drill?"

"There's no fire," I said calmly, "we just wanna get this over with so Preston can move on with his life."

"And are we sure Preston here is gonna be able to keep his nose clean from now on?"

It took a second for Preston to realize he was actually supposed to answer this time.

"Trust me reverend," he said shakily, "this is a one time thing for me."

We said our goodbyes and within five minutes were in the backseat of our town car, on the way back to the hotel.

"You hungry?" I asked.

"I could eat, I guess."

"Well there's an Italian place next to —"

"Alright stop dammit!" he cut me off, "you gonna tell me what the hell just happened?"

"You really think you should be cursing so soon after being in the house of the lord?"

"Julie I swear to god —"

"AH!" I gasped dramatically, breaking out my southern accent again, "how dare you take the lords name in vain?!"

He just glared at me.

I tried to keep a straight face but couldn't stop myself from bursting out laughing.

"Fuck off."

"What?!" I laughed some more.

"You need to tell me what —"

Before he could finish, I grabbed him by the face and promptly stuck my tongue down his throat. When I knew I had his attention I leaned in and whispered in his ear.

"Not here."

I tilted my head in the direction of the driver and he nodded in recognition of what I was saying.

I smiled, shifted my weight and turned around so I could lie back and rest my head in his lap.

"Ok," he said quietly, "but at least answer one question for me."

"What's that?" I said, softly running my fingers up and down his legs.

"Are we good?"

I looked up at him and smiled.

"Baby, you have no idea."

I was on cloud nine and ready to hit the town to celebrate in style but, as luck would have it, my twenty-one year old boyfriend decided we should "chill" and grab a burger in the hotel bar. He gave me some crap about there being a DJ that night and not wanting to be out late since we had an early flight out in the morning. Seeing as it was his birthday, I didn't fight him, but I knew damn well the only reason he didn't want to go out was because he couldn't wait for me to translate what went down with Drake and why I was so giddy about it. In truth, the former would be much easier to explain than the latter.

"Ok," he said after the waiter took our order, "spill it."

I thought about torturing him for a while longer but decided against it.

No need to be mean...

"Ok, so on the surface, you are about to make an eight figure donation to Pastor Drake Benson's 'Each One Teach One' urban education foundation."

"On the surface?"

"Yes," I leaned forward so he would hear me over the music, "the truth is, you are about to funnel all of your illegal funds through the largest, most successful money laundering operation in the history of the United States."

It was true. Drake Strong sat at the head of a consortium of more than fifteen hundred black churches and religious organizations across the country that specialized in transforming large amounts of illicit cash into legitimate assets. It was a network that dated back to the pre-civil rights era south, a time when there were two economies in that part of the country, one black and one white.

It was a little known fact that, because of segregation, there were thriving black owned businesses all over the south before the civil rights movement. Grocery stores, hardware stores, restaurants, you name it. There was even a black wall street in Oklahoma and, eventually, several black owned banks. Before those banks, however, black businesses and entrepreneurs had nowhere to turn for capitol. That's where the churches came into play.

It started off with individual churches here and there making small loans to local businesses and investing in things that would benefit their communities. As the civil rights movement picked up steam, churches across the south began communicating with each other, organizing and coordinating their efforts. That much is taught in most grade school history classes. What's not taught is that the organization and coordination of the various congregations in support of the civil rights movement, included the organization and coordination of their financial resources as well.

The civil rights movement was much more than just a series of peaceful protests and marches. It was a massively successful PR campaign. Protests and events and all of the logistics and communications involved with those things cost money, and those churches banned together to make sure cash got to where it was needed, when it was needed. It was an amazing behind the scenes success story that's not been told nearly enough.

It wasn't all good news however. In one of the great ironies of American history, the success of the civil rights movement destroyed the thriving black economy that existed in the south. Those black owned businesses existed to serve a community that didn't have access to the more 'main-stream' establishments. Once that access was 'won', those businesses and entrepreneurs were no longer needed.

The churches however, would remain the hub of the black community for years to come. And the framework that was built to allow them to communicate with each other during the height of the movement stayed in place as well.

The pastors of these churches now knew, first hand, the benefits of talking to each other and organizing their efforts together. So they knew it would only help them, in the long run, to keep their network alive. No one knows exactly who or how, but at some point someone figured out how to take advantage of that network and then, to expand on it.

"Wait a minute," Preston said, sounding like an eager undergrad challenging his professor, "you're telling me that whole church thing was just a front like that hair salon in Winnfield?

"Well, yes and no. It's not quite the same thing."

"What's the difference?"

"Well, for one, you're not talking about a single church. There is a network of religious organizations across the country, all working together to process large sums of money."

"How does it work?"

"The same as the salon, but better," I smiled, "and bigger."

"What do you mean?"

"The first, most basic thing you need is a business that exists primarily on cash income, no credit cards, few, if any, checks, etcetera."

"Ok."

"And," I continued, "nobody would expect a hair salon in a place like Winnfield to accept checks or take credit cards right?"

"Right. That's pretty normal for a place like that."

"Exactly, so you can set up shop and run your business without deviating from the standard business model. No reason for anyone to be suspicious."

"Alright, I get it. But why is the church thing better?"

"Think about it," I smiled, "all churches exist on donations, primarily cash donations."

The waiter arrived with our food before Preston could say anything else. Just as well, he needed marinate on that last bit of info before continuing.

"Ok," he said after our waiter was a safe distance away, "I think I get it."

"You sure?"

"I mean, I get how it works, sure. Since everything, or almost everything, is in cash, you can get your dirty money into the system easily. You just mix that money in with whatever legit donations you have and nobody knows the difference. I still don't see how the church is any better than the salon though."

"Well, the first thing you need is a cash business. The second is a business that can justify large variations in revenue from week to week or month to month, without raising any red flags. A hair salon can work like that only to a point. A church? Well a church is a charitable organization, so variations in income are expected. Not only that, because a charity's sole source of income is based on the generosity of others, there is a built in justification for any swing in revenue."

"Wow. Ok, this is really cool."

I laughed.

"Seriously," he said, as he took a bite of his hamburger, "who knew this kinda thing was even possible?"

"I guess it is kinda cool huh?" I smiled and started on my salad.

"Ok, wait. I understand how the dirty money gets in, but how do we get the clean money out?"

"You have any cash on you?"

"What?"

"Cash. Do you have any cash on you?"

He looked completely confused, and annoyed, but checked his wallet anyway.

"I have a twenty."

"Give it to me," I said, "for the tip."

He gave me a confused look but handed over the twenty. He looked at me as if he was waiting for me to say something but I went back to my salad without speaking. He shook his head.

"So anyway," he said after a moment, "what I was ask—"

"Wait," I interrupted and handed him a five dollar bill, "take this."

"What the hell?"

"Use that for the tip when the check comes."

"I just gave you twenty dollars for the tip."

"No, you gave me five."

"Julie, I just handed you a twenty dollar bill."

"Prove it."

I smiled and watched as the lights slowly went on for him. He just shook his head and laughed.

"Wow."

"Yes, wow is right," I smiled, "the absolute best thing about cash donations is that no one knows how much they are until you tell them. You just gave me twenty but I'll only give five to the waiter. He has no idea what you gave me and has no reason to question what I gave him."

"Then you pocket the fifteen and no one is the wiser."

"Not only is no one the wiser, everyone is happy with the transaction."

"Wow."

"The key is patience."

"Patience?"

"Preston if we showed up tomorrow and dropped ten million dollars in cash in the collection plate somebody is going to notice. I don't care how big the church is."

"Ah," he said, now fully grasping the concept, "so you spread it out over an entire network of churches and break it down into smaller amounts that make it into the system over time."

"And?" I asked, allowing the student to become the teacher.

"And," he smiled proudly, "you do the same in reverse for the withdrawal. You skim smaller amounts incrementally off the top so that no one notices anything."

"Close," I smiled.

"What?"

"Well, it's not that nobody notices anything Preston. There is nothing to notice. That phantom ten mil that made it into the system fattened up the coiffeurs, but that was only temporary. The skimming for the withdrawal balances the books for anyone looking for a long-term trend or pattern. Minus the processing fees of course."

"What is a processing fee?"

"You remember the notes Drake and I were passing back and forth?"

"Yeah, it was in some kind of code or something right?"

"Well, yes and no. The first was just the amount, so I wrote the number 10 which really isn't in code, but it's just a number with no context so it doesn't need to be. After that he wrote TnT, which stands for Timing and Terms. To which I responded with the numbers 30 and 5."

"And what's that?"

"You have thirty days to provide the cash and his organization gets a five percent processing fee for doing the job."

"So they keep five cents off every dollar they process?"

"Hence the term, processing fee."

"How do you know all this?"

For a brief second I was tempted to give him an honest answer. I decided against it.

"That's a tale for another day," I smiled shyly and went back to my salad.

Chapter Twenty-One

We finished our dinner with no more talk of money laundering or any other illicit business activity. In fact we didn't do much talking at all. Amazingly enough, it wasn't an awkward kind of silence. It was the comfortable kind you don't feel compelled to fill with meaningless small talk.

I had definitely turned a corner where Preston was concerned. I don't know exactly how, or when, but at the end of the day, it didn't matter. He met me at my absolute worst and had just gotten his first glimpse of me at my best. Through it all, he stood by my side, happily going along for the ride.

And yes, I was fully aware he was much too young and my life way too complicated for this to be anything more than a fling. I knew, in my head, that he was just starting out and didn't need to take on me and my problems before he had the chance to build his own life and make his own mistakes. I knew all of that. I just didn't care.

When we met, I was on my ass, desperate with no clear way out of the mess I had created. And now, a few weeks later, my life had done a complete one-eighty and Preston had been with me the entire time. How could I not feel close to him?

Because of him I felt like myself again and not the weak-minded, fragile, scared version of me that I had become so familiar with over the past three years. I felt strong and smart and capable. I felt like the best version of myself had been reborn and all I wanted, in that moment, was to share that with him.

"You ok?"

"Excuse me?"

"Where were you?" he laughed.

"I've been sitting right next to you genius."

"You looked like you were a million miles away. What were you thinking?"

"That's none of your business." I smiled shyly.

"Hey, no fair keeping secrets on my birthday."

"It is still your birthday isn't it?"

"It is."

"Well, don't you think we should go upstairs and celebrate properly?"

"You know what I wanna do?" he said excitedly. *MMMM...*

"I'm afraid to ask."

He stood up.

"Dance with me."

"What?"

"Let's dance."

Shit...

"Um, Preston I, I'd rather not."

He smiled and sat back down.

"Are you seriously not gonna dance with me?"

I looked at him, only this time he was looking right back at me. Our eyes locked. My heart melted.

"Preston, I'm sorry, it's just I'm not a real good dancer."

"Oh please, come on," he took my hand and led me to the dance floor "What kind of music you like?"

"I like everything." I mumbled awkwardly, as we made our way to toward the DJ.

"That's what everybody says," he said dismissively, as he stopped in front of the DJ table and turned around to face me, "now tell me what kind of music do you really like?"

My heart felt like it was going to beat out of my chest. I'm not sure if I had ever been so nervous.

"I'm not being evasive. It's just that anything I like was probably recorded before you were born so —"

"Julie stop," he cut me off, "you know what an excuse is?"

"What?"

"A well dressed lie."

I laughed and shook my head.

How the hell do I get myself out of this???

"Now," he continued, "it's my birthday and you are going to dance with me and you are going to like it."

"But Preston I wasn't joking. I really don't know how to dance."

He took both of my hands and looked me in the eye.

"Then you're just gonna have to trust me."

I swear the way he said it made my knees weak. It was all I could do to stop from tumbling into his arms right then and there.

"Whatever you want," I said, "let's just get this over with."

"Cool, you like Craig David?"

"Never heard of him."

"Ok, well trust me, this song is perfect."

He asked the DJ to play something called Hypnotic and led me to an empty dance floor. I scanned the room and, fortunately, there were maybe ten people in the entire restaurant and most of their attention was focused on one of the four big screen televisions hanging over the bar.

The song started and, unfortunately for me, it wasn't a ballad. It was some sort of mid tempo R&B thing.

Shit I'm done...

My heart sank. I could see in his face that he wanted to do this and I wanted to do it for him, but I was lost. I just stood there, frozen in place. I had zero idea what to do.

"Preston, I —"

"Shhh," he said softly, grabbed my hands and put them on his chest, "let me take care of you."

He put his hands on my hips and smiled at me. His hands gently, smoothly, moved my hips left and right to the beat of the music. All the while, his eyes never left mine.

I trust you...

"Take a step to your right."

Before I could process his command, he moved me to my right.

"Now bring your left foot over."

I did as told and he mirrored my movements perfectly.

"Now step with your left. Bring over your right."

After a few awkward stumbles we were step-touching in tandem to Hypnotic by Craig David.

With each movement, with each step, I gained confidence. Not in my ability to dance, but in Preston's ability to take care of me. I wasn't fighting him anymore. I was going where he wanted, when he wanted and how he wanted. He was leading. And I found myself wanting to follow.

As each eight count passed, I fell deeper. I fell harder. I never took my eyes away from his, not because I was scared but because that's where I felt safest. Out of nowhere, my body started moving more freely. My hips loosened up and I started to find the rhythm on my own. All we were doing was moving from side to side, but within that simple two step movement was a whole world of wide open space to express what I was feeling, what I was seeing, what I was hearing.

I took my hands from his chest and placed them on his shoulders. Each time I stepped left or right, I let my hips swing a little more emphatically in that direction, as if I was channelling some sort of inner belly dancer I never knew was there.

Just as I was finding a groove, my partner stopped me in place. Before I could protest, I felt his hands shifting my weight left and right as if we were walking in place.

I was completely confused, until I looked in his eyes. The instant we made eye contact I knew what he wanted. As I was leaning against him, walking in place, the only things moving on my body were my knees, my hips, and my ass.

This what you want??

Once I knew what he wanted, I worked it. And kept working it, until he moved me to my right and we were back two stepping again.

His transitions worked perfectly with the music, and each time we went through it, I needed less direction.

Step Right.

Step Left.

And Walk.

By the third or fourth time through I was pretty much moving on my own, but his hands never left my waist. He wasn't letting me go. He wanted me to know I was safe. And that's what I felt. My eyes never left his.

Step Right.

Step Left.

And Walk.

His hands kept me in place but I was in charge of how much movement to give as I followed him. It was up to me, how much sexy to show. I didn't hold anything back.

Step Right.

Step Left.

And Walk.

I was seriously working the *'walk'* by this point, not worried anymore about what anybody might be thinking. As long as he was happy, that's all that mattered.

I have never felt so sexy. Ever. I had never felt so exotic or sensual. It was completely empowering in a way I didn't expect to ever feel on a dance floor.

Step Right.

Step Left.

And Walk.

He winked at me and darted his eyes to my left. I glanced over my shoulder to see we had a mini audience of three middle aged white men sitting at the bar.

You boys want a show??

Taking a cue from my man, I walked my hips more slowly and seductively than before. We let them see clearly, vividly what they were missing, what my man would be getting. Now that I knew we had an audience, I wanted them to have their moneys worth.

As we started stepping left and right again, I took my hands from his shoulders and reached into the sky. My whole body flowing up and down, left and right, following Craig David's voice in a powerful display of femininity. It was seductive. It was sexy. It was hypnotic.

the perfect song...

We were so lost in the moment, we didn't realize the music had stopped. We might have still been dancing if not for the spontaneous applause from my admirers at the bar.

Chapter Twenty-Two

"Hey Julie! Ready to rock it today?!"

Somebody had too much coffee...

"Hi Ira," I smiled weakly, "you're full of spunk this morning."

"Live each day on purpose right?"

"Whatever you say."

"We'll get that energy up, trust me. Wanna try some free weights?"

"You're the boss."

One of the benefits of not being tied to a desk for eight hours a day is being able to go to the gym in the morning, when it's less crowded.

"It always like this?" I asked, looking around the near empty gym floor.

"Calm before the storm," he smiled and checked his watch, "there's a Zumba and a soul-cyle at 10:30."

"Am I supposed to know what any of that means?"

He laughed.

"It means this place'll be swimming in soccer moms in less than an hour."

"Well we better get to it then."

"Let's do it! Sit down here and let's knock out some bicep curls."

He handed me two wimpy looking dumbbells and positioned himself behind me.

As if I'd need help lifting these...

"I think I got it," I laughed.

"No need to be a hero," he smirked, "it's all about your form."

I started working my way through the first set, under the watchful eye of my *'trainer'* who, oddly enough, seemed genuinely focused on my form.

"Nice Julie, Really nice!"

I finished the first set of ten, set the weights down and took a quick sip of water before being instructed to start my second.

"How'd everything go?" he asked.

Finally...

"We're all set. You deliver the cash some time in the next thirty days, and ninety days later it's done."

I finished set number two, dropped the dumbbells at my feet and took another sip of water.

"Nope," he said loudly, gesturing for me to put my water bottle down, "no breaks. Three more sets, let's go!"

I did as told and went back at it for set number three, burning biceps and all.

"How do we get the legit funds out?"

"Well," I grunted, struggling to get the weight up, "we still have to work out the exact details but, because of the amount, I can tell you it'll have to be a mix of things."

I dropped the dumbbells by my feet after struggling through that third set. Without missing a beat, Ira grabbed two even smaller dumbbells and handed them to me.

"How much do these things weigh?" I asked, stalling for time.

"Enough," he demanded, having none of it, "two more sets Julie. Let's get it!"

I don't know why I didn't just drop the weights and admit I was spent. I guess my pride wouldn't allow it. Plus, I had noticed some subtle changes in the mirror lately and, seeing as I was sharing my naked body with someone on a regular basis, I had extra motivation to keep the results coming. I pushed through.

"What kinds of things are we talking?" he asked.

"How much do you wanna know?" I was barely able to form the words through the pain.

"I want it all," he said as I started the fifth and final set, this time without dropping my weights to the floor in between.

He encouraged and assisted me through those last few reps.

"Nice!" he shouted as I finished the last rep, "now that's what I'm talking about!"

As Ira was clapping, I jumped up out of the chair and started pacing back n forth. Not because I was excited or motivated, but because I was literally trying to run from the insane burning sensation pulsing through my arms.

"Have some water," he said softy, handing me my bottle.

"That freaking hurts," I said, between sips.

"We just getting started," he smiled.

He wasn't lying. We spent the next twenty-five minutes working through a series of upper body exercises, destroying everything from my biceps to my shoulders. When he was finished turning my body into mush, we went over to the stretching tables to cool down.

"So," he said as walked me through a few upper body stretches, "break it all down for me."

"Well, everything will work through a series of shell corporations I've set up. Like I said before, the cash will take about ninety days to process, but after that, the recoup should be quick."

"Define quick."

"Two to three weeks."

"And are these shell corps charities or what?"

"The less specifics you know, the easier it is to shield you from any blowback."

It always helped to make the client feel important and like everything you were doing was to protect them. The truth is, while I certainly didn't mean Ira any harm, protecting him wasn't anywhere on my list of priorities. I didn't share those details with him because I had decided, after my meeting with Drake, that I didn't need him.

The commission I was making off this one job for Ira and Preston, was more than enough to build and establish this network on my own. There was no longer a need for any partnership.

It wasn't a control thing or a money thing, nothing like that at all. It was more about self preservation and longevity. Every person with knowledge of what I was doing represented, at best, a liability. At worst, they were an outright threat that would, at some point, have to be eliminated. Where did I learn that? From Pastor Drake Strong himself.

I had no desire for my life to be any more dramatic than it already was, so I decided to go into this alone. Ira would know what he needed to know, and that's it. The only person with ownership and full, working knowledge of the entire network would be yours truly. I would treat Ira as a client, an important client, but a client nonetheless.

Would he have agreed to that arrangement? Probably not, but that didn't matter. The fact is he wouldn't even know it happened until it was too late for him to do anything about it.

"Ok," he said, "that makes sense. As long as you have it all under control."

"I do," I assured him, "the network will take the payments and receive all revenue under the guise of various legitimate transactions. Each one of the corporations in play will then funnel that money back to you through another series of legit transactions. Once that happens, the income is yours, free and clear."

"What about taxes?"

"Excuse me?"

"Taxes," he said, "what about the taxes that have to be paid on this income?"

Are you kidding me???

"Ira," I said patiently, "in this country, anybody making over seven figures that's still paying taxes needs to fire their accounting firm."

He laughed.

"Were you testing me?" I asked, mildly annoyed but too tired to get angry.

"Hey," he smiled, "I have to make sure you know your shit."

Asshole…

"Ira, if you do what I say, you and your money will be at least three times removed from anything even remotely questionable at all times. You're welcome."

"Alright alright, calm down," he smiled, "I was just trying to have a little fun. So what's next?"

"Well, everything will be in place by the time you are fully recouped from this first transaction."

"And then it's on to new business."

"Exactly."

I had my own ideas on how to find clients, not that I had any intention of turning down whatever new business Ira could bring my way. I needed to take on as much work as I could, as fast as I could, for as long as my network could safely handle it, which I knew wouldn't be forever.

And that was just fine with me. The idea was to make a splash and get out. To make the largest amount of money possible, as fast as possible and then get as far away from the money laundering business and the network as I could. In order to do that I needed an exit strategy.

Time to mend a fence...

Chapter Twenty-Three

"What are you doing here?"

"It's good to see you too Gregory."

It was true. He'd put on a little weight and was wearing glasses, but he still looked like the same old Gregory to me.

Short and stocky with an aggressive, confrontational nature and a seemingly permanent scowl on his face, Gregory Strong was never big on charm. He was the kind of black man that made white women clutch their purses and cross the street when they saw him walking in their direction, but he didn't mind. He figured if his physical appearance was intimidating, it created something else for his opponent to be focused on that might distract them. And distractions, he knew, made you sloppy.

Sloppy is not what you wanted to be when going up against a man like Gregory. Physical appearance and bad attitude aside, he was a ruthless shark of a litigator with a competitive drive that bordered on manic. He was also pretty much the smartest person I'd ever met.

It'd been close to four years since I'd seen my old partner but, apparently, that was too soon for him.

"I'm serious Julie. What are you doing in my office?"

He hung his coat on a rack by the door and sat down behind his desk, glaring angrily at me the entire time.

"I have an appointment."

"Seriously," he said, "you needed an appointment for me to tell you to go fuck yourself?"

The hostility didn't surprise me. Much like everyone else from my past life, things didn't end well between Gregory and I. His beef with me was legitimate but still, he was the only person in the world I trusted to handle this and I was not leaving his office until he agreed to help me.

"Gregory, I'm not here to rehash the past. I need your help."

"Are you high?"

"I'm serious."

"You're seriously insane. What part of your warped brain woke you up this morning and told you, you could come to me for help?"

"The part that can count? The part that can see you're in a windowless office in a shitty little firm where nobody even knows you exist?" I leaned forward and placed a folder on his desk.

"So," I continued, "you can hop down off that high horse, open that folder, see I'm offering you seven figures in bill-ables over the next five years, and start making yourself relevant again. Or you can tell me to go fuck myself."

As much as he would hate to admit it, there was no denying I knew Gregory Strong almost better than he knew himself. He had been my best friend, and more, since we met as first-year associates at Governalli and Stern, and he was the only person I'd ever met whose ambition matched my own.

And that's the thing about extreme ambition, you never really grow out of it. The voice in your head is always there, telling you you're not good enough, imploring you to do more, insisting that you be more. I knew what that was like because I'd lived with it my whole life. Gregory knew it too.

And so as much as I missed my best friend and hoped there would be a kind of water-under-thebridge vibe to our meeting, I knew I had a trump card to play if I had to.

"As usual," he shot back stubbornly, "you have twice the attitude with only half the information."

Nice try...

"How long have you known me?" I asked.

"Long enough to remember when you still had a fucking soul."

"Long enough to know I didn't come all the way down here without doing my homework. So forget your fucking pride Gregory and look at the folder. I'm not here to beg for your forgiveness or to be lectured. I'm here because you are the best lawyer I know, period. This is business."

What I was asking wasn't purely about business, but he could find that out for himself by looking over what I gave him. He paused for a moment and stood up to leave.

"Don't be here when I get back," he said coldly, as he walked past me. He paused at the door only long enough to put on his jacket.

"Leave the folder," was the last thing he said before turning off the lights and walking out into the hall.

• • •

Ok, so I didn't mend any fences that day. That's ok. The main objective had been to convince Gregory to look at my file, which I did.

Still, I'd be lying if I said I wasn't disappointed. Gregory had been by my side for almost my entire adult life. Through every up and down, both professionally and personally. From my first trial victory to my wedding day, from multiple miscarriages to the birth of my daughter, Gregory was always my constant.

More than that he had always been the one person who could talk me down when I was about to go too far, which wasn't exactly a rare occurrence for me. He had been my confidante and my sounding board through virtually every major decision I had ever made and now, as I was embarking upon the riskiest, most perilous venture of my life, the silence that replaced his counsel was deafening.

I certainly thought of myself as a strong, capable woman, but I had long since disavowed myself of the illusion I was perfect. I was far from it.

But when you're risking everything, there's no such thing as good enough. I had no choice but to be perfect because the consequences of even a small misstep would be devastating, not only to me, but to the people I loved.

In my past, I could take comfort in the fact that I had bounced whatever crazy idea I had off of the smartest person I knew. Someone who always, always, had my best interest at heart.

But that was then. I was on my own now, and the sooner I accepted that, the better it would be for everybody.

Relax Julie...Focus...

I was going to have to check and double check all of my plans and assumptions myself. There wouldn't be anyone working with me to tell me what I'd missed, so I just had to make sure I didn't miss anything. And to do that I had to quiet my mind. I had to be more focused and single minded than at any point in my life, because distractions made you sloppy. And being sloppy, in this case, meant losing everything.

Chapter Twenty-Four

"Mom did you see us?!"

"Oh my god Ashley, you guys were so good!"

She jumped into my arms, nearly knocking me over. I don't think I'd ever seen my daughter so excited.

As usual, the dressing room after a performance was a massive heap of discarded costumes, makeup and toiletries. The winter recital had gone off without a hitch and the dressing rooms was absolutely buzzing with youthful energy and excitement. Even Theo was smiling.

"Congratulations chica." Cassandra said as she came backstage to join us.

"Thank you Cassie! Thank you so much for everything! This was so amazing!"

"Make sure you thank your mother. She's the one who made this happen."

"Mom," she said, giving me another hug, "you're amazing!"

"Thanks sweetie but, and I want to say this to all you girls, tonight is about all of you. You guys worked really hard and it showed. And I know I speak for Theo and Cassandra and Preston and every one of your parents and families when I say we couldn't be more proud of you."

The room erupted in applause that took several minutes to die down. I watched Ashley as she and the other girls from the advanced class hugged and high-fived each other. It was truly a magical moment for her and I cannot describe how happy it made me to see her like that. My little girl was truly in her element. She was confident and poised and, most of all, she was happy. My heart felt like it was about to explode with joy as I watched my baby girl come of age.

"I know, right?"

I turned to see a tall, attractive woman handing me a tissue. I was so caught up I didn't even notice my own tears.

"Thank you," I said and wiped my eyes.

"No problem," she smiled, "they grow up so fast."

"Tell me about it. I still remember when Ashley cried every time I left the room."

"Now they scream whenever we walk in."

We laughed.

"And I just have to tell you, your daughter is a doll."

"Oh, well thank you very much. I'm Julie."

"Hi, I'm Stephanie Pavani, Sylvia's mom."

"The Sylvia?" I smiled, "well it is a pleasure to meet you finally. Ashley can't stop talking about your daughter."

"Same here," she laughed, "they're becoming inseparable, which is actually the other reason I wanted to introduce myself. I know you're busy, but could I steal you aside for a quick chat?"

"Sure."

We stepped outside the dressing room.

"What can I do for you?"

"Well, I felt like I should tell you that I didn't officially meet your daughter at the studio. I am a friend of Brian's."

"Really?"

"Actually, we're dating."

Before that instant, I couldn't have picked Stephanie Pavani out of a lineup if my life depended on it. As soon as she said the words, I noticed her smooth olive skin, shoulder length black hair and the silk, Eli Tahari blouse she was wearing. With the exception of the fact that she was obviously of Indian or Persian descent, Stephanie Pavani had 'City of Aldan' written all over her.

"Oh," I started stammering after a long pause, "I, I um, I appreciate your letting me know."

"I felt like you should hear it from me, especially since the girls are becoming so close."

"And I appreciate that, I really do."

"And you're ok with it?"

"Stephanie listen," I said as I started to find my bearings, "yes, you caught me a little off guard, but who Brian chooses to bring into his life is entirely his business. I'm fine with it as long as Ashley's ok."

"Thank you for saying that, really. I know this is kinda awkward, but it's better to get everything out in the open and avoid any drama, you know?"

"I couldn't agree more. Now I do have to get back to work."

"Absolutely, and by the way, Cassandra tells me you put this whole thing together yourself?"

"She gives me too much credit, I had a lot of help."

"Well, congratulations, it really was an amazing night."

We said our goodbyes and I snuck off into the green room to collect my thoughts. As perfectly pleasant as it was, I just had a conversation with my ex-husbands current girlfriend. I needed a moment.

After a few minutes alone, it turns out I really was ok with it. Stephanie seemed genuinely nice, if annoyingly mature, and her daughter was Ashley's new bff. It seemed like an ideal situation for Brian to ease himself back into the dating world. I was happy for him.

"Here you are."

I turned around to see Cassandra walking into the room followed closely by a short, heavy set, latin woman with cropped brown hair and black, horn-rimmed glasses.

"We've been looking all over for you. Is everything ok?"

"Yes, I'm fine Cassandra. Just needed a moment to catch my breath."

"Well good, I want to introduce you to someone. Annie Velasquez, this is Julie Sharpe."

I extended my hand.

"Nice to meet you Ms. Velazquez."

"Please," she smiled, "call me Annie."

"Julie."

"ok," Cassandra said, "I need to go make sure the girls aren't destroying the dressing room. You two can talk in here."

Cassandra excused herself, leaving Annie and I to stand in awkward silence.

"Um," I smiled, "what just happened?"

"Ok," she laughed, "I've been asking Cassandra for weeks if I could have a meeting with you and this seemed like as good an opportunity as any."

My radar instantly clicked on. Even under normal circumstances, I wouldn't have liked anyone enquiring about me without my knowing who they were or what they wanted. And my circumstances, at that moment, were anything but normal.

"Um, Ms. Velasquez, I'm afraid you have me at a disadvantage."

"How do you mean?"

"Well, you obviously know who I am but I have no idea who you are or, more importantly, why you wanted to meet with me."

"I can explain that."

"Please, but first tell me, why the subterfuge? You could have easily called my home or my office or just come by the studio. I'm not terribly difficult to find."

"Well, to be honest, if we met in the open, someone might notice and I wanted to feel you out first."

"Feel me out?"

"Yes, I have a proposition for you."

WTF?

"Ok Ms. Velasquez, I don't mean to sound impatient or rude but you're gonna have to fill me in right now, or this conversation is over."

"I'm so sorry, can we sit down? I promise to tell you everything."

"Why don't we talk standing up."

My room, my real estate...

"Ok fine," she smiled, unfazed, "let me get right to the point. I work for the Democratic National

247

Committee and we would like for you to consider coming to work with us."

Needless to say, that's not what I was expecting to hear. It actually took a second or two for it to fully register in my mind.

"You work for the DNC?"

"Yes."

"And the DNC wants to offer me a job?"

"Why do you sound so surprised?"

"It's just a little out of the blue, that's all."

"You don't give yourself enough credit," she smiled, "You've been on the radar of some very important national voices ever since you defended Michelle Smith. On a local level, Cassandra is an active member of our voter registration committee and has been talking you up non-stop for weeks. I did some of my own research and it seems you're exactly the kind of strong, intelligent woman we need on our team."

"That's nice of you to say but, if you've done your homework, I assume you must know about *all* of my past, not just one case."

"I do and that's why I'm here."

"What do you mean?"

"Julie, there are a lot of women who believe, as I do, that the work you've done in support of women's reproductive rights is nothing short of heroic. And not just what you did for Michelle which, by the way, might have been the most courageous thing I've ever heard of."

"It cost me my license."

"And yet, from where I sit, you seem to have put your life back together quite nicely. You're a survivor Julie. You are exactly the kind of strong, capable woman we need working with us."

I was intrigued. I still had questions, lots of them, but based on what I just heard, it sounded like Annie Velazquez was offering me a chance to reclaim the narrative of my past and start writing the narrative of my future. For me, that was as close to an offer I couldn't refuse as you could get.

I had lots of regrets that were going to be with me for rest of my life. The mistakes that ended my marriage and destroyed my family were childish and selfish and I had to own them because, as much as I would have done anything to take them back, I wasn't going to have that opportunity.

I knew that and I had come to accept it. But this *horrible thing* I had done for Michelle Smith? The unthinkable act that cost me my license to practice law and the ability to provide for my daughter? That was something I was in no way shape or form ashamed of. In fact, I would do it again in a heartbeat.

"What do you have in mind?" I asked.

"Well, as you can imagine, your name brings with it a certain amount of attention. The first thing we want to do is re-brand you so that the attention you attract is beneficial for our cause."

"Re-brand?"

"We want to be able to spin the announcement of your joining the DNC as a woman's personal triumph over a male dominated judicial system. In order to do that, we have remake your public image."

"And how do we do that?"

"You've heard of the Worthington Foundation?"

"The Super PAC? Yes, of course."

"Well, they need a CEO."

Wow...

A Super PAC is an organization that can raise unlimited amounts of money and spend it however they damn well please in support of whatever political candidate they like, or against whatever candidate they don't like. The only rule is they can't give the money directly to said candidate.

The Worthington Foundation is not only the largest, most influential liberal Super PAC in the nation. It is technically the largest organization of its kind, regardless of political affiliation.

"And you want me for that job?"

"Yes, based on your background, you're certainly qualified. And I know the title is CEO, but the primary responsibility of the office is to make sure the coiffeurs stay filled. Looking at what you've put together here tonight, I'd say you definitely have the ability to bring people together and get them to open their wallets."

"Well," I smiled, "at least that explains why we're meeting in secret."

"I have no idea what you're talking about," she laughed.

"So, the DNC is not actively recruiting the next CEO of the worlds largest Super PAC?"

"Nope," she smiled mischievously, "that wouldn't be even a little bit kosher. I'm just here to see my thirteen year old niece's ballet recital."

Chapter Twenty-Five

For the first time in years, it felt good to go home. My schedule, between the recital and setting up a new business, had been insane for the past few weeks and I needed to recharge my battery.

One of the benefits of my new found financial status was the ability to upgrade a few small things around the house. All I could think about when I left the theater was pouring myself a glass of wine and spending some quality time with my insanely comfortable new sofa. I had it delivered the week before but, unfortunately, I'd barely had a chance to sit in the damn thing. That was about to change.

Mind you, I didn't go crazy with purchases. The sofa and some wardrobe upgrades were about as extravagant as I dared go. Everything else amounted to small things to make our house and our lives more comfortable. And yes, those things

I considered luxuries when money was tight, felt more like necessities now that I was flush with cash. I'm sure Im not the only one.

In my defense, I resisted the temptation to upgrade my vehicle, at least for right now. I restricted my splurging to things like a new bed for myself and a new laptop for Ashley, who was spending the night at the home of her fathers new girlfriend.

As bizarre as it felt to consider that particular reality, I quickly shook off the thought. The important thing, I reminded myself, was that I had our newly decorated home to myself for the night, and that was exactly what the doctor ordered. Especially considering I had no intention of spending the evening alone.

"I have something for you."

"I bet you do."

"Preston, can you keep your penis in check for the next five minutes?"

"What fun is that?"

"A lot more fun than the blue balls you will experience if you don't stop screwing around."

"Fine," he smiled, "watchu got for me boo boo?"

"Don't do that."

"Do what?" he laughed.

"Make me regret inviting you over."

"You know you love it."

Actually I do...STOP. SMILING.

"Are you ever going to shut up?"

"Alright fine," he laughed, "what would you like to give me?"

I handed him a plain white envelope.

"What's this?"

"Open it."

When he saw the contents, he did a double take.

"Julie, what is this?"

"It's a check Preston."

"For seventy-five thousand dollars?"

"Those are the proceeds from the festival."

To call it a recital was misleading. That's how it started but, under my direction, it morphed into Bristol's first annual performing arts festival. A three day celebration of the arts culminating in a performance by the students of Bristol's most beloved dance studio, Victor's Academy of Dance. Amazingly, every single dance workshop, seminar and performance over the course of the three days was completely sold out. A fact that would have been a little less amazing if people knew I had purchased all of the tickets myself.

"But," he asked, "why is this check mine?"

"Because it was your money I used to purchase all of the tickets and give them away."

He gave me a confused look.

"You did what?"

"You heard me," I smiled.

"Wait," he said, "I don't get it."

"Think about it Preston. Your money goes into the box office to buy the tickets."

I paused and waited for him to finish the thought.

"And then," he said after a moment, "that same box office writes me a check for the proceeds from the sale. Wow."

"Dirty money goes in." I smiled proudly.

"And clean money comes out."

"Minus?" I asked, testing him.

"Minus any fees and venue expenses. The processing fee."

Nice Preston. Very nice...

"Exactly. So what's in your hand is a perfectly legitimate check from the venue for tickets sold to an event you promoted."

"Wow," he said quietly, "I don't know what to say. You really are a genius."

Stop! Smiling!

"Like I said, there's absolutely no reason for you to hide that money. You can spend it however you like. You could even open a hair salon if you wanted."

"Wait. Is that —"

"You said you wanted to help your sister," I shrugged.

He just looked at me but I knew what he was thinking. I knew because it's exactly what I was thinking in Chicago. Just like I knew the moment I turned the corner with him, I could see him going through the same process of recognition.

It was one of the most perfect moments of my life. After everything I had been through, much of it self inflicted, I had finally come full circle. I was once again at peace with where I was, who I was with and, most importantly, the person I was becoming.

"You ok?" I asked, wondering why he wasn't kissing me.

"I don't think I've ever been happier."

"Good," I smiled softly.

I'm sure I was glowing. The fact that I could give him something that meant so much to him felt incredible. The fact that he wanted so desperately to take care of the only family he had, made me relate to him in a way I didn't think would ever be possible with someone so young. I leaned back into my sofa and soaked in the utter perfection that had been that day.

What he did next was nothing short of amazing. Instead of tearing my clothes off and making passionate love to me for the rest of the night, my twenty year old boyfriend got up and poured me a glass of red wine, without me even asking.

"What are you doing?" I asked through yet another huge smile.

"You've been saying all week how you wanted to enjoy your new sofa. So let's enjoy your new sofa."

He handed me the glass, sat down beside me and patted his legs. I took the cue, and lied my head in his lap as he took out his phone and put on some music.

"What's that?" I asked as we settled into position.

"A Shade of Blue."

"More Craig David?" I teased.

"No smartass, Incognito. You want me to change it?"

"No, it's nice," I said softly, "where'd you get your taste in music?"

"My dad was a musician."

"Really? I guess there's a lot about you I don't know huh?"

"We have plenty of time," he smiled.

"Yeah, we do."

I closed my eyes and lost myself in the music as he started slowly, gently stroking my hair. It was the kind of moment that could only have been diminished by talking. So, we said nothing.

Then, as those seconds turned into minutes, the sublime state of relaxation I found myself in slowly began building into something else.

I sat my glass on the table and started lightly running my fingernails up and down the front of his legs.

I felt my pulse quicken.

My body temperature began rising and I could sense a subtle tingling in my legs.

mmmmm...

As if reading my mind, Preston's subtle stroking of my hair extended to my shoulders and arms. The tingling in my legs spread to my entire lower body with every movement of his hands.

No longer content with lightly running my fingers over his legs, I was now firmly rubbing up and down his shins with my whole hand. As I came up past his knee, I would reach between his legs, finding his inner thighs and then back down again.

His hands knew no limits at this point. He had come to know my body and it showed. He wasted no time, reaching for and finding my spots. When he grabbed my ass, I instinctively arched my back to grind into his hand as he reached around and found me, wet and ready for him. I arched my back more and that subtle movement changed my body position just enough so that I was face down in his lap.

It's time...

I never had an opinion, one way or another, when it came to performing oral sex. To me, it was just something you did to make your man happy.

But in that moment, I suddenly knew what all my college girlfriends were talking about when they said how much they loved it.

Taking Preston in my mouth wasn't some selfless expression of love. Feeling him inside me that way, being in such complete control of what he was feeling, made me feel like I owned him. Like he was mine and I never wanted to let him go.

I kissed him, gently, lovingly, all over. Front, back, top, bottom. My lips had a mind of their own as they explored every inch. I let no part of his hardness go unloved.

Then, I slowly took all of him in my mouth.

"OOHHH."

He moaned and squirmed, but I was determined to take my time. I sucked and licked and kissed him in every way imaginable, but I did it slowly, methodically. I savored him, not to make him mine, but because he was mine.

I wrapped my fingers around the base to hold him in place. Slowly but surely, I found a smooth, up and down, rhythm that worked and he started to move with me.

His eyes were shut tight and he had the most exquisite look of pure pleasure on his face. A look that only made me want to devour him more.

I kept working at my pace. Whenever I felt him stiffening and moving with more intensity, I backed off and stroked him lightly with my hand. I wasn't trying to torture him. I just wasn't ready for this to end.

When he settled down, I would go back to work, slowly, rhythmically taking him to a place I wanted him to never forget.

Trust me Preston...

This time, when he stiffened, he didn't try to move faster. Instead he just settled into it and let me continue to work him slowly, rhythmically, up and down with my mouth.

That's it baby...let me take care of you...

His eyes stayed shut, his legs straightened and his moans were low and guttural, but his disciplined body resisted the temptation to move.

Let it go baby...

I kept moving with the same slow, methodical rhythm, but applied more pressure with my tongue. That sealed the deal. He started pounding his fists on the sofa and tossing his head back and forth. I never increased or changed my pace in any way, so when he released himself into my mouth, it wasn't a single explosion. It was a prolonged stream of ecstasy that, judging by his reaction, he had never experienced before.

Chapter Twenty-Six

Some call it the sleep of the just, others refer to it as sleeping like a baby. For me, I was just so happy to feel fully rested I didn't care what they called it. Suffice it to say it was the best nights sleep I had in a long time. I was so rested, in fact, I decided to try my hand at breakfast in bed.

There was one problem with that idea. I'm a terrible cook. It's not that I'm not able, at least I don't think so. It's just that I never learned.

I'm a career woman and have been ever since I could remember. For all those years I was out building my career, I had little to no use for domesticity in my life. I had more important things to spend my energy and focus on.

Having said all of that, I didn't see how scrambled eggs and pancakes could be beyond even my meager capabilities. I was wrong.

"Wow."

"Not a word."

"I'm just saying, did you get any flour in the bowl?"

I couldn't help but laugh as Preston surveyed the damage.

"I had a little problem with the mixer."

"A little problem?"

"You wanna give it a try big mouth?"

"Yeah, gimme that," he said, taking the hand mixer, "I think we should leave the kitchen tools to the professionals."

"Professional huh?"

"Ok, maybe I'm not a chef de cuisine, but I can manage a pancake."

I started cleaning up my mess while Preston went to work on our breakfast. It was hard to believe how relaxed we were around each other, considering how we met and my state of mind at that time.

Not that I wasn't open to meeting someone, as evidenced by my whole online dating fiasco, but I certainly wasn't looking to meet and fall for a twenty-something hip hop dancer. And that wasn't even the most incredible thing about the situation.

The most unbelievable part of the whole thing was that, by every indication, this twenty-one year old choreographer was every bit as into me as I was him.

Not that I was complaining. Aside from everything else, he was like some sort of walking good luck charm. Things had been turning around for me from the day we met, and all I could think about as he was standing in my kitchen with no shirt on, was how excited I was to see what was going to happen next.

"Here," I said and handed him a glass of orange juice, "don't say I didn't help with breakfast."

"I guess you ambitious career women don't have time for things like cooking," he smiled as he took his glass.

I went over to the counter, sat on a stool and watched with joy as my man cooked us breakfast.

"I was always too busy for that kinda thing," I said after a moment.

"Busy conquering the world?"

"Something like that, speaking of which, can you keep a secret?"

"I think we're way past that point aren't we?"

"Point taken," I smiled, "anyway, I got offered a job last night."

"Seriously? How'd that happen?"

"I can't get into too many of the details right now, but it's an amazing opportunity."

"That's awesome, but what about the thing with Ira and all that?"

"Well, that kinda thing is not meant to be permanent Preston. You always need an exit strategy and this could be exactly that for me."

"So it sounds like the timing's perfect," he smiled and turned on the stove, "that's really cool."

"It kinda is." I smiled and stood up.

To hell with pancakes...

"In fact, I think it's cool enough to be cause for a celebration."

"What'd you have in mind?" he asked, still too focused on his pancake batter to notice I had dropped my robe to the floor.

"Are you kidding me?"

"What?" he asked, still not looking up from his bowl.

"I'm naked you asshole."

He looked up and promptly knocked the bowl off the counter, spilling pancake batter all over my floor. I didn't care.

"You're cleaning that up," I smiled.

"I'd say that's the least I could do," he replied and turned off the stove.

He walked over to where I was standing, but just as he put his hands on my naked body and his lips on mine, my phone started buzzing.

I thought, for a fleeting second, about ignoring it but the mommy in me wasn't having any of that. Ashley had spent the night away from home, so not answering wasn't an option.

I reached clumsily into the pocket of my robe and checked the number,

Unknown Caller

Hmmm...

"Gimme a sec," I said, still unwilling to risk not answering, "hello?"

"Julie Watson, as I live and breath."

WTF?

"Drake?"

"I catch you at a bad time?"

"Well, actually I am kind of in the middle of something."

"Ok, then let me get right to it. It was really good seeing you the other day."

"Thanks, it was really good to see you too."

"We have to do it again some time."

Uh oh...

"I don't know about that Drake. We don't make it out there to your neck of the woods too often. That was kind of a one time thing for us."

I waited for him to respond. Nothing.

Shit...

"Hello? Drake you still —"

"That's too bad Julie. Like I said it was REALLY good seeing you and I REALLY think we should do it again some time, soon."

Fuck...

"Alright well, lemme see what our calendar looks like and get back to you. I'm sure we can —"

"Will you be coming alone?"

"Excuse me?"

"I was just wondering if you'd be coming by yourself next time."

"Um, yeah I think that would probably be a good idea."

"Yeah I agree," he responded coldly, "easier to schedule that way."

"Ok, well let me see what I can do and let you know, ok? I promise I'll get back to you soon."

"I'm sure you will Julie. Take care and god bless you and the family."

SHIT...

Chapter Twenty-Seven

What I remember most from that morning is how cold it was. An admittedly odd takeaway, considering the meeting that was about to take place started a downward spiral that ended up nearly costing me my life.

But I'm not talking about cold in a 'could you turn up the thermostat' kind of way. I'm talking about a shivering, nose running, see your breath kind of cold that would have made no sense inside an office building if I were meeting anyone but Gregory, who couldn't have been pleased with the way our last discussion went. This deep freeze was his way of re-establishing control.

We were also meeting in a dingy, sparsely furnished conference room that was barely big enough to fit the single table and three chairs that were in there. I had been in my share of interrogation rooms and, if not for the cheap artwork adorning the walls, that's exactly what that conference room felt like. I knew Gregory well enough to know that was no accident.

He obviously felt I was too comfortable and in control last time. So between the sub arctic temperature and the rigid, impersonal setting, he was going out of his way to make sure I was much less so this time around, and that could only mean one thing.

He wanted me to be focused on my surroundings instead of on the conversation we were about to have. He wanted me to be distracted.

What are you fishing for Gregory?

Of course had he known my state of mind coming into that morning he could have saved himself the effort. I was already about as distracted as I could be.

"You're kidding me right?" he asked, finally entering the room after letting me sit alone in that ice box for what seemed like an eternity. He took his seat across from me.

"About what?" I answered tiredly. I hadn't slept at all the night before.

He just glared at me for a moment before speaking.

"Lemme ask you something Julie. Is it physically impossible for you to tell the truth? I mean, is every single word out of your mouth a damn lie?!"

"Gregory come on, I don't have time —"

"Did you THINK I wouldn't find it?!"

"Find what?!"

"See?!" He stood up. "That right there! That is exactly the problem with you Julie! It always has been!"

It was beginning to feel like a cross examination which, I knew, was the whole point. Had I been my normal self, I would have been able to deal with it easily, but I wasn't at my best. Not even close.

"Gregory, let's not do this right —"

"No, let's," he cut me off and sat back down, "you've spent your whole life believing you were the smartest person in every room you were in. That you were always two steps ahead of everybody else."

"Do you have a point?"

"When's it gonna stop Julie?"

"When is what gonna stop?!"

"When are you going to stop playing games with your life as if you have nine to lose?! That bullshit you pulled with Michelle Smith didn't cost you enough?"

"Here we go with Michelle Smith again," I said, rolling my eyes.

"It's the truth and you know it."

"What I know is that Michelle was my client and it was my job to —"

"To perjure yourself?!"

"It was my job to protect her!"

"And lose your license in the process?!"

"You think I wanted that?! I did what I had to do for my client!"

"That what you tell yourself at night, when you can't buy food or clothes for your daughter, that you did what you had to do for your client?"

Now he crossed the line...

"Don't you fucking dare sit there and pretend you have any idea what my life is like! You walked out on me just like Brian and everybody else, and yeah you might've had your reasons, but at the end of the day you still chose to turn your back on me. So how I choose to pay my bills and take care of my daughter is none of your fucking business!"

He picked up the folder.

"You made it my business when you came to me with this shit. Just like you made Michelle Smith my business when you brought that crazy bitch into my office."

"I think you mean OUR office, you arrogant prick! And while you're sitting there all high and mighty and in judgement of everything and every one, let me remind you that Michelle Smith wasn't the problem. Her psycho mother was. Michelle was just as much a victim as —"

"She fucking shot you! She walked into OUR office, pulled out a gun and shot you and —"

"She snapped Gregory! She had a breakdown and she made a mistake!"

"So that justifies you lying under oath that her mother did it?! Jesus Julie, it's a miracle your ass isn't in jail already, and now this?!"

I stood up to leave.

"I could fill a library with everything you don't know about that case. Unfortunately I don't have the time to educate you right now."

"You wanna know what I do know?"

"Please Gregory, enlighten me."

"I know Anna Smith played you like a fucking drum from the beginning of that whole mess. She treated you like a puppet on a string and, at the end of the day, your pride wouldn't allow you to let that shit go. That's why you did what you did for her daughter, not because you were standing up for what you believe in or protecting some innocent, abused girl. That's all bullshit. You just couldn't live with the fact that somebody actually got over on the great Julie Watson. That shit ate at you and your mountain sized ego until you were willing to risk everything you had for the chance to put Anna Smith in her place."

The scariest thing is, I don't know whether he was right or not. There were so many things Gregory didn't know about that case, things he could never know. But he knew me and, as much as I told myself I was protecting Michelle when I decided to lie under oath, I would be lying yet again if I said the thought of sticking it to her evil witch of a mother never crossed my mind.

"Gregory, I am not about to sit here and relive my past with you."

"Good, because I could give a shit about your past. I'm talking about today and how even now, even after losing everything, your fucking pride is

273

about to lead you into making the same dumb ass mistake all over again."

"Would you mind skipping the lecture and just telling me what the hell you're talking about?!"

"Fucking money laundering Julie?! Seriously?!"

I just stood there, stone faced.

"That's the difference between me and you," he continued, "see, I know you're not stupid. But did you seriously believe I wouldn't take a second look at any of those transactions? Did you honestly —"

His voice trailed off at the end, as I tried to look away, too embarrassed to make eye contact. From the beginning, I had a feeling where all this was going, but the route he took to get there caught me off guard. He had me so rattled I could barely keep up with the conversation, which I knew was his plan all along.

Nicely done Gregory...

The problem now was, I was too distracted with my own emotional state to tell how much he had deciphered from my file or what questions he still had. Judging by his reaction, this latest tidbit was clearly a new revelation.

"Mother fucker," he muttered, under his breath.

"Gregory, it's not what you think," I asserted calmly, sitting back down.

"You knew damn well I would figure it out. That's why you made an appointment the other day, so the meeting would be on record."

"I needed to make sure I was protected," I said softly.

"You mean you needed our conversation to be privileged," he shook is head, "what the hell is happening to you?!"

Even as the words came out of his mouth, I wanted to crawl into a shell and hide. It wasn't that anything I'd done was unethical or over the line. It was a perfectly legitimate ruse that had gotten me into Gregory's office and that, I had to admit to myself, was the problem.

The fact that I needed a ruse to ask him for help was something difficult for me to wrap my mind around, and it should have been the surest sign yet that I was heading down the wrong path. This was a man who, at one time, would have literally given his life for me, and I would have given mine for his.

We were perfect for each other in so many ways. As first year associates, we were required to put in sixteen hour days on occasion and, while everyone else was complaining, Gregory and I loved every minute of it and even volunteered for extra duty whenever the opportunity presented itself.

We ended up spending so much time together we could finish each others sentences. And neither of us found it odd that those sentences were usually about some obscure precedent, controversial ruling or antiquated piece of legislation.

But while our passion for the law might have been what initially brought us together, we soon found ourselves bonding over things that had nothing to do with work.

He was the only person in my life who understood me. We worked tirelessly and laughed effortlessly together, sharing our lives in a way that would have made most married couples envious. Gregory and I shared everything for those years and, in hindsight, we were kidding ourselves thinking we wouldn't eventually share each other. Which would've been fine except for the fact that, for most of that time, I was married to his best friend.

"I'm sorry."

"Screw your apology Julie. And screw you for getting me involved in more of your bullshit."

"I needed your help."

"You need more than help. Do you have any idea what you're getting involved in?"

"I know exactly what I'm getting into. Why do you think I came to you?"

"The question is why didn't you come to me sooner, before this shit got out of hand?"

"Nothing's out of hand Gregory! Most of what you saw in that file isn't even real. They're theoretical transactions put on paper to see if they would stand up to a certain level of scrutiny. I came to you because there's no one better at this kind of analysis and if there was a hole in my thinking, I knew you would find it."

"So what, you wanted me to help make you a better criminal?!"

"I needed your advice on how to build a network like this in a way that would protect me and my family."

"You needed?"

"Yes, things have taken a turn and I have an opportunity to get out of this thing before it ever really gets started."

"What opportunity?"

"It's a job but I can't get into the details right now. Suffice it to say, I would be able to earn a semi-honest living."

"Well," he smiled, "that's a start."

It was good to see him smile.

"And what about all of this?" he asked, referring to the file I had given him.

"Well, at first I was thinking of going ahead and setting things up, just for short term operations."

He looked at me and, for a second, I honestly thought his eyes were going to pop out of his head.

"I know, I know," I said, before his head could explode, "I wasn't thinking straight."

"And now?"

"Now I just want to close this thing out and move on."

"Close what out?"

Shit...

"I'm just saying, I wanna move —"

"Wait," he interrupted me, "you said most of the transactions weren't real. What did you mean?"

I walked right into that and now had no idea what to say. The last thing I wanted was to get him any deeper involved than he already was.

"Julie, what did you do?"

"Gregory, I told you I wasn't thinking straight ok? There were a few small things that came my way and I honestly didn't feel like —"

"Dammit Julie, stop stalling! What did you do?"

I looked up to see him staring intensely at me. Only this time I didn't sense anger, he was genuinely concerned.

Careful Julie...

"A little over ten million dollars."

This time I really do think his eyes popped out of his head. Only, I couldn't be sure because I quickly looked away once the words came out of my mouth.

"Tell me you're kidding."

I just shook my head.

"But how?" he asked, "I checked and none of what you have in the file is real."

This caught me by surprise.

"You knew?"

"The effective dates on the corporate ID's were all too close together to be a coincidence. So I checked a few of them and found they were either pending or didn't exist at all."

He really was good...

"Dammit, I never thought about that."

"Exactly," he said impatiently, "so if none of this is real, how the hell did you —"

"Wait," I interrupted, needing to distract him since I wasn't ready to answer his next question, "how did you even know to look at the effective dates?"

"I didn't. It's not so much something you check as it is something you notice. There is no such thing as a fool proof transaction in this business. That's a myth that gets people arrested. And since there is no transaction that can stand up to every level of scrutiny, the key is to never attract any scrutiny."

"To not get noticed in the first place."

"Exactly. What you have here is good Julie. It's very good, in theory. The problem is not so much what you did as the way you chose to do it. You have to build these things incrementally, which means you need capitol to fund legitimate operations for a period of time before anything remotely illicit takes place. Money laundering is the long game. It requires a different kind of mindset than your typical criminal enterprise. It takes a lot of patience and resources up front."

"I can see that."

"Good, but none of that speaks to the penalties of which I know you are aware," he stood up, walked over and sat on the table next to me, "now, as your lawyer, I need to know exactly what you've done, and don't even try to bullshit me. This aint my first rodeo."

"I know that."

"Good," he smiled, "spill it."

"I know it's not your first rodeo Gregory."

It wasn't what I said that got his attention. It was the way I said it. I watched as the look on his face went from annoyed to pissed off to horrified in a matter of seconds. He stood up, grabbed the folder and flipped hastily through the papers until he found what he was looking for.

"Son of a bitch," he said softly, as he handed me a piece of paper with the letters E.O.T.O. at the top, "tell me you didn't."

"It's not as bad as you think."

"You went to my cousin?!"

"It was just a one time thing."

"You're unbelievable."

"I'm serious Gregory. It's not like we're partnering or anything. This thing came up, I had to move quickly and so —"

"And so you went to church in Chicago."

"Yes, but it was only that one time ."

He shook his head and looked at me like I was a naive child.

"Julie, it's not possible that you're this smart and this stupid all at the same time."

"I know what I'm —"

"There is no such thing as one and done with a guy like my cousin! Once he has his claws into you —"

"Gregory, I can handle Drake," I said, unconvincingly.

"Wait," he ordered, noticing the small, rolling suitcase sitting beside my chair, "where are you going?"

I thought about lying but quickly realized there was no point.

"I have to go to Chicago."

"Like hell you are!"

"Gregory, I just have to close this thing out. One more trip and I'm done, I swear."

He studied me for a moment before speaking. His eyes were soft and welcoming. It was the way he used to look at me. It was a look I hadn't seen in a long time, and thought for sure I'd never see again.

"He called you didn't he?" he said, after a long moment.

"Why does that matter?"

Without responding he took out his cell phone and made a call.

"Carey, cancel all my appointments today and tomorrow."

"What are you doing?" I asked.

"I'm going with you to Chicago."

Chapter Twenty-Eight

I tried, briefly, to talk him out of coming but got nowhere. Gregory was determined to "put an end to this bullshit" and didn't trust me to do that on my own. Truth be told, he was probably right.

It was clear by this point that I was out of my element. I knew Drake from working with him in the past, but Gregory was his cousin. They grew up together and were, in their own words, as close as brothers for most of their childhood.

So while I had no idea why Drake summoned me to Chicago or why he insisted I come alone, Gregory seemed to know exactly what was going on. I felt better having him with me.

The flight to Chicago was only about half full, so getting an extra ticket wasn't a problem. Neither was the drive to the airport. Traffic was light and, with NPR playing in the background, the silence between us wasn't quite as awkward as it could've been.

We managed to make it through security, onto the plane and into our seats without so much as a syllable of conversation. Once we were settled into our seats, I closed my eyes and tried to think of something I could offer by way of explanation for the mess I had gotten myself into. I had nothing.

Gregory just sat down and stared out the window with a worried look on his face. I knew he was running through all of our options and working through every possible scenario for our meeting with his cousin. He was doing his job as my lawyer, and my friend, to protect me.

"I really am sorry Greg. Not just for all of this, for everything."

"What were you thinking Julie?" he asked quietly, still staring out the window.

"I don't know. I guess I wasn't.

"Not good enough."

"I don't know what you want me to say. I guess I was desperate."

"But why though? That's what I don't understand. Why were you so desperate? Is living in a huge house and driving a fancy car really that important?!"

"It has nothing to do with any of that. It has to do with paying rent and tuition and buying food —"

"Julie stop. If things got that bad you could've gone to Brian."

"Yeah and then he goes after full custody."

"And so what if he does? Brian lives what, ten minutes away from you? There is no scenario where you aren't still seeing your daughter every single day of the week, regardless of what address she calls home. I'm sorry Julie but there is NO excuse for your being this reckless."

"You don't understand."

"Oh but I do understand. I understand you and how your mind works and how every crazy thing you've ever done traces back to your fucking pride."

We had been estranged for so long I'd forgotten how important his opinion was to me. Hearing him say those words hurt, as the truth often does. But even though it felt like I was being hit over the head with a blunt instrument, I knew I needed to hear every word he was saying.

That's the thing about being an intelligent person. Most smart people have the ability to talk themselves into or out of anything, if left to their own devices. I was no different. Without any input from the outside, the narrative playing in my head always found a way to justify whatever I was doing. Gregory had a way of countering that narrative with direct, objective, unfiltered fact. His voice had often been the governing device that kept me from going completely off the rails.

"Tell me this," he said after a moment, "didn't you ever get cold feet? I mean, how many times did you try to talk yourself out of this? How many chances did you have to back out of this thing before pulling the trigger?"

"Why does that matter now?"

"I'm trying to understand how you let things go this far. You're smarter than this."

"Gregory, I cant give you an answer I don't have."

"Try."

"Alright fine, first of all, there's no one answer. Of course the money was attractive, it seemed like it would be an easy fix to some financial issues I had and, if I'm gonna be completely honest, I was bored."

"Bored Julie?" he laughed and shook his head, "are you shitting me?"

"Did you know I was working in a fucking call center?"

This, he found hilarious.

"I'm serious! You try sitting in a cubicle answering phone calls from angry sick people all day. I'm not built for that."

"No," he laughed, "you're absolutely right about that."

"I missed the action. I missed feeling challenged and so I guess I just got caught up."

"And you don't think that'll happen again?"

"Well, if the job opportunity I told you about comes to pass, there's no chance I won't feel challenged."

"What is this mysterious job anyway?"

"I really shouldn't say, at least not yet. But if and when it happens I'll absolutely be back in the game in a major way."

"Sounds like it came up at exactly the right time."

"Like a lot of things lately," I smiled

"Ladies and gentlemen, welcome to Chicago's O'hare Airport. Local time is..."

The ride from the airport to the church was quiet. That doesn't mean it wasn't stressful. I still had no idea what was going on and that bothered me. I didn't like going into anything this blind, much less a meeting with a man like Drake Strong, who'd made it clear over the phone that this wasn't a social call.

When I first met Drake he had been charged with manslaughter in the beating death of two teenage drug dealers accused of sexually assaulting a teenage girl from his old neighborhood. There was little doubt he had actually done what he'd been accused of and, justified or not, he was looking at spending fifteen to twenty years in federal prison if found guilty.

He had a decent lawyer who pleaded with him to make a deal, which was good advice considering the circumstances. Drake refused.

He eventually fired that attorney and turned to Gregory who, because of the closeness of their relationship at the time, didn't feel he could remain objective enough to do the job. So he did the next best thing and pawned his cousin's piece of shit case off on me.

And when I say it was a piece of shit case, that is exactly what I mean, and not just because it was un-winnable. The client, in the words of his first attorney, was an absolute nightmare. A stubborn, self-righteous jerk who was guilty as sin but refused to take a deal. Oh and by the way, he was flat broke.

Fortunately for him, I could understand Drake's stubborn insistence to stay the course, even when advised to surrender. He was, in essence, betting on himself and that was something I could definitely relate to.

Turns out, Drake and I shared a lot of the same qualities, so we hit it off from the beginning. That doesn't mean I had any better idea how to keep him out of prison than the first guy. It just means I was willing to stand and fight for him if that's what he wanted. He respected that and I respected his desire to fight as opposed to taking a deal, even if there was no way in hell we could win. It was his life so it was his call. The only problem for me was the money.

Murder trials are notoriously expensive and, as I said, Drake had no money back then. As willing as I was to put it all on the line for him, I needed to get paid.

I explained this and he assured me it wouldn't be a problem. Sure enough, the next day, he gave me a ten thousand dollar check as a retainer. When I asked him where the money came from, he said it was a donation from his church. Apparently the girl who was assaulted was the niece of his pastor and so the church took up a special collection for his defense.

It all sounded perfectly plausible to me so I saw no need to look into it further. Even had I been suspicious, everything he told me was the truth so it would have all checked out. Of course, in hindsight, I know there was more to it but that wasn't my focus at the time. I had the money and happily took the case, fully prepared to fight tooth and nail for my new client.

I spent most of my time interviewing Drake, deposing state witnesses and devising some sort of desperation based strategy. There were countless hours spent sifting through evidence and probing for some sort of strand to pull on that might begin to unravel the states' case. We found nothing. The only thing useful to come from spending so much time together, was I felt like I got to know a side of Drake that a jury could relate to.

He was smart and articulate and disarmingly self deprecating. In a lot of ways his personality was the exact opposite of what you would think based solely on his imposing physical appearance. If I could actually get a jury to see what I saw, we might have a chance of pulling off a miracle once we went to trial.

Only Drake's case never made it to trial. When I took over the case, the prosecution had as many as seven eye witnesses. Within six weeks, they had none.

One by one, each recanted their earlier statements until, eventually, the prosecution could no longer effectively place Drake at the scene of the crime, much less present any evidence of his guilt.

When I told Gregory the charges had been dropped and that we had been paid, in full, I assumed he would be thrilled. I was wrong. He just shook his head in disgust and told me I needed to stay the hell away from his cousin.

Apparently when he first heard about witnesses recanting their testimony, he got suspicious and did the kind of digging that only he was capable of. He got ahold of the church financials and started doing his own, off-the-record, investigation. In less than a week, he knew everything and broke down for me exactly how the church came up with the money to not only pay for my legal services but to buy off all of the states' witnesses as well.

He also told me why the church did all of that. They did it because that was the deal the pastor made when he hired Drake to kill the two dealers who assaulted his niece.

This was the man I chose to do ten million dollars worth of business with. Yes, he was charming and engaging and funny and all of those things. But he was also a killer for hire, and not one who sat a couple hundred yards away in a tree with a rifle. This was a violent man who didn't mind getting up close and personal with his victims.

Brilliant Julie...brilliant...

I shook my head at the ridiculousness of it all. Gregory was right. How in the hell could I have been so reckless?

In my defense, as much as Gregory always warned me he was dangerous, I never saw Drake in that way. Not until I got his phone call.

Chapter Twenty-Nine

"Waddup D?"

I studied Drake closely as he walked into his office and could tell immediately he was surprised to see Gregory. We had definitely caught him off guard.

Good...

"What's goin on cuzzin?" Drake greeted us cautiously, "when did you get in town?" he was speaking to Gregory but never took his eyes off of me. The look on his face gave me chills.

"Oh we came together," Gregory responded smoothly, "and I have to get back so we need to move this along."

I didn't need a doctorate in human behavior to tell Drake wasn't used to anyone speaking to him like that. Gregory, for his part, was playing it straight, showing no emotion at all. He knew he had the upper hand but didn't want to push it too far.

Drake made his way over to his desk, sat down and forced a smile.

"One of y'all wanna tell me what's going on here?"

"That's just it," Gregory answered quickly, "there's nothing going on here, not anymore."

"Excuse me?"

"D, whatever this meeting was about, whatever venture you had in mind that involved my client —"

"Your client?" Drake interrupted with a laugh, "that what they callin it nowadays?"

"The point is, it aint happening. Not today, not tomorrow, not ever."

Drake looked over at me.

"This you talking? Or is it him?"

"Drake," I answered shakily, "I told you this was a one time thing for me."

"And I asked you to come alone."

Now it was Gregory's turn to laugh.

"Drake, save that scarface bullshit for somebody else. You don't get to keep this one dawg. This fish you gotta put back."

"Says who?"

"D, you and I both know I could end you and there's not a damn thing you could do about it."

"You think so?"

"I don't think anything," Gregory boasted. The change in his tone was striking but calculated. He had obviously been waiting for the conversation to get to this point and was ready with his response.

"It would take me fifteen minutes to get a warrant opening your books, and less than twenty to find enough irregularities to have every forensic accountant in the country combing through each and every transaction you've ever authorized. You'd be doing twenty to life within eighteen months, and that's if you make a deal. And for what? So you could have Julie funnel a few extra zeros your way? It's not worth it homie."

"Nobody asked you to evaluate my risk for me *homie*."

"Oh but it's not a risk," Gregory smiled as he corrected him, "see, what I laid out for you is exactly what's going to happen if my client so much as cleans a quarter through you or anyone you're associated with ever again. I will collapse this piece of shit empire of yours like the house of cards that it is and you, better than anyone, know I'm not bluffing."

Drake didn't respond right away. He just leaned back in his chair and rubbed his hands over his forehead. You could almost feel the wheels turning in his brain.

"You guys hungry?" he asked after a moment, "I think Jumbo's BBQ is open."

"Good to see you cuz." Gregory, ending the meeting, stood up and grabbed his coat. "Have to take a raincheck on lunch though. We have a plane to catch."

He put on his jacket and walked out without saying another word, leaving me sitting there with his cousin. Talk about awkward.

"Drake, I'm really sorry about all this."

He just looked at me and, surprisingly, gave me a warm smile.

"Julie," he said calmly and leaned forward as if to tell me something private, "get the fuck out of my office."

Chapter Thirty

"So what now?"

"What do you mean?"

"I mean, what happens now? Do I just go home and act like none of this ever happened?"

"Have you wrapped up whatever business you had with my cousin?"

"Yes, all funds have been recouped and all customers happy."

"Then what happens next is you go home, look under your bed or behind your sofa or anywhere else you can think of."

"And what am I looking for?"

"Your mind, which you obviously lost some time ago. You're gonna find it, put it back in your head and do your best impression of a normal person for the next fifty years."

"Sounds boring," I smiled.

"Well," he whispered as we boarded our return flight, "I'm sure you negotiated a decent payday for your lone adventure in money laundering. Take some time, get yourself a hobby, preferably something legal, go back to school, do some volunteer work —"

"Boring, boring and more boring."

We took our seats.

"Well, I don't know what you want me to tell you," he mused as he fastened his seatbelt, "a life of crime ain't for everybody."

"I don't know, I think I could've been good at it."

The look he gave me told me it was too soon to joke about it.

"Fine," I conceded, not wanting to set him off, "boring it is."

"Thank you," he yawned as he reclined his seat and closed his eyes, "besides, boring is underrated."

The flight attendants went through their take off routine which, of course, included the instruction to place all seat backs in their upright and locked position. A command Gregory acknowledged only long enough for our attendant to do a walk through the aisle and return to her seat.

He was obviously tired and wanted to rest. If I had to guess, I would say he'd been up all night going through everything I gave him and piecing together the nightmare that was about to become my life. Looking back, I now know he came into our meeting that morning determined to save me, and that is exactly what he did, from myself.

I suddenly found myself feeling sad.

"And what about you?" I asked before he could fall asleep.

"What about me?"

"You just gonna crawl back under your rock and disappear?"

"Maybe I like it under there."

"Good luck convincing yourself of that one."

"Julie, believe it or not, there are people in the world who do not share your obsession with self destruction."

"You saying you're one of them?"

"I'm saying even if you had nine lives, which you don't, you'd have to be pretty close to running out by now. Maybe it's time you gave normal a chance?"

"If I didn't know better I'd say you're worried about me?"

He paused for a moment before responding.

"Lord help me but, regardless of anything I might have said in the heat of the moment, I've never stopped caring about what happens to you."

Hearing him say those words sent my heart off to the races. It was all I could do to keep from crying.

"And I would imagine," he asked, "you feel the same about me?"

"You even have to ask? Of course I —"

"Then would you mind shutting the hell up and lettin a brother get some sleep?"

• • •

The rest of the flight was uneventful as Gregory was out like a light and didn't wake up until we were at the gate.

I didn't even try closing my eyes. I was too busy replaying his words over and over again in my head.

"You need a ride?" I asked as we de-boarded the plane. I wasn't quite ready to say goodbye just yet.

"Nah, I'll grab a taxi. I have a few errands to run."

"You sure? I don't mind —"

"I think you need to go home and start thinking about what you're gonna do with the rest of your life now that you're not gonna be an international fugitive."

We both laughed as we stepped out of the concourse and into the cold, winter air. The taxi stand was directly in front of us, while the parking lot was to the right. We made our way to the side so that we weren't impeding traffic as we said our goodbyes.

"You sure you want me doing that much thinking?" I asked, "I mean, if you go back into your cave and abandon me again, who's gonna talk me out of my next crazy idea?"

He looked me in my eyes and smiled.

"Nobody's going to abandon you Julie. You know where to find me."

"Finding you was never the problem. The question is, do you want to be found?"

"What are you saying?"

"I'm saying I need you around to keep me out of trouble."

He laughed.

"Since when have I ever been able to stop you from getting into trouble?"

"Ok, fair enough," I smiled, "let's just do lunch next week then. Hopefully by then I can tell you all about my new job and we can officially catch up."

"Lunch huh?"

"Strictly off the clock. No elaborate ruse, no work, just two friends having lunch."

"Fine," he smiled, "I do have to admit my life is much more interesting with you in it."

"I'm nothing if not entertaining."

"I'll call you this week to set a time. And Julie?"

"Yes?"

"I think it's time for us both to admit we've never been *just friends.*"

His candor caught me off guard, but I honestly don't know that I've ever heard a more perfect sounding sentence.

"I suppose you're right," I said softly, through a huge smile, "timing was never our strong suit."

"That's the understatement of the decade."

"Well," I smiled, "things can change."

"I guess we'll see won't we."

● ● ●

"You ok?"

"Yeah, why?"

"I dunno, you haven't seemed like yourself since you got back from Chicago."

"I'm fine Preston. Just have a few things to figure out."

"Like what?"

"Like how I can get you to stop interrogating me."

"Fine," he laughed, "be that way. But don't say I didn't offer to help."

"I know, and I do appreciate it. This is just something I have to deal with on my own ok?"

"Does it have anything to do with what happened in Chicago?"

"No, actually that went better than I expected."

"That's good, anything I need to know?"

"Just that I decided to quit while I was ahead."

"Meaning?"

"Meaning I'm retiring from the money laundering business."

"Seriously?"

"Yeah, it's not for me."

"But you never really even got started. Why the sudden change of heart?"

"The thing about living that kind of life Preston, is it never really ends well. Eventually, no matter how careful you are, it catches up to you. So I went to Chicago and told Drake I'm hanging it up before things have a chance to go bad."

"Wow."

"Are you really that surprised?"

"No, I mean, everything you're saying makes perfect sense. It's just you sound like a totally different person than yesterday."

"Well, I did tell you this was gonna be temporary, I just didn't realize how temporary until I went to Chicago."

"No, I guess you're right. I just, I dunno, it's just something about the way you said it maybe? You just don't seem the same. You sure nothing else happened?"

"Preston, I'm the same person I was yesterday and the day before. I just realized the direction I was going in wasn't right for me."

"Alright," he sighed unevenly, "as long as you're ok."

"I am," I smiled weakly, "now can we please talk about something else?"

The waiter brought us our dinner, giving me a welcomed opportunity to clear my thoughts before things could get any more awkward. Preston was right. As far as he was concerned my change in attitude was completely random and, without context, he had every right to feel that way.

But I couldn't exactly tell him the real reason behind my change of heart. It's not that I wanted to be distant or evasive, I just hadn't had enough time to process everything that happened with Gregory before he called and insisted I join him for dinner. Thankfully I had to go and pick up Ashley from Sylvia's so I had a built in excuse to make this an early night. All I had to do was get through dinner without making things worse.

"So," he said, as he settled into his burger, "what do you wanna talk about?"

I didn't have much of an answer or an appetite.

"I don't know," I responded as I moved my salad around on the plate, "have you given any thought to what you're gonna do with your new found wealth?"

"I guess I should make some plans huh? Any suggestions?"

"Well, I'm not exactly an investment advisor."

"I'm not just talking about the money though."

"What do you mean?"

"I mean I've never really given much thought to what I'm gonna do when I finish school."

"You mean like a career?"

"Well, yeah. I always just figured I'd keep dancing as long as I could and then maybe get a permanent teaching job somewhere."

"And, what's wrong with that plan?"

"Nothing, but now that I can actually spend the money I have, I was thinking maybe I should look at some other options."

"Like what?"

"Like maybe opening my own studio or something."

"There's nothing wrong with that. As long as you're smart with your money and live within your means, you shouldn't ever have to worry about paying your bills again. Which means you can choose a career you love and not worry about how much money you'll be making."

He gave me a funny look.

"What?"

"You sound like my guidance counselor."

"I'm sorry, I don't mean to. It's just that's a kind of freedom most people will never have Preston. You should take advantage of it."

"You're right. I guess I'm still getting used to the idea of having options. None of this seems real yet."

"It'll seem real soon enough," I reasoned, "until then, hold onto those options and try not to make any decisions or commitments that limit what you can do down the road."

"Meaning?"

"Just that it's important to keep your options open. The great thing about being young and unattached is you can do whatever you want, whenever you want, without asking permission."

"Um," he said softly, "unattached?"

"Preston stop, you know what I mean."

"I guess."

I honestly didn't mean anything by what I'd said, at least not consciously. It didn't matter because the damage was already done and I could see it on his face as he went back to his burger. We finished our dinner in silence.

Thankfully, the drive to pick up Ashley gave me time to quiet my mind and collect my thoughts. It had been five hours since I left Gregory at the airport and what was going on in my head would best be described as a confused, convoluted mess. And if that's how I felt, I can only imagine what Preston was thinking.

So yes, I completely understood why he responded the way he did. He was picking up on changes in my attitude that even I didn't fully understand yet. Was that fair? No, but there wasn't anything I could do about it.

Either way, the point is he wasn't far off base with anything he was picking up from our conversation and I felt horrible about being in this position with him. Preston hadn't done anything to deserve being placed, as an unwitting participant, in my pathetic little Shakespearean love triangle and yet, here he was with a leading role.

Clearly, the right thing to do would have been to tell him what was going on. If nothing else, that would have allowed him to make whatever decision he felt was best for himself, while I figured out what I wanted.

The problem with giving people options though, is they don't always make the choice you want. If I told Preston about my reconnecting with Gregory, he could have easily walked away and never looked back. And as much as I knew what we had wasn't necessarily meant to be forever, I was, in no way, ready for it to end.

I had just started to develop the kind of feelings of him that made me want to explore something deeper than a casual fling. There was no denying how good we were together and a part of me was genuinely excited to see where that could lead. Even the age difference turned out to be a positive. While he was able to benefit from my experience, being with someone so young, in a weird way, made me feel younger and more vibrant.

There were too many positives to just shut the whole thing down and yet I had learned, from experience, not to try and ignore my feelings where Gregory was concerned.

He and I were connected, there was no denying that. And, regardless of whatever might be going on in either of our lives, that was never going to change. We were the yin to each others yang and, as much as we fought and challenged and pushed each other, at the end of the day we saw the world the same way.

That shared view was the direct result of a shared history. We survived the carelessness of youth together. We shared all of our most important moments, from our biggest triumphs to our worst defeats. Our bond had been cemented through a lifetime of ups and downs experienced at each others side, and those memories had proven impossible to ignore and difficult to compete with. They even trumped my marriage.

So now, after all this time, was I honestly considering putting all of that to the side yet again? Now that Gregory and I finally had the opportunity to openly build upon that history and add to those memories, was the potential of what I could possibly build with Preston enough to make me walk away?

Even as the words made their way through the circuitry of my brain, I knew how ridiculous they

312

sounded. Preston was a great young man, amazing even. But he was just starting out in his life and had yet to experience so much of what Gregory and I had already lived, together. And while a part of me wondered at the possibility of living through all of that, for a second time, with someone as amazing as Preston, a bigger part of me knew what I would be sacrificing.

I parked in the driveway and walked up the steps to Sylvia's front door having made my decision.

"Hey Stephanie," I smiled as she opened the door, "is Ashley ready?"

"Just about, come on in."

"Thanks."

I followed her into the foyer just far enough to see my ex husband sitting on the sofa in the living room. I must have been so caught up in my own thoughts that I missed seeing his car in the driveway.

"I'll go let her know you're here," Stephanie said and excused herself.

I stood there silently, not sure if I should say anything and risk setting him off. The last thing I wanted to do was cause a scene in his new girlfriends home.

"You ok?" he asked, after a few moments.

I almost thought I was hallucinating, until I looked over and saw Brian staring at me.

"Yeah, yeah I'm fine," I answered awkwardly, "just have a few things on my mind. How about you?"

"To be honest, I don't know yet."

He looked down at the ground and put his head in his hands.

WTF??

"Everything ok?"

He looked up and stared at me for a long moment before speaking.

"You don't know?"

"Know what?"

"Julie, Greg's been shot."

Chapter Thirty-One

Acute stress reaction, or ASR, is a psychological condition arising in response to a traumatic event. Symptoms include things like detachment, selective amnesia, severe depression and continued re-experiencing of the event through dreams or flashbacks

The key thing to understand about the symptoms of ASR is that they can occur anytime within four weeks of the triggering event. So, in hindsight, it's not all that surprising I was able to make it out of Stephanie's house and all the way home without melting down. Brian, on the other hand, was a complete mess from the moment he received the call from Gregory's mother.

Like me, he had been estranged from his former best friend since the day our affair came to light.

But you don't just erase over a decade of friendship, no matter how serious the betrayal, as evidenced by the fact Brian was among the first to hear from Gregory's family. I expected no such call.

I found what information I could by looking on the internet when I got home. Details were sketchy with little more than a carefully worded police statement copied and pasted on a dozen different local news sites. The police had no suspects or witnesses in what they were calling an attempted home invasion.

I thought about calling Brian to see if he'd heard anything else, but before I could reach for my phone, I saw something at the end of the article that made my heart freeze.

<u>Shooting Victim Pronounced Dead At</u>
<u>The Scene</u> | CITYNEWS.com

For most of my adult life I was an attorney, and a damn good one. As such, language was my battlefield and words my weapons of choice. So it was an entirely unique experience for me to be, quite literally, speechless. There is not a single word or phrase in the entirety of the English language that could adequately do justice to what I was feeling in that moment.

I stared at those seven words for what seemed like an eternity, my eyes burning a hole in the screen as if I was unable to look away. As if looking away would somehow cement the moment into my reality.

I kept my fingers lightly positioned above the mouse pad so that whenever the screen dimmed, I was able to touch it and keep it from going completely dark. It was an oddly therapeutic dance done with just one purpose, to keep those seven words perfectly in place until I was ready to deal with whatever came next.

There's no telling how long I would've sat there if my phone didn't ring. It was Brian but there was no reason to pick up. I knew what *news* he was calling to share and I could already feel myself becoming infuriated at the inadequacy of whatever series of pathetic platitudes was about to fall from his lips.

No, I didn't need to hear anything he had to say. I didn't need to hear anything anybody had to say. I just needed to sit there and...

NO!!

Everything changed for me the moment I saw that black screen. I'd been distracted just long enough for the screensaver to kick in and now, the wave of despair I had managed to keep at bay for those precious few seconds was officially unleashed. I had nowhere else to hide.

At first, it felt like a panic attack. My heart started racing, my entire body was shaking like a leaf and it was difficult to breath.

Next came a surge of desperation that was as intense and relentless as anything I'd ever experienced. It felt like the moment you go over the apex on a roller coaster, only to find yourself on a ride with no bottom. I just kept falling and falling, deeper and deeper into an abyss I instinctively knew I would never be able to climb out of.

I could feel my body shutting down but had no idea what to do or how to stop what was happening. I'm not sure I even wanted to. It was like I was under attack, while simultaneously losing the will to fight back.

There is a saying in the bible that the truth shall set you free. Well, in my case, the truth was an insatiable virus eating away at my insides. And I'm not talking about the violent assault that took the life of someone I loved. No, that was an undeniably horrible fact, but there were some truths behind that fact. Truths that Brian, Gregory's family and even the police didn't know.

And right now, those truths were roaming around inside my body like a cancer, seeking and destroying every organ that impacted my will to live.

But I didn't fight. I couldn't. Because even as I continued my descent into darkness, I realized the only way to fight the truths attacking my soul was to face them. And the only way to face them was to accept and release them, setting them free in the three dimensional world so that they would no longer be trapped inside me, eating away at the core of my being.

But how could I do that? How could I accept the fact that my best friend, my soul mate, my protector, was gone? How could I face the world with the truth that the only man I had ever truly loved was dead, and it was me who killed him?

I collapsed to the floor, curled up into the fetal position, and cried an unending stream of tears that felt neither cleansing nor therapeutic. Wave upon wave of inconsolable sadness left my body, but none carried with it the real source of my sickness.

The truth stayed where it was, hidden from the world, but far from dormant. As I lay there on my floor, in between each violent sob, I could feel the virus diligently, patiently going about the business of eating away at everything left inside me, determined to keep going until there was nothing left.

I didn't fight.

I couldn't.

I closed my eyes tight and welcomed the darkness.

Chapter Thirty-Two

The worst thing about what came next was the silence.

It is a time honored american tradition to have old friends and rarely seen relatives gather together in support of someone who'd suffered a death in their family. I'd seen it more than once in my own, extremely dysfunctional family unit. And the more sudden and tragic the loss, the more people tended to crawl out of the woodwork.

So when I woke up on my floor at 3:30am that next morning, I was certain, even at that hour, that Gregory's mother and sisters were immersed in a swarm of concerned humanity.

I was envious.

I never understood how it could be particularly helpful having virtual strangers lingering around in a time of crisis, but like so many other things in life, experience informed my perspective. I would have given my left arm, at that moment, to be distracted by an army of well wishers delivering casseroles and baked goods.

I had nothing.

I had no one.

And without anything or anyone to occupy my mind, all I was left with was the nightmare that kept replaying over and over in my head.

And the silence.

An oppressive, relentless, deafening silence that filled the room and assaulted my senses.

"Hello?"

"Hey, it's me."

"Julie??"

"Can you come over?"

"Are you ok? What time is —"

"Preston, I need you to come over now, please."

He must have heard how shaky my voice was because less than thirty minutes later, I was in his arms, holding onto him as if I was drowning and he was a life preserver. That wasn't too far from the truth.

"Are you cold?"

"No," I whispered shakily, "why?"

"Baby you're shivering."

"Just hold me."

We lied back on the bed and I got as physically close to him as possible with our clothes on. It still didn't feel close enough.

"Please don't leave me."

I don't know where the words came from. I hadn't told Preston what happened so I'm sure he thought I was losing my mind. I didn't care. I didn't have the will or the strength to care what anybody thought at that point.

"I'm not going anywhere."

I would love to say his words comforted me or made me feel safer, but they didn't. To be honest, I don't think anything could have.

I searched my brain for the words to tell him what was going on, but I couldn't find them. Or maybe I didn't want to. Either way, there was no explanation coming from me that night.

So I just squeezed him tighter, rested my head on his chest, and cried myself to sleep.

Chapter Thirty-Three

"Mom?"

Ever had the experience of over sleeping and waking up completely panicked and disoriented? Imagine going through that with a moody, judgmental teenager staring down your throat. You haven't lived until...

SHIT!!!

"Ashley," I shrieked, frantically looking and feeling around my bed, "get out of my room!"

"You overslept!"

"Alright fine, go get breakfast and I'll get up now."

"I already ate."

I shot her a panicked look

"How long have you been up?"

"Normal time, why?"

"And everything's, um, normal?"

"Everything except you."

I started looking around the room again. I tried to be subtle but couldn't shake the feeling that I had just woke up in an alternate universe.

"What are you looking for?!"

"Nothing! Ashley please, I'm sorry for yelling but I just need a minute to get myself together ok?"

"Fine, weirdo."

That last comment came under her breath as she walked away. Normally that would have been a punishable offense, but I had bigger things on my mind. Like where the six foot two inch, one hundred ninety-five pound man that was in my bed had disappeared to.

• • •

"Did you know dads friend?"

"What?"

"You know, his friend that was shot."

Her words felt like a punch in the stomach. I had been so distracted trying to figure out what the hell happened to Preston that, until then, our ride to school hadn't included many thoughts of Gregory or what happened.

"Yes," I answered quietly, "and you did too."

"Really?"

"You were too young to remember but yes, Gregory and I used to work together."

"And I met him?"

"He was at the hospital the night you were born," I laughed, "he used to come by our house all the time."

"You make it sound like he was almost a part of our family."

"Yes," I whispered, almost to myself, after acknowledging the truth in what she said, "we were all very close at one time."

"Wow," Ashley responded after a moment, "I'm sorry mom. Are you ok?"

The concern in her voice was genuine and made me feel better.

"No, but I'll be ok sweetie."

"I had no idea."

"Like I said, you were too young to remember." I actually found myself smiling at some of the memories. Despite the state of things over the last few years, we certainly had more than our share of good times.

"What happened?"

"Excuse me?"

"You said you were all close 'at one time'. Why not anymore?"

"Baby, sometimes people just grow apart. Gregory was always single, never had any kids and once your father and I had you, our lives just changed."

The ease with which the lies fell from my mouth might have been surprising, especially considering my state of mind at the time, but the truth is I had rehearsed those particular misdirections for years. I knew eventually Ashley would have to be told what really happened, but eventually didn't mean right then and I had every intention of putting that off for as long as humanly possible.

The rest of our ride was quiet and uneventful. I dropped her off and was on my way home when the phone rang. It was Brian.

"Hey."

"I tried calling you last night."

"I know. I didn't feel much like talking."

"I didn't know if you'd heard."

His voice trailed off at the end and there was a brief pause before either one of said anything.

"Yeah," I whimpered softly, "I know."

There was another, more awkward, pause this time. I could only imagine how difficult that call must have been for him, on several different levels. The fact that he was reaching out to me at all showed the kind of man he was.

"Are you ok?" he asked, and actually sounded as if he meant it.

"No," I answered honestly, "but I will be."

"Listen Julie," he started stammering, "I don't know how to say this, but with the way things were there at the end, I don't, I really don't know if it's a good —"

"Brian, it's fine." I interrupted, "I have no intention of crashing the funeral."

"I know it's not fair."

"It is what it is Brian," I replied, cutting him off, "I know the score."

"But still —"

"Can you pick up Ashley today?"

"Um, sure. Everything ok?"

"Yes, I just have something I need to do. I'll come get her after dinner."

I hung up without saying goodbye or giving him a chance to respond. I wasn't trying to be rude, I just needed to get out of that conversation before I lost it. My ex-husband just told me I had been banned from attending the funeral of someone I loved, depriving me the chance to say goodbye. As much as I understood the reasons, it still hurt like hell.

When I got home, Preston was sitting on the steps waiting for me.

"You ok?"

"What the hell happened to you?" I asked, purposely avoiding his question even though I'm pretty sure the answer was written all over my face.

"I figured I needed to be out before 6:00, so when you were still asleep at 5:00, I snuck out and got you some coffee."

He smiled proudly and handed me a cup.

"Look at you," I grinned and took the cup, "I guess you thought of everything. Come on in."

"No," he stood up and blocked me from going inside, "let's go for a walk. Something tells me you could use some fresh air."

It wasn't the worst idea in the world and, even if it was, I was way too exhausted to argue.

We walked down my block in silence and, I have to admit, it was nice. There's something soothing about a crisp winter morning. The sun was shining and the air was cold, but not freezing, with just enough bite to awaken the senses yet not enough to send you running inside.

The feel of the hot coffee going down gave my body an exquisite jolt of warmth that played perfectly off a slight breeze coming at us from the front. Young Preston was right, this was exactly what I needed.

We walked in silence, save for the ambient noise of the morning commuters doing their thing. I kept waiting for the inevitable interrogation to begin, but by the time we turned the corner onto Clifton avenue, it was obvious he was going to wait until I collected my thoughts and was ready to talk. I resolved then and there to never underestimate Preston Richards again.

"I got some pretty bad news yesterday," I volunteered after a sip of coffee, "and I couldn't stand the thought of being alone, so —"

"So that's when you called," he finished my thought, "I get it. I'm glad I could be there for you."

"I am too."

We walked in silence to the end of Clifton.

"Wanna talk about it?" he asked as we turned the next corner.

"A close friend of mine was shot and killed yesterday."

"Shit."

"Obviously I was pretty shaken up."

"Jesus Julie, I'm so sorry," he took my hand, "any idea what happened?"

I had a very good idea what happened, but wasn't going to share those details, not yet.

"The police are calling it a home invasion. Don't know much more than that right now."

Before he could ask anything else, my phone rang. I didn't recognize the number.

"Excuse me a second," I said and put the phone to my ear, "hello?"

"Julie hi, this is Annie Velasquez, did I catch you at a bad time?"

Shit...

"No, not at all, and I am so sorry for not getting back to you. I've had a lot going on."

"I completely understand," she responded pleasantly, "so have you given any thought to my offer to come and work with us?"

"I have and I'm sorry but I'm going to have to decline."

There was an awkward silence before she spoke.

"I'm really sorry to hear that," she said evenly, "we could use someone as talented as you."

"Thank you for saying that, but it's just not a fit for me right now."

"Do you mind if I ask why not?"

"To be honest, I have some personal things going on that require my full attention. Bad timing I guess."

"Well listen, before you officially close the door, why don't you come to a fundraiser we're having at the foundation next week? The board of directors will be there and you should at least meet them and talk to them before making a final decision."

I had no interest in attending a party of any kind, much less a stuffy, black tie, thousand dollar a plate, liberal guilt fest. But I had a pretty good read on Mrs. Annie Velasquez and she was not the type of lady to accept rejection over the phone.

"That's fair enough," I replied, "but please understand I have no intention of changing my mind."

"Julie, sitting on the Worthington board of directors are the smartest, richest, most accomplished liberal minds in the country. If they can't convince you to join our cause, then this truly isn't the job for you."

"Fine," I conceded, wanting to get off the phone, "I'll be there."

"Excellent. I'll have my assistant send the details."

She hung up and I put my phone back in my purse.

"Was that about the job you told me about?"

I almost forgot Preston was walking beside me.

"Yes it was."

"Sorry for listening in, but did I just hear you turn it down?"

"Yeah."

"Why?"

Because any day now I was going to get a call from a psychotic criminal, blackmailing me into running his money laundering operation...

"I'm sure you heard the part where I said it's not a good time for me."

"But you seemed so excited about it before. I don't understand."

"Preston, do I look like a person ready to take on a high pressure job right now?"

"If you're asking if you're a mess, the answer is yes."

"Then you do understand."

"What I understand is you're allowed to be a mess right now. Jesus, Julie your friend was just murdered. Don't you think you deserve more than twenty-four hours to recover from that before making any kind of permanent decision to turn down a job you were super excited about less than a week ago?"

"I don't see how dragging this out is going to make any difference. I've made up my mind."

"Because you're not thinking straight."

"Well," I sighed, tiring of the conversation, "if it'll make you feel any better I agreed to talk to them some more next week."

"What'll make me feel better is you finding a way to relax and clear your head."

I stopped walking and glared at him.

"Preston," I scolded, "if you're trying to get laid, I'm sorry but it ain't happening."

"No," he laughed, "believe it or not I'm thinking only about you."

"I'm fine," I said, and started walking.

"You're a basket case and I think you need to take a minute to get yourself together."

"And how do I do that?"

"Start by letting me help you relax."

"Well, if not with your penis, what else do you have on your mind?"

"You have any plans today?"

"Nope, and Ashley's dad is picking her up after school."

"Cool," he smiled, "follow me."

"Are you fucking kidding me?!"

"Would you calm down and hear me out?!"

"No fucking way!"

"Could you just please trust me?!"

"Preston Richards, I am a grown woman!"

"A grown woman whose life is spinning out of control."

"I had a bad night and I just told you why."

"It's not just one night! Did you forget you damn near had a nervous breakdown right where you're standing?! And that was long before what happened with your friend."

"Ok fine, I'm a mess. We can agree on that much. But you seriously think the answer to my problems is to sit here and smoke a joint with my boyfriend?!"

He took me by the hands and walked me over to the sofa.

"Julie listen," he insisted, "you are the smartest, strongest person I know, but the woman I saw last night? The woman who was crying hysterically and had to be picked up off this floor and carried to her room? That woman is melting down."

"You're being dramatic," I waved my hand dismissively.

"Am I? Whatever it is you're going through, whatever you're dealing with, it's eating away at you and if you could see things from where I'm standing you'd know I'm right."

"Ok, then let's open a bottle of wine and talk or something! But Preston come on, I can't have you walking around my house, where my teenage daughter lives, with a bag of marijuana in your pocket!"

He laughed.

"Is that funny to you?"

"Julie, do you seriously think I'm some kind of pot head?"

"I don't know, are you?!"

"Look, after last night I was worried, ok? I could see you were having a tough time and I wanted to help."

"How exactly is this helping me?"

"You don't just need to relax, you need to forget. You need to take your mind completely off of everything that's bothering you and yes, as ridiculous as it sounds, getting baked is about the best way I know to do that."

"A bottle of merlot works just as well."

"So you can be drunk or hungover when you have to pick up your daughter later on? Trust me, you smoke a little weed, get something to eat, maybe watch a movie, take a nap even, most of all you get to turn that hyper active brain of yours off for a few hours."

He certainly made his case with passion, I'll give him that. A part of me was tempted but, to be perfectly honest, the whole idea just seemed ridiculous. Like most people, I experimented with drugs in my youth, mostly pot and once or twice with the harder stuff, but I hadn't smoked anything since high school or done any kind of drug since I graduated college.

The flip side of that, Preston was right. My brain needed a break and if it didn't get one soon, lord only knows what I would do. When I thought about it that way, I didn't have anything to lose

"Look," I asserted after a moment, "this is not something I want to make a habit of."

"Nobody's suggesting that."

"And you're doing it with me."

"Are you scared?" he laughed.

"No asshole," I smiled, "I'm just not some pathetic loser who gets high by myself."

Chapter Thirty-Four

I was so not in the mood for a party. It had been a week since Gregory's murder and, while I wasn't curled up in the fetal position anymore, I still felt like my world had been rocked to its core and was showing no real sign of recovery.

Fortunately, it'd been an uneventful few days, so I was able to get through my daily routine pretty much on auto-pilot, aided of course by a healthy dose of Preston's marijuana therapy.

Turns out he was right, mostly. It wasn't so much about forgetting. I don't think a drug's been invented that could've made me forget the image of my best friend lying lifeless in a pool of his own blood. For me it was more about dulling my senses. I felt numb when I was high, so even though I had all the same demons and nightmares wreaking havoc in my brain, being buzzed made them easier to ignore.

I was half tempted to smoke before the fundraiser, but thought better of it. I decided I needed to be mentally sharp and, with the dual distraction of a huge event and meeting the board of directors, I figured I'd be able to keep the demons at bay, at least until I returned home.

The spread was impressive, as was the venue. Without dividers, the Clinton room at Worthington Plaza was the size of an airplane hangar, and there were no dividers in place that night.

Before the evening was through, every inch of space would be filled with the best and brightest progressive minds in the country. And those luminaries would be treated to a display of decadence worthy of royalty.

The food was prepared by an army of the best chefs in the world, table settings included exotic floral arrangements imported from as far away as South America and there were gold rimmed champagne glasses on all of the tables, intended for the guests to take home as gifts. To top it off, there was close to ten million dollars of original artwork being auctioned off in a makeshift art gallery at the far end of the ballroom. Those were just a few of the things I noticed within fifteen minutes of arriving.

I treated myself to a black, sleeveless Herve Leger for the occasion and was concerned I might be overdressed. Not even close. On that night, I actually fit right in with my progressive colleagues wearing a two thousand dollar designer gown and a twelve hundred dollar pair of Valentino's.

In hindsight I should have expected nothing less. The Worthington foundation was originally formed as the liberal response to a legion of conservative Political Action Committees (PAC's) springing up all over the country. That was then.

Now the foundation raised more money annually than the next ten PAC's combined, and it was growing because of events such as the one I was attending, which were intended to seduce the rich and powerful. How is that possible?

The key is to create a buzz. To reach the one percent, you have to convince them that something significant is happening, that decisions, deals and connections are being made that they can't afford to miss out on. That's what these events are really about, convincing a bunch of wealthy decision makers to get together and open their check books.

And that's the dirty little secret of American Politics. As much as we like to scream and holler and accuse the other side of being the party of corporate interests, speaking only for the rich, the truth is liberals have just as many, if not more, millionaires and billionaires supporting our team as the other guys. We just don't brag about it.

In fact, most of the biggest donors give to both parties. They hedge their bets that way because they're not supporting an ideology or a platform, they're buying influence. And there is just as much of that for sale on the Democratic side as the Republican.

God, I would have owned this job!!

Obviously I have some definite feelings about what I was seeing that night. My mind was swimming with changes I would make and different policies I would implement, policies that would make events such as this a thing of the past.

But I had to put all of that aside and focus on what I was there to do. While there was no question the CEO position was a perfect fit for someone with my experience and passion for liberal issues, I was there to turn it down.

It was killing me, it really was, but at the end of the day I had no choice. My fate was sealed the day I made my deal with the devil. All I could do after that, was bow out as gracefully as possible.

To that end, I forced myself to do a bit of research before the fundraiser, mostly so I wouldn't come off like an idiot when I met the board. Oddly enough, I wasn't able to find much of anything online. Granted, I didn't put a whole lot of effort into my search, but it was obvious information about the Worthington Foundation Board of Directors was being closely guarded for some reason.

That made me curious. Try as I might, I couldn't imagine why that information would need to be confidential. I was about to find out.

• • •

"I'm so glad you could make it."

"Thank you Annie," I smiled, "I appreciate the invitation, and don't worry, I brought my check book."

We both laughed.

"I'd protest," she joked, "but I wouldn't think of denying you your first amendment rights."

"As well you shouldn't," I smiled and looked around, "how else are you going to pay for all of this."

"Impressed?"

"Who wouldn't be? Although I have to be honest, I'm not sure if I like the message an event like this puts out there."

"How do you mean?"

"It's too over the top Annie. This kind of excess doesn't represent the core values we, as progressives, are supposed to stand for."

"Spoken like our next CEO if you ask me."

It couldn't be...

At first, It felt like all the blood in my body stopped moving and I was sure I was hallucinating. The voice was unmistakable, but there was no way it was who I thought it was, no way.

I must still be high from earlier...

All I had to do was turn to my left to see, but I couldn't bring myself to do it. Not even for a quick a peak. As much as I knew the person walking up behind me couldn't have possibly been who I thought it was, I couldn't force myself to look.

Even though I knew there was no way in hell it could be...

"Ah, right on queue," Annie smiled and turned to meet our mystery guest, "Julie Sharpe I would like you to meet Pastor Drake Strong, one of the most influential members of the Worthington Foundation board of directors."

● ● ●

The fact that I managed to excuse myself and make it to the bathroom without throwing up was a major accomplishment. That I found my way into a family friendly restroom with a locking door was just dumb luck.

I'd love to say I was sitting there, calmly assessing the situation and developing some kind of strategy to deal with it. I wasn't. The truth is I had never felt so afraid in my life and the only thing I was doing was staring in the mirror, trying to will my body to stop trembling.

There were so many things I should have been considering, so many questions I needed to be asking, but I couldn't get my brain to focus on any of that. As far as I was concerned, Drake was there to kill me like he did Gregory, and no one could have convinced me otherwise. At that moment, all I could think about was getting the hell out of there and as far away from that monster as humanly possible.

Calm down!! Think...

I took a deep breath and tried to compose myself. Whatever he had in mind, he wasn't about to do anything dramatic in a room full of people and press. I would be safe as long as I was out in the open, but one look in the mirror and I realized I couldn't go back out into the ballroom looking like I did. I needed to fix my makeup, unfortunately my hands were shaking so badly I would have ended up looking like Jackson Pollack.

That's when I remembered Preston had stuffed half a joint in my purse before I left the house. He said it was in case I got bored, his idea of a joke that I didn't think was all that funny. At that moment though, I could've kissed him.

I lit up, took a deep drag, closed my eyes and let the narcotic do it's thing. Anywhere else and I would've been taking a huge risk, smoking in a public bathroom like that, but this was a liberal fundraiser. If anybody caught me, not only would I not have been arrested, I'd probably have been given a standing ovation.

Within a few minutes, and after a few more puffs of smoke, I was relaxed enough to adjust my makeup and reasonably compose myself.

My brain was too fuzzy from the high to recall exactly how long I'd been in there, but it surely had to be long enough for Annie and Drake to have moved on to mingle with the rest of the guests. All I had to do was make my way to the front lobby, get in my car and be done with this. Here goes nothin.

"Hey."

"Don't fucking touch me!" I snapped and whirled around as I felt his hand on my shoulder.

"What the hell is your problem?!"

My heart felt like it was going to beat its way out of my chest.

"Don't come near me Drake," I warned, taking a step back, "or I swear to god I'll scream."

"We need to talk."

"Fine," I replied, my voice shaking horribly, "start talking."

"Not here," he whispered, looking around, "too many people."

"Well I'm not going anywhere with —"

Before I could finish he gave me a hard shove, knocking me back into the bathroom. I would have screamed but by the time I found my footing he had entered the room, closed the door and had his hand covering my mouth.

"Look dammit," he growled into my ear, "I don't know what you think you know, but you need to calm down and get your —"

He stopped himself and looked around the room, pausing for a second before realizing what was out of place.

"Are you high?!" he asked, glaring at me angrily

I don't know if was the weed or pure adrenaline, but my fear started turning into anger. I knocked his hand away from my face.

"Keep your filthy fucking hands off me!"

"Jesus," he said, studying me closely, "you are high!"

"Get out of my way."

I tried to walk past him to the door but he was having none of it.

"Are you crazy?! Are you trying to blow this whole thing?!"

"Drake, get the fuck out of my way!"

"You ain't goin nowhere until you get your shit together! We have entirely too much at —"

"We?!"

"Julie," he grunted impatiently, "why do you think you're here?!"

"Because I had no idea you would be! I don't like being this close to animals outside of the zoo."

"When you're done making jokes you might realize you're here because of me! Who do you think got you the job offer in the first place?!"

"Bullshit."

He laughed and shook his head. "It's impossible you're this naive. The Worthington Foundation is a *democratic* organization supporting *democratic* causes and candidates. I speak for the largest collection of *black* churches in the country. Do you seriously not see how those two things go together?"

The only thing I was thinking at that moment was how badly I didn't want to be high anymore. I needed my brain functioning at full capacity if I was gonna justify being stupid enough to not see this one coming a mile away.

"So here's what's gonna happen," he continued, "you're gonna dust yourself off, sober up, get out there and make friends with the rest of the board. Then, before you leave for the evening, you're going to accept their offer and become CEO."

"And if I don't?"

He stepped back and rolled his eyes condescendingly. "Nobody's trying to control you Julie. At the end of the day it is entirely up to you to determine the best way to take care of you and your daughter."

He didn't say anything else. He didn't need to. We both knew he had made his point loud and clear.

"I'm gonna leave you to put your face on. I'll cover for you with the rest of the board for fifteen minutes but after that, I need you out there pressing flesh understood?"

He turned to leave without waiting for me to respond. "Oh and by the way," he pointed out before opening the door, "the position pays eight figures. You're welcome."

• • •

Have you ever done something really dumb? I'm not talking about forgetting to turn in a homework assignment or forgetting to pay your credit card bill. I'm talking about something so colossally stupid, with such severe consequences, that you spend days trying to figure out what you were thinking. If so, then you have a good idea how the next forty-eight hours of my life were spent.

I must've been out of my mind. I willingly brought a homicidal psychopath into my life and, because of that, someone I loved was gone and everyone else I cared about was at risk.

It would probably take years of psychoanalysis to figure out why I made some of the decisions I'd made, but with everything at stake, I didn't have the luxury of time. After my little *talk* with Drake, I knew what I needed to do, and it was going to be the hardest thing I had ever done in my life.

Chapter Thirty-Five

"Hey mom."

Seeing Ashley fly through the door after school was a relatively new routine for us. Stephanie and I had started alternating weeks driving the girls to the studio and, as usual, my teenage daughter forgot something she needed for class.

"Bye mom."

"Ashley wait." I stopped her before she could run back out the door. "Tell Ms. Pavani to go ahead. I need to talk to you about something."

"Why can't we just talk later? I have —"

"Ashley please," I cut her off, "tell Ms. Pavani I'll drop you off myself today. "

Like most teenagers, Ashley had a mechanism in her brain telling her when it was time to argue, and when it was time to just do as she was told. She correctly assessed this as being the latter.

After sending Stephanie and Sylvia on their way, she came back in, flopped down on the sofa, and waited for me to join her in the living room.

"What's so important?" she asked with just enough attitude to let me know how my change in plans had ruined her life.

"You remember that job I told you about?"

"The CEO job?"

"Yes, well it looks like they're going to make the offer."

"Oh my god mom, that's great!"

Before I could say anything, she lunged at me to give me a hug. The force of her body weight knocked me back on the sofa where she ended up on top of me.

"Wow," I smiled and sat back up with her still draped all over me, "I didn't expect you to be so excited."

"Mom, why would you say that?!" she replied, sounding genuinely insulted.

"I don't know, I guess I just —"

356

"Of course I'm excited for you!" she shouted, cutting me off, "this is a really important job huh?"

"Yes, I suppose so."

"So you'll like be on TV and stuff?"

"Anything's possible."

"Mom, that is SO cool, congratulations!"

Her attitude was throwing me off. I figured I'd get a hug and, maybe, a kiss on the cheek, but not much more. Teenagers are programmed to be self-centered and, as much as I love my daughter, Ashley was no different in that way. In her world, if it wasn't happening to her then it wasn't happening, at least that's what I thought until I sat there and watched her be genuinely excited for me. If I had any doubt before, I didn't after that. I had been blessed with a truly amazing child.

Baby please don't make this harder...

"There's something else," I mumbled softly, ashamed of what I was about to do, "this position requires quite a bit of travel and so, I um, I spoke with your dad yesterday and, well we agreed it'd probably be best if you went and stayed with him for a while."

The look on her face as she realized what I'd said is one I will never forget. I could literally see the color draining from her cheeks as she made the transition from excitement to confusion and then to sadness right before my eyes. I immediately knew I would be living with that image for the rest of my life.

I braced myself for the inevitable explosion of teenage anger but instead, all I got was a single word.

"What?"

There was a shaky desperation in her voice that told me everything I needed to know about what she was going through. My baby girl felt like she was being abandoned.

"Honey listen," I said, trying to be as reassuring as possible, "it's not like we won't be seeing each —"

"But," she interrupted quietly, fighting back tears, "I don't understand. Why can't I just stay with dad when you're traveling?"

"Because that would mean too much back and forth Ashley. You need a consistent place to call home."

"My home is with you."

"I know baby."

I hugged her and held her as tightly as I could, trying desperately to think of something, anything, I could say to make this easier.

But there was nothing left for me to do or say. It wasn't safe for her to be anywhere near me and, as much as it was killing both of us, I had to do what I could to protect my little girl, even if that meant losing her.

"Mom You promised! You promised you would never leave me! You said we would always be together!"

Tears would have been enough to push me over the edge, but her words cut so deeply I felt they were being carved into my heart with a knife.

I wanted to fall apart. Every instinct in my body wanted to collapse to the floor and cry uncontrollably for hours. But I held it together. I had to. My little girl needed her mother at that moment, and I was determined to do my job, maybe for the last time. "I'm so sorry baby, but this is just the way it has to be for right now."

"But why?! I don't wanna live with daddy, I wanna stay with you! Why can't you just get another job that lets us stay together?!"

"It's not that easy. Your father and I have to work to pay for things like school and new —"

"Then I'll go to another school!" she suggested, excitedly wiping her tears as if she sensed an opportunity, "send me to Truman or Pennington!"

"Ashley, come on, you love going to Bristol."

"Not if it means we can't stay together! No school is worth that!"

I couldn't tell you much about the rest of our conversation. Only that, for weeks afterwards, those five words played over and over again in my head like the bass line of some obnoxious techno song.

No school is worth that...

One simple sentence, from a thirteen year old, that perfectly summed up the insanity that had become my life. It wasn't all that long ago that my biggest fear was not being able to pay her tuition. I was willing to sell my soul and betray my friends to keep her at Bristol Academy because failing to do so would have given Brian enough reason to seek custody.

Everything I had put myself and my daughter through, every single thing, had been justified, in my mind, because of my determination to keep us together.

And not only had I failed to do that, which would have been bad enough under any circumstance, but her world was being torn apart specifically because of the things I'd done to keep it together.

No school is worth that...

Chapter Thirty-Six

"Aren't you worried they'll give you a drug test for your new job?"

"It's not the CIA Preston."

"Alright fine." He handed me a plastic bag filled with pot. "This should last you a good while, at least until I get back."

"What time's your flight?"

"We decided to drive. My sister hates flying and she invited her boyfriend, so now we have too much stuff, blah, blah, blah. You sure you can't come, even for a few days?"

"I don't ski so Wyoming in the winter is not my idea of a party, but thank you for the invitation and thank you for this." I took the bag and dropped it on the counter. "Where do you get this stuff from anyway?"

"A kid I went to high school with named Benny. Why?"

"Just want to make sure you're not getting into trouble."

"It's fine," he assured me, "Benny's Ira's cousin. I've known him forever and he only deals with soft stuff like weed and ex."

"As long as you're being careful." I was about to offer him something to eat when I noticed him looking around. "What's wrong?"

"Nothing," he replied, "something just feels different in here."

"Oh," I said softly and opened the refrigerator, "Ashley's gone to stay with her dad for a little while."

"What?! When did that happen?"

"Last week. With the new job I'll probably be traveling a lot and Brian will be able to give her more stability."

"And you're ok with that?"

"It's for the best," I replied curtly, "now, if you don't mind I have to get ready for a conference call."

"I thought we were gonna do lunch?"

"I'm sorry babe, this came up right before you got here, and from the sound of it, it's going to be a long meeting. Let's go to dinner when you get back ok?"

• • •

Preston was a life saver. There's nothing better at turning off your feelings than a nice long hit of pot. I knew this because I had been spending quite a bit of time *managing my emotions* since the day Ashley moved in with her father.

Turns out I was also pretty good at the whole joint rolling thing, which I found to be an oddly therapeutic exercise requiring steady hands and a laser like focus on the task. As ridiculous as that sounds, I honestly enjoyed having something to do with my hands. Focusing on something, anything, physical allowed me to put off any thought of the world outside of my kitchen. It was better that way. I wasn't ready to deal with anything that was taking place outside of those four walls.

So, there I sat. A thirty-eight year old woman with an Ivy league education, soon to be CEO of the Worthington Foundation, patiently rolling joints and lining them up neatly on my kitchen counter.

Oh how the mighty have fallen...

When I was about half way through with my bag, I decided it was time for a smoke break. I lit up one of my perfectly rolled specimens and took it over to the sofa.

Unfortunately, just as I was about to sit back, relax and enjoy the fruits of my labor, my phone rang.

"Hello."

"Ms. Sharpe?"

"Who's calling?"

"My name is Crystal La Rue. I'm calling from Care Systems, the firm contracted to do your background check."

"Ok," I said, calmly taking a drag, "and what can I do for you Ms. La Rue?"

"Something came up in your financials I'd like to chat with you about. When can you come into our office?"

"Can't we just talk about whatever it is over the phone?"

"I'm afraid not. Can you make it in this afternoon?"

"Do I have a choice?"

"Does 4:30 work for you?"

I guess not...

"Fine."

I hung up, tossed aside my phone and finished smoking my joint.

Chapter Thirty-Seven

I purposely arrived at Care Systems offices fifteen minutes late, and not just because I was still buzzed. I didn't appreciate Ms. La Rue's tone from earlier and felt I needed to establish some authority. Regardless of how or why I got the job, I was about to become CEO of the most powerful political organization in the most powerful nation on earth. I could't have just anybody telling me what to do or where to be.

The elevator opened directly into their suite on the fourteenth floor. Their receptionist, a heavy set, middle aged white woman with short dark hair, recognized me right away and greeted me warmly.

"Thank you for coming in Ms. Sharpe, can I get you some coffee or a bottle of water?"

That's more like it...

"No thank you," I replied brightly, "what's your name?"

"Bethany" she smiled and extended her hand.

I could have easily read the nameplate on the front of her desk, but I always found people appreciate it when you take the time to engage them directly.

"It's a pleasure to meet you Bethany. Please let Crystal know I'm here?"

I stepped to the side while Bethany dialed the appropriate extension.

"You're all set," she smiled after hanging up, "I'll take you to the conference room now."

I followed her down a narrow hall, past a series of small, nondescript offices with matching furniture.

Middle management...

At the far end of the hallway was an executive conference room adjacent to a large corner office. It was obvious the occupant of that office sat at the top of the food chain at Care Systems.

I tried to get a quick peak at the name on the door, but we were moving too fast. I'd have to check it on the way out.

To my surprise, there were five, young, intense looking gentlemen in the conference room when Bethany led me in, none of whom appeared to be waiting or looking for me.

Associates...

Even in my mildly inebriated state, I could spot a young lawyer a mile away. Judging from their intensity and level of concentration, these five were probably the best of the associate pool at whatever firm was enslaving them, and they were now working together on something big, at least something that felt big. Which means they were in a life or death struggle to impress the client at the expense of their four co-workers.

Each of them had a laptop and a stack of papers in front of them and, from what I could tell, seemed to be working feverishly.

Good boys...

"Excuse the chaos."

The voice came from a tall, athletic looking red head at the far end of the conference room.

"Crystal?" I asked, intentionally addressing her by her first name.

"Yes," she replied as she made her way over to shake my hand, "it's a pleasure meeting you Ms.

Sharpe. Thanks for taking the time to meet with us."

"You made it sound important."

"That depends, we just have a few questions about something we found."

"We?" I asked, looking around the room at the five robots who had yet to acknowledge my presence.

"Oh no," she smiled, "my partner is waiting for us in my office. Shall we?"

I followed her through the door into her corner office and was immediately relieved of any illusion I might have had about who was in control.

"I believe you know Pastor Strong."

My stunned silence said it all.

"Julie," he remarked evenly, "why don't you have a seat."

"What's this about?" I asked cautiously, suddenly feeling a lot less sure of myself.

"It's nothing major," Crystal replied and handed me a manila folder containing a single sheet of paper, "at least we don't think so."

The office was big enough for a desk with two visitors chairs and a small conference table with four other chairs in front of a large bay window overlooking the city. Drake was seated in one of the visitor chairs across from Crystal's desk. Not wanting to be anywhere near him, I took the folder and sat at the conference table.

"What's this?" I asked, opening the folder.

"We found, in your financial records, that you recently purchased a dance school. Victor's Academy of Dance I believe?"

"Yes, that's true."

"Well, in doing your due diligence before the purchase, did you notice anything irregular."

The language she used set off alarm bells in my head. "No offense Crystal but would you mind just getting to the point?"

"Of course," she responded calmly, unfazed by my attitude, "in doing our internal review of your assets, we noticed some questionable transactions specific to the dance school."

"Define questionable."

"We printed them out for you."

She pointed to the folder she had given me. I took out the piece of paper and, sure enough, it listed all of the money laundering transactions I'd done for Preston through the studio.

Fuck...

While I was looking it over and searching my pot-damaged brain for some sort of explanation, she handed me another folder, this time with two pieces of paper inside. I briefly glanced at the one on top and immediately recognized it as an affidavit.

"What's this for?"

"As you can see," she answered, "all of the listed transactions took place prior to you taking ownership of the studio. That is your sworn affidavit stating you knew nothing about them and had nothing to do with them. Underneath that is a letter of intent to sell the studio."

"Excuse me?"

"I'm sorry Ms. Sharpe, but the team agreed your best course of action going forward is to sell the studio. That's the only way we can limit your exposure."

"I see, and I assume by team, you are referring to the five glorified interns in your conference room right now?"

"Crystal," Drake chimed in, having heard enough, "can you give us the room please?"

It sounded more like a command than a request. Whatever it was, Crystal was out of her office in under thirty-seconds.

"What the hell are you doing?" I asked as soon as she shut the door.

"What am I doing?! I'm cleaning up your fucking mess is what I'm doing!"

"Cassandra had nothing to do with any of those transactions and you know it!"

"Well," he quipped dismissively, "I hope Sandra, or whatever her name is, has a good lawyer. Her and your little boy toy for that matter."

"What?"

"You know how this works Julie. Once we alert the authorities, both the owner and the recipient of the funds will come under investigation."

SHIT!!

"You can't make me do this."

"Make you?! Jesus Christ, you should be thanking me!"

"I won't sign it."

"Excuse me?"

"They're innocent Drake! It was all my idea! Cassandra knew nothing about it and Preston was

373

just doing what I told him! You can't ask me to sell them out like this!"

"Let's get something straight," he snapped, "I'm not *asking* you to do anything! Quite frankly I'm getting tired of fixing the shit you break!"

"Nobody's asking you to! How many lives are you willing to destroy for this?! How many —"

"Don't you say another fucking word! You wanna talk about what I know? Fine, here's what I know. I told you to come see me, alone. You brought my cousin. Now he's dead. You used your friends dance studio to launder money for your teenage boyfriend and you used him as an excuse to come to me to launder more. Notice a theme?"

I shook my head, not because he was wrong, which he wasn't, but because I was desperate. All I wanted him to do was leave my friends alone and it was killing me that I couldn't find a way to make that happen.

Think goddammit...

"None of that matters now," I offered lamely, "the point is, all of this drama is bad for everybody, you included."

"I think I'll survive."

"Are you really willing to put your entire operation at risk for this?"

"Since when do you give a shit about my business?"

"I don't! I just want you to leave my friends alone, but that doesn't change the fact that the reason you are where you are today is because you don't draw attention to yourself. That's not going to last if you do shit like this."

"Yeah well," he responded, thoroughly unimpressed by my argument, "who's really gonna care all that much about an old lady and a hip hop dancer? As long as you don't keep fucking things up, I'd say the risk is worth the reward."

"You can't be serious!"

He shrugged and sat back in his chair. He was dead serious.

"You really are a fucking animal."

"Oh please," he waved his hand dismissively, "why don't you save the righteous indignation for someone who doesn't know that YOU are the reason your friends got mixed up in this bullshit in the first place?"

"Don't do this!" I pleaded, out of ideas but still desperate to get through to him, "you know this'll never stand up to any kind of investigation, much less a trial! It wouldn't take any half decent detective more than five minutes with Cassandra to know she didn't do this on her own, and —"

"You have a point," he interrupted thoughtfully, "all the more reason for it to never come to that."

It took me a second to realize what he had just suggested. "Don't even think it!"

"How much of that shit have you been smoking? Do you seriously still not know who's in charge?!"

"Drake please," I begged frantically, "I'll do whatever you want. I swear on my life I will do anything you ask. PLEASE just don't do this."

"I'll do what I have to. Now I'm tired, I'm aggravated and I'm in no mood for your pity party. You're the one who walked these people into my world without knowing the rules, so whatever happens to them is on you. I suggest you put your big girl panties on and deal with it." He stood up to leave. "Now I need your signature on both of those forms before I leave, and I have to leave now."

The look on his face told me all I needed to know about how serious he was. As far as he was concerned, this conversation was over.

I picked up a pen but my hand was shaking so badly I was having trouble writing. "Please don't do —"

"SIGN!"

His voice was loud enough to almost knock me out of my chair. Completely defeated, I did as told and watched helplessly as he took the forms, put them back in the folder and walked toward the door. "I'll tell Crystal you need the office. Stay as long as you need to get yourself together."

Chapter Thirty-Eight

I left Crystal's office that day officially at rock-bottom. Drake had all but promised to kill two of the kindest, most loyal friends I'd ever known and the best I could do was sit there, begging him not to do it.

I thought about going to the police, but had nothing to offer besides a weak theory on the death of my friend and an unsubstantiated story about some veiled pseudo threat issued by a prominent religious leader with no criminal record or documented history of violence. I would've sounded like a delusional, paranoid lunatic and had already learned, the hard way, that Drake was not the kind of target you got two shots at. If I was going to go after him, I needed to make it count. The only thing I would have accomplished by going to the cops with what I had, is to piss him off even more, and probably put a target on squarely my daughters back.

The more I thought about it, the more pathetic I felt. Sure, when my biggest problem was a bounced check and a late tuition payment, I was the queen of crisis management. My brain could run backwards through an obstacle course, at full speed, if all it was tasked with was finding a creative way out of a fucking overdrawn checking account.

But now, when the stakes were real and the people I loved needed me the most, I was nothing more than a scared little white girl from South Jersey who shook like a leaf just being in the same room as the big bad gangster from Chicago.

I was sick to my stomach. The reality of everything that had just transpired was beyond what my already fragile psyche was equipped to deal with, and all I could think about was escaping. But I had nowhere to run to.

So I sat in my car for what seemed like an eternity before I started driving. With no real destination in mind I, somehow, found myself pulling into a Mercedes dealership. I got out of my car and was approached immediately by a skinny, middle eastern looking gentleman.

"May I help you?"

"I'm looking for a CL65 coupe, black with grey leather interior."

"That's pretty specific," he smiled.

"It's the car I used to drive, and I miss it."

"Let me check our inventory. You looking to lease or purchase?"

"Purchase, cash."

Ninety minutes later I pulled out of the dealership in my new car.

I wasn't done.

I drove my new Mercedes over to a high end mall in Aldan and walked into the Valentino store on a mission. Thirty-thousand dollars later I hit Armani, then Coach and topped it off with a visit to my old friend Louis Vuitton.

All told, I spent close to fifty-thousand dollars in the mall. Between the clothes and the car, I was out of more than a quarter of a million dollars in the few hours since I left the Crystal's office, and I still felt completely empty.

There weren't enough designer dresses in the world to mask the miserable, pathetic mess of a human being I had become. Drake was right, I'm the one who did this to my friends. I'm the one who did this to my daughter.

It didn't matter if I was driving the same kind of car or wearing the same kind of shoes, the impressive, proud, accomplished, talented woman I used to be was gone. Replaced by a self destructive monster who destroyed everything and everyone she came in contact with.

Back in my car, draped in thousands of dollars in designer clothing and accessories, I still desperately needed something to fill the cavernous black hole where my heart and soul used to be.

• • •

Cruising a two hundred thousand dollar car through Winnfield after dark is not a recipe for anything good to happen. A white woman, driving alone, hoping to happen upon a drug dealer, is downright suicidal.

I turned off the radio and my phone, not because I needed to pay attention to my surroundings, but because I wanted to immerse myself in them. Looking out at block after city block of boarded up windows, abandoned buildings and broken street lights, I could smell the stench of hopelessness and desperation beginning to leak in through my custom ventilation system. But I didn't turn around and I never even considered driving away. I welcomed it all. I breathed it in hungrily.

Because this was where I belonged, in a place where all of the damage had already been done. Where crippled, vacant souls like mine could safely feed on already broken dreams and ruined spirits without having to find new lives to destroy. I drenched myself in silence because I didn't want to mask the bleakness of where I was, any more than I could continue masking the darkness of who I had become.

Drake was an animal, but he was also right. Whatever was about to happen to my friends would be on my head. And I knew exactly what was coming next, just like I knew there wasn't a damn thing I could do about it.

I parked myself in front of the salon and waited. Even though I knew nothing I needed or wanted would find its way to that location, I also knew a two hundred thousand dollar Mercedes parked in front would attract attention. From what I remembered, this was a key location for the Cartel and so it was certainly being watched by someone, probably a local kid who would call someone else to report the fancy car sitting out front. This would elicit a drive by and, shortly after that, a knock on my window, and that would give me what I needed.

I had been sitting there for maybe ten minutes when I was startled by bright headlights shining behind me. I looked back and noticed it was the police.

Nicely done...

"Ma'am, you mind telling me why you're parked out here?"

"I'm so sorry officer," I said, voice trembling as I let my window down, "I'm looking for my little brother."

"Your little brother hangs out around here?"

"He's had some problems."

"Drugs?"

"Yes," I admittedly shyly, "heroin, but that's all in the past. At least I thought it was until my mother called saying he hadn't been home for two days. I know he was picked up once for possession somewhere close to here so I figured I'd come look around for him."

"Well, if he was lookin to buy, it wouldn't be here."

"Where then?"

"Tell you what, follow me and I'll drive through the neighborhood where I think he would've gone. If you see him, point him out and I'll pick him up."

"Ok."

"But I can't have you parked out here, so if you don't see him, I need you to go to the station and give a description."

Two minutes later, officer Russell Hamm escorted me and my quarter million dollar car through two of the most notorious drug corners in Winnfield. I made note of the intersections before informing the patrolman I didn't see my brother anywhere and would be on my way to the station to file a missing persons and give a description.

In reality I hopped on the freeway for one exit and turned around. Yes, I had been resupplied with enough pot to last several weeks, but what I needed at that point was way beyond the medicinal benefits of marijuana.

"How can I help you?"

The girl couldn't have been more than fifteen and sounded like she was working the drive through window at MacDonald's. Not at all like you see on TV. I remembered enough from the cartel affidavits not to say anything in response. I just handed her two hundred dollars and drove up the block where I was met by yet another teenage worker, this time a boy who unceremoniously dropped my purchase onto the passenger seat and walked away without ever once making eye contact.

And just like that it was done. A transaction that was as efficient as it was uneventful and had me back on the freeway less than ninety-seconds after pulling up to the corner. Only now I had a couple hundred bucks worth of heroin sitting on my passenger seat.

The thought of going home to an empty house seemed unbearable. So instead, I drove back to Aldan and checked myself into the Presidential Suite at the Four Seasons.

Chapter Thirty-Nine

"Heroin Julie? Are you fucking kidding me?!"

The voice sounded like it was coming from far off in the distance. Still, it was familiar and soothing and made me want to find my way back to consciousness. I slowly opened my eyes, but was having trouble remembering where I was. I could see it was morning and, for some reason, I was wearing an expensive dress.

"What the hell is going on with you?!"

I turned to see Preston sitting on the edge of the bed. Seeing him sitting there violently thrust my brain back into reality and I immediately started to panic.

"No," I stammered incoherently, "no, no, you, you can't be here!"

"Why? Because your ex-boyfriends' cousin wants to have me killed?"

I just looked at him, completely confused.

"You told me everything last night, at least as much as you could in your altered state."

I wanted desperately to respond, but my brain was useless at that moment. I flopped back down on the bed and muttered aloud the only relevant thought I could come up with.

"I need coffee."

"It's noon."

What?!

"Coffee. Please."

An hour, a pot of coffee and a shower later, and my brain was still mush, though not quite as bad as when I first woke up.

Apparently, Preston walked in on my trip down heroin highway and I told him everything that was going on, and I mean everything. That was as much as I could piece together before our lunch arrived.

We ate for a few minutes in silence before I decided I was ready to deal with the elephant in the room.

"How'd you find me?" I asked quietly.

"Your iPhone."

"What?"

"Remember that Friend Finder app I told you about for Ashley? Well, I downloaded it to your phone and you never deleted it."

"Ok, but what happened to Wyoming?"

"I was worried about you after you told me about Ashley, so I told my sister and her boyfriend to go ahead without me. I wanted to make sure you were ok."

"And how'd you get in the room? Or did I open the door?

"Ira knows the general manager. I had him make me a key."

"Of course."

"Speaking of which, why the hell are you here anyway? Why didn't you go home?"

"Go home to wha? I couldn't handle an empty house on top of everything else going on, so I checked myself in here. By the way, you didn't tell anyone where we are right?"

"Only Ira."

"I guess that's ok."

"Well, considering he was the only person I could find last night, it's gonna have to be. Now are you done with your questions? Because I have a few of my own."

"I'm pretty sure I told you everything already."

"Everything except how or why you ended up with more than two hundred bucks worth of heroin!"

"Preston, do you seriously think that's the most pressing thing we need to discuss at the moment?"

"The other day you bit my head off for offering you a joint, and now you're shooting up?! How do you even know how to do that?!"

"It wasn't my first time," I admitted quietly.

"What?!"

"Once in high school and again —"

"Are you an addict?"

"What?! No! I did it once at a high school graduation party and again when I got into law school. That's it!"

"Bullshit Julie. Nobody does heroin twice."

"Well, I don't know what to tell you. I did it twice in my life."

"Until last night."

"Fine, I was out of my mind! Is that what you want to hear?! I felt defeated and out of control and I made a really dumb decision! Are you happy?! Now, can we please drop this and talk about something we both know is more important?!"

"If you're referring to the psycho preacher who wants to murder me and Cassandra, we'll get to that."

Shit!

"Don't worry," he said before I could freak out, "Cassandra went to visit her daughter in Texas for a few days, which gives you about forty-eight hours to figure a way to convince this nut job friend of yours to leave her alone."

"He's not my friend."

"Whatever," he scoffed impatiently, "you need to fix this."

"You think I don't know that?! Jesus Preston if there was something, anything, I could do I would be doing it!"

"So that's it? This preacher from Chicago is suddenly the most powerful man in the world? Bullshit! He's not some untouchable super villain who gets to do whatever the hell he wants Julie. He's a fucking bully. A guy with money and a few friends, well guess what? We have money and friends too."

"So what do you suggest, we go to the mattresses like some kind of silly gangster movie?!"

"Don't you dare fucking condescend to me! You're the one that brought this fuck into our lives so you need to figure out how to make him go away! That's what you should've been doing last night, instead of sitting on the floor with a fucking needle in your arm!"

"I already told you that was a mistake."

"You were shooting heroin! That's not a mistake, that's suicide!"

"I wasn't trying to kill myself."

"Then what were you trying to do?!"

"I don't know."

"That's not good enough Julie, not anymore! You're the smart one remember?! The ivy league lawyer! Are you seriously telling me that some low life thug has you beat to the point where all you can do is shoot yourself up full of drugs and pass out?!"

"Did you forget what happened to Gregory?! That was his cousin Preston! They were best friends! If he can do that to someone in his family —"

"You don't have to be afraid of him! All he did was show you how far he's willing to go, and guess what? That was his only advantage! You have money, you have friends, you have everything you need to fix this! Why are you letting this guy win?!"

"Because I can't protect you! I can't protect you or anyone else that matters! I don't know what I'd do if anything happened to you or Cassandra or, god forbid, Ashley!"

"Then instead of frying your brain with this shit, you might wanna figure out a way to stop this guy from hurting anyone else you care about! You're the smartest person I know Julie. You've forgotten more ways to work the system than this fuck will ever know! There is no way you can't figure this out!"

I put my head down and looked away, not wanting to risk eye contact. I was afraid if he saw my eyes in that moment he would see the truth about me, and then he would realize how wrong he was. Not that it mattered. He was about to find out anyway.

"I'm so sorry," I whimpered pathetically after a long pause, "I'm sorry for everything."

Without responding, he stood up to leave.

"Where are you going?"

"I'm done here," he hissed angrily, "I'm going to meet my sister and her boyfriend."

He grabbed his stuff and was out the door in less than a minute. I wanted to stop him, to tell him I had a way to fix this and all I needed was more time, but I had no way of making him believe any of it. I had no more lies left to tell.

I felt humiliated and not just because of what I'd done the night before. I just had to admit, to Preston and myself, that he, much like Ashley, was better off, and safer, without me.

As I sat there, feeling utterly useless, I heard a knock. Before I could make the conscious decision to ignore it, I heard the door opening.

"Housekeeping," she announced herself cheerfully before I could panic, "everybody decent?"

"Yes," I answered evenly, "I'll be out of your way in a second."

As I walked past her to get my shoes, I could feel her eyes on me. That's not to say she was staring, it's just that the presence of another human being at that moment was the last thing I wanted. The thought of anyone looking at me made my skin crawl. The presidential suite at the Four Seasons is over fifteen hundred square feet, but her being there made me feel cramped, almost suffocated.

I managed to find a pair of shoes and make it down to the gift shop without having a panic attack. The problem is there were people there too, lots of them. All I wanted to do was disappear and yet I found myself navigating a sea of humanity, all of whom felt as if they were staring a hole into my soul.

I purchased a pair of sunglasses and a newspaper to hide behind while I waited for my room to be ready. I also bought a bottle of water and some ibuprofen to combat the massive tsunami of a headache I felt coming on.

I sat myself down on one of the oversized leather chairs in the main lobby and opened my copy of the Aldan Gazette only to find my dreams of anonymity shattered beyond repair.

Sources confirm Julie Sharpe to be named CEO of the Worthington Foundation

Apparently some *anonymous* sources saw fit to announce my new job to the world without consulting me. To make matters worse, the Gazette is a small, local paper with no real reporting talent. The only way they could get a story like this would be to pick it up off one of the wire services, which meant it was national.

Great...

I quickly folded my paper and headed back to my room. There was no way housekeeping could be done this quickly but I needed to get out of the lobby before somebody saw through my pseudo disguise. The last thing I needed was to be stuck fielding a bunch of inane questions.

I figured I'd go upstairs, call for my car and go for a drive. The car was new, so no one would be looking for it, making it my best option to remain hidden for the time being.

"It's just me," I announced as I made it back into my room without incident, "I need to make a call."

"You need me to give you some privacy?"

"No, no," I assured her as I dropped my paper on the bed, "I just need to call for my car."

She went back to her work but I noticed her eyes lingered on the newspaper for an extra beat or two as she walked past the bed. I wasn't worried about it though. I planned on being long gone by the time those seeds of recognition were able to fully take...

"Is that you?"

Wrong again Julie...

"Excuse me?" I mumbled softly as I hung up the phone, hoping she would get the hint that I didn't want to talk.

"In the paper," she persisted, "is that you?"

No such luck...

I took note of her expression and sensed she was asking out of more than random curiosity. Either way, I was in no mood to deal with her agenda, whatever it was.

"I'm sorry," I replied gently, "I'm kind of in —"

"Did your name used to be Watson?"

"I'm sorry, do we know each other?"

"I wouldn't expect you to remember."

She said it with an attitude that implied some sort of elitism on my part which, to be honest, if she knew the old me, would not have been all that far off base.

I studied her closely. She was a middle aged, heavy set, black woman with a caramel complexion and short, curly hair. If we had, in fact, met, I had absolutely no recollection of it.

"Ma'am, I think you have me mistaken for —"

"You're a lawyer right?"

"I used to be, yes."

"A defense attorney?"

"Look, I really don't have —"

Before I could finish my sentence, she slapped me in the face hard enough to knock me over onto the bed.

Chapter Forty

"What the hell is —"

"That," she snarled hatefully before I could continue, "was for my nephew."

The old me wouldn't have tolerated being slapped. In fact I would have probably lunged back at her already. Of course there was no part of the old me that felt I deserved to be hit in the face. That was the old me.

"You better leave," I told her, tiredly, as I sat up on the bed, "before I call security."

"I aint goin nowhere."

"Ma'am," I pleaded, my face still throbbing, "I don't want any more trouble ok?"

"I aint movin until you tell me why."

"Why what?"

"Why that boys life aint mean enough for you to do your damn job!"

I could see she wasn't budging, so either I was prepared to brawl with the fucking maid, or I would have to deal with whatever injustice she felt I had done to her and her family.

"Have a seat," I conceded with a sigh and stood to pour myself a drink, "what's your name?"

"Patrice."

"Well Patrice," I said, still smarting on the left side of my face, "you've got a pretty good right hand on you."

"I raised three boys all by myself," she stated proudly, "mama don't play."

"Was one of them your nephew?"

"No, he lived with his mother, my sister, in Illinois."

"What was his name?" I asked, sitting back down with my glass of merlot.

"Calvin. Calvin Harris"

"Am I to assume he was a client of mine?"

"You seriously don't remember?"

"I mean no disrespect, but no, I'm sorry I do not."

"Let me ask you this," she scoffed, "do you remember *any* of their names?"

"Patrice, I had hundreds of clients in my years as a practicing —"

"The victims!" she shouted, "the people hurt by the animals you call clients after you put them back on the street!"

And there you have it. Over the years I defended countless criminals and would be lying if I said I thought all of them to be innocent. To the contrary, I was fully aware many of my former clients deserved to be in prison for the crimes they were accused of.

But I also knew what professor Olivares taught me, what every lawyer understands. That our system of justice guarantees everyone a defense, not just the good guys.

"Patrice," I began smoothly, having had this conversation once or twice in my life, "I'm sure you can understand that, as an attorney, I do not determine anyones' guilt or —"

"Calvin didn't touch that girl."

"Excuse me?"

"They say he raped her, but that was some bull shit. I know my nephew since the day he came into this earth and he aint rape nobody."

"But he was found guilty?"

"He aint never have no trial!" she snapped angrily, "y'all let that grown ass man beat them two kids to death and then YOU made it so he wasn't gonna never have no trial neither!"

The disdain in her voice only marginally masked the pain. It was obvious these wounds were still very raw, even after all this time, and I couldn't blame her. Her nephew and his friend never got their day in court. They never got to make their argument while the man who murdered them never had to make his. It wasn't fair. Life wasn't fair, at least not always.

Now that I remembered her nephew, I felt worse than before. I put my head in my hands and tried to find the right words. "Patrice," I started slowly, "I am so sorry for your loss and you're right, what happened to Calvin was not fair and it was not right and for whatever part I played in it, I am deeply sorry."

"Is that supposed to make me feel better?"

"No," I went on, "nothing I say could possibly do that, just like nothing I do or say is going to bring

Calvin back. You should know a few things about me though, like the fact that I'm not a lawyer anymore. I lost my job and my license a few years ago."

"Seems like you landed on your feet," she retorted, looking around my fifteen hundred dollar per night suite.

"None of this is what it seems. The truth is I've lost everything that was of any importance to me. All this is just a pathetic mask."

"Mask?"

"I've made so many mistakes Patrice. I've hurt so many people…people I love dearly. And now I'm just gonna have to learn to live with that because, unfortunately, life doesn't always afford you the opportunity to right your wrongs."

"So you saying I should get over what happened? Just forget what that man did to my family?"

"Actually no, that's not at all what I'm saying."

"What then?"

"Look, I can't undo the past and I may very well have to live with all of the damage I've done to my family, but I *can* do something for you and yours. I just need you to give me a little time."

I have to admit it felt good to be telling the truth for a change.

Chapter Forty-One

"Thank you for seeing me on such short notice."

"Absolutely, what can I do for you?"

"Annie, I hope you know how excited I am to be the next CEO of the Worthington Foundation."

"I'm happy to hear that Julie. The board absolutely loved you."

"Well, that's why I'm here. There's a problem with one of our board members and I'm afraid if I'm going to be CEO, I'm going to have to address it."

She was predictably cautious about what she said next. "May I ask who?"

"Drake Strong."

I studied her body language closely and, surprisingly, she didn't become defensive at all. In fact, she seemed relieved.

"What did the good reverend do now?" she asked.

"I'd rather not get into specifics, let's just say if his exploits are ever made public, his seat on the board will be a problem."

"And let me guess, you have reason to believe that some of these exploits will, in fact, be made public."

"I cannot predict the future Annie but yes, that is what I am afraid of."

"Well, I appreciate your honesty Julie and I'm going to return the favor. Let me start by saying Drake Strong is a piece of shit and everybody knows it. The flip side of that is he brings a significant amount of money into the organization every year. Money we need to compete with the likes of the Koch brothers and Tea Party America."

"And you don't care where the money comes from?"

"No we don't," she answered bluntly, "I know how that sounds but you have to understand, every dollar that comes into the foundation does good. How it gets there is not something we feel we can do anything about."

"Can't or won't?"

"I respect your passion Julie, I really do. And a part of me agrees with you, but the bottom line is the bottom line. You will be hard pressed to get enough votes to remove Drake from the board simply because of the amount of money he brings to the table. I'm just being honest."

"I'm not asking for votes."

"What then?"

"Just don't catch him when he falls."

She considered that for a moment before responding. "That's doable, but then there is another problem."

"Which is?"

"Well, for a lot of reasons we need your tenure as CEO to be seen as a rousing success. It's not helpful to start off by losing our biggest benefactor."

"I have a plan to replace Drake's support within six months. The foundation will not miss a beat without him."

"If that's the case, why don't you leave him in place for a year or two to solidify your position with the rest of the board?"

Nice try...

"Let me be clear Annie. Drake Strong is going down. Neither you or the board can stop that now. The only reason I'm here is to protect the foundation. The question for you is whether you are going to let that piece of shit, as you call him, take you and everything you've worked to build down with him."

"Fine," she smiled, "I had to ask."

I stood to leave. "You'll be contacting the rest of the board?"

"Yes, I will ensure there is no safety net for the so-called pastor."

"Time is of the essence Annie. This could go down sooner than you might think."

"I better get to it then, and Julie?"

"Yes?"

"Remind me never to piss you off."

• • •

That went exactly as expected.

My next stop would, undoubtedly, be a lot more complicated.

I managed to make it to Aldan without hitting much traffic, which was good because being late wasn't an option for my next meeting. In fact, I made it a point to ring the bell five minutes early.

"What can I do for you?"

"Hi Kim, can I come in?"

Chapter Forty-Two

The flight to Chicago was downright relaxing. Things had moved faster than I expected which left me scrambling for time to get everything done. I'd spent the past few weeks running around like a crazy person, fielding interview requests and introducing myself to a never ending stream of new colleagues and well-wishers. Through some fairly impressive time management, and a little luck, I managed to do what I needed and make my flight with a few minutes to spare. Once we took off I realized, for the first time in months, there was nothing for me to do. So I sat back in my seat and welcomed the ninety minutes of calm.

Annie suggested I hire an assistant, and she was right. But since I hadn't officially been announced as the CEO, I wanted to hold off on building my staff. Not that I had any doubt or second thoughts about my new job. There was just one last piece of old business I needed to handle before I could make my move on to bigger and better things.

• • •

"Hey Drake."

"Julie Sharpe," he beamed confidently, "to what do I owe this unexpected pleasure?"

"Just wanted to touch base."

"You look good girl," he observed as we sat down at his desk, "I see you've been getting some rest."

"I've been trying to get it together."

"Well, it's working. Keep it up. Your announcement is next week right?"

"Actually that's why I'm here. We pushed things back a few weeks."

That got his attention and he leaned forward in his chair. "Really?" he said cautiously, "why is that?"

"Needed more time for due diligence," I responded nonchalantly, "turns out there are some problems with the board we need to address before I step in."

He leaned back, rubbed the side of his face and studied me closely. After a long moment, he reached for his post it pad, wrote something on it, and passed it to me.

WTF

R U Doing?!!

I handed him back his note, picked up his pen and wrote one of my own.

For Gregory

He took it, read it and looked up just in time to see two of Chicago's finest enter his office without knocking. "Drake Strong?" they asked, as a mere formality.

They knew exactly who he was...

"What the hell is going on?" he protested, looking at me.

There was only one thing left for me to say, though I didn't think I needed to say it out loud, lest the two detectives think this was personal. So I looked back at him, smiled and mouthed the words *'Fuck You'* as Reverend Drake Strong was placed under arrest for the murders of Calvin Harris and Kevin Young.

My return flight was peaceful but not quite as relaxing as my earlier trip. It wasn't as if I didn't take extreme pleasure in putting that animal in his cage, because I did. It's just that the whole thing came at such a high cost to me and the people I love, I would never be able to say it was worth it. Ever.

There was a long road waiting for me when I got home, but I was determined to deal with it. I had to. I'd made such a mess of, well, everything, but there were people at home waiting for me to get my shit together. People who needed me to do better, to *be* better.

Whatever it takes…

I had a new found resolve to fix what I'd broken. It wouldn't be easy, but nothing worthwhile ever was. There are no free rides in life and every choice comes with consequences. It was time for me to face the music.

Chapter Forty-Three

"Do you have your homework?"

"Yes."

"Would you mind reading it out loud for me?"

"Are you serious?"

"You don't have to if you don't want."

"No, it's fine."

I opened my book to the marked page and began reading aloud:

As I look back at my life, I see a history of heartache and frustration...But that's only when you aren't looking.

When I look into the mirror, I see broken promises and broken dreams, I see missed I opportunities despair and desperation, I sense weakness and isolation...But that's only when you aren't looking

When you are in the room, my faith does not waiver, I remain a humble servant to my savior and I stand firmly on the rock of my convictions.

I defy you, any of you, to name a time, a single time, when as you looked In my direction, you got any sense of my deception or saw me not loving another as myself. I have always kept the truth near me and spoken it clearly for those who would hear me and have NEVER forsaken my soul in search of wealth

It was not until your eyes were closed, that I allowed mine to open and I felt the true measure of my defeat

You see, I needed your eyes and your attention, for they were my refuge, my protection and without them, all that is left is my deceit.

If death were a man I would call him to save me from this lie, this lie which I confront at the end of each and every day, you see the truth is, I'm a fraud...but none
of you would ever know it, for this truth comes...only when you look away.

"What is the title again?"

"Regret by Claire Worthington."

"Powerful stuff. Thank you for doing that."

"No problem, although Dr. Schultz I have to be honest, I'm not sure why it was so important."

"You can't see it?"

"No."

"Julie, every time you mention his name you become anxious."

"Yes, and I've already told you everything about our relationship and how he died. Don't you think that explains my anxiousness?"

"No, I don't. At least not fully."

"So you think there's more to it?"

"I do, yes."

"And reading you my favorite poem is supposed to help me recognize whatever else is going on?"

"Do you remember why you said you liked this particular piece of writing so much?"

"Because I identify with it."

"You said the words perfectly capture how you feel."

"Forgive me Dr. Schultz, but I don't see what that has to do with Gregory."

"I think a big part of the reason you cling to your past is because you don't think you deserve a future. I think you blame yourself for —"

"I blame myself for things that are my fault. Do I think I should be living happily ever after? No I do not. Not after getting my best friend killed."

"Yet you are intelligent enough to realize you have to move on."

"Tell me how to do that! Tell me how I'm supposed to just forget everything I've done and go on with my life?! A man I loved lost his life because of me! Tell me how I'm supposed to forget that!"

"You can't forget Julie, that's impossible. Unfortunately you will live with that regret for the rest of your life. But living with regret doesn't mean living with guilt. You have to let go of the guilt Julie, and to do that you have to forgive yourself. Only then will you be able to say goodbye."

I sat silently and stared out the window, composing myself, for a long moment before speaking. "Why do I have to say goodbye?"

"There are many reasons why saying goodbye is important, but only two that matter. Number one, because you have no choice. And number two, because your friend deserves it."

"What do you mean he deserves it?"

"Julie, if everything you say is true, and I have no reason to believe otherwise, this is a grown man who made a conscious decision to protect you. And that decision, as much if not more than anything you did or didn't do, is what cost him his life. Put simply, the man gave his life to protect you, and the only way you can honor that is by living."

"I see."

"Julie, I'm going to ask you a question and I want you to think about it before answering."

"Ok."

"Are you ready to move past this?"

"Honestly," I said through tears, "I don't know. A part of me feels like the guilt is all I have left of him and letting that go means I will have nothing."

"These things must happen in their own time. But when you are ready, you have to talk to him. Open yourself up completely and that's where the poem comes in. You said those are feelings no one would associate with you, even your own mother correct?"

"Yes."

"Then that sounds like a wonderful place to start. Our time is up for today."

I walked him to the door. As he put on his coat and hat, he looked at me and smiled. "For what it's worth, I believe you are ready to move on."

"Is that your professional opinion?" I smiled.

"It is."

"Then I'll think about it."

"That is all I can ask. Until tomorrow?"

"Looking forward to it."

• • •

I've always thought there was something magical about Switzerland, especially in the winter. There's something therapeutic about enjoying your meals with a view of snow-capped mountains in the background and, as a city girl, no other place I'd visited offered the same effortless combination of quaint and cosmopolitan.

When I apologized to Preston, he refused to speak to me until I checked myself into a drug treatment program. I resisted, for a lot of reasons, but when he found an exclusive facility outside of Zurich, I changed my tune. After everything we'd been through, a trip seemed like exactly what we needed to reconnect. And even though I'm not technically an addict, after looking at the mess I'd made of my life, some therapy honestly wasn't the worst idea in the world.

We rented a Chalet close to some ski resorts for Preston and his sister Amanda to busy themselves with during the day, while Dr. Schultz came and worked with me to exorcise my demons in the privacy of our residence. Brian and Stephanie even allowed the girls to miss school and come stay with us for a week. Between ski lessons, snowboarding and shopping, I don't think either of them slept more than eight hours total since they arrived.

My announcement as CEO came with some fanfare and more than a little scrutiny, but not nearly as much as the outing of my relationship with Preston. Annie certainly wasn't happy as I took some hits publicly, but my family was surprisingly ok with it.

Brian was fine once he actually met Preston. Ashley, well she just thought the whole thing was weird, and hilarious. And Stephanie, whom I had become increasingly friendly with, went so far as to give me a wink and a high five, when Brian wasn't looking of course.

It felt good to be living my entire life out in the open again. No secrets hiding in the shadows. No more lies waiting to come back and bite me in the ass. Just me, my new job and my amazing family.

There was only one thing preventing me from being as happy as I'd ever been. Unfortunately that thing was a huge hole in my heart I wasn't sure could ever be filled.

"Sylvia," I called upstairs, "don't forget to call your mother before it gets too late."

"Roger that Mrs. S!" she yelled downstairs between giggles, "as soon as the movie's done."

"Now please."

"Ok Mrs. S."

"Thank you."

"Don't be such a tyrant."

I turned to see Preston standing in the doorway.

"Shut up little boy, before I send you to bed with no supper."

"Whatever," he laughed, "hey, Amanda wants to take the girls on some bus tour."

"That's fine, you joining them?"

"Unless you need me to stick around. I know how you need your alone time after your sessions."

"Preston," I smiled, "I seriously don't know what I'd do without you."

"Let's not try and find out ok?"

"You got it."

• • •

When they were off and I had the house to myself, I poured a glass of wine, sat back and gazed out over the mountains at sunset. This was my favorite part of the day and I treasured the opportunity to experience it in solitude. Watching the orange glow slowly disappearing behind those snow capped peaks truly captured the essence of Zurich in a way that words could not do justice.

I allowed myself to get lost in the moment and tried to clear my head to think about what Dr. Schultz said. Was I ready to let go of the guilt I felt over everything that happened? Was I ready to move on?

I wish you were here to see this with me. Though you'd probably be too busy with your head in a book to even notice.

I miss you Gregory, so much more than I ever thought possible. Everything is so different now and I feel like I don't know who I am anymore. Even in those years when we weren't speaking, you were never this far away from me. You were always right there in my heart, even when you didn't want to be. I never, not for one-second, considered what my world would look like without you in it. Well, I'm living it now, and it sucks.

I should have told you all of this before. I wake up every morning wishing I had found the courage to open myself up to you. And yes, I realize you knew how I felt but I still should have let you hear me say it. You deserved that. You deserved so much.

Thank you for saving me. Those words sound ridiculous and small next to the reality of what you did for me, but those words are all I have right now. I will never forget what you did. Ever.

There is some good news too though. You would've been proud of how I kicked your cousins ass.

Gregory, it was a thing of beauty and it all started when I got slapped in the face by the fucking maid at the Four Seasons.

Stop laughing.

Anyway, it turns out her nephew was one of the kids Drake killed and, as soon as I heard her story, I knew we had his sorry ass.

When I defended Drake all those years ago, his case never went to trial because the witnesses all recanted. The key thing though, is it never went to trial. No trial, no double jeopardy. And since it was murder, no statute of limitations. If enough of those old witnesses decided to come forward with what they saw, the case would be reopened. The only problem was, as his attorney of record, I couldn't be anywhere near it or the whole case would get tossed out.

So I went to your old buddy Kim. You know she's not my favorite person, but she loves you as much as anybody and so if I could get her to hear me out, I knew she would help. Her job was simple, convince enough of the old witnesses to come forward, by any means necessary.

It took her less than a week.

How she did it, I'm smart enough not to ask. Maybe she played on their guilt as good christians. Maybe she paid them off. Whatever the case, Drake Strong is locked away where he belongs.

I made so many mistakes baby, and I hurt so many people, but because of you I get to try and fix some of that. Because of you I get another chance and I promise you with all of my heart, I will do better this time.

I will love you always.

Bye for now...

The tears flowed freely and I didn't try and fight them. I knew this was all part of the process and, as painful as it was, I had to let go and prepare myself to move on.

My sessions with Dr. Schultz had been incredibly helpful in so many ways, but today especially. He reminded me constantly of all the things I had to live for, a great job, plenty of money and a strong family standing behind me. Most of all, he convinced me that I was formidable again, not some powerless middle class dance mom who had to sit back and take what the world was dishing out.

And today he helped me to see how my life had finally come full circle, and how I owed it to Gregory to live it fully. While I can never again be what I was, I know now that I can be something different, something even better. From this day forward, it will be my goal, every day, to live my life in a way that honors the man who meant more to me than anyone. Today, with the help of Dr. Schultz, I found my purpose and, in that, I found some peace.

I closed my eyes, breathed the incredibly clean mountain air into my lungs and waited for my family to join me after their tour. On cue, I heard footsteps coming down the hall.

That was quick...

"What happened? You guys forget something?"

"Hello Mrs. Watson."

The voice was like a bolt of lighting that knocked me out of tranquility and sent my heart racing down the mountain.

I stood up, whirled around and couldn't believe my eyes.

"Michelle?!"

THE END

It is said those who don't know their history are doomed to repeat it…

Turn the page and take a look back in this excerpt from

'Choice'

(The case that changed everything)

To say she was skinny would have been like comparing the Olsen twins to Oprah Winfrey. The poor thing was emaciated, tiny enough that she could fit her entire body into the small steel chair I found her in when I entered the room. She sat on the chair with her knees to her chest and arms wrapped tightly around them as if she was freezing, or petrified. Either way I couldn't blame her.

The interview rooms at the Dates Correctional Facility were soulless concrete boxes. Prison cells without bars, that had a table and two chairs bolted into the ground instead of a bunk and a toilet. They were cold, harsh reminders, for the occupants, that the world as they knew it, did not exist anywhere within these walls. Whatever status or stature they carried in 'the world' did not translate in here. This was a cold and scary place for all but the most seasoned criminals, which this girl obviously was not.

She was pale as a ghost with long, straight black hair that looked like it hadn't been washed in weeks. It was hanging down, sloppily concealing her face so I couldn't see much else, not that it mattered. I would have plenty of time to fill in the blanks.

She didn't seem to notice when I walked in and sat down across the table. She just sat there, looking down, slowly rocking back and forth in her chair as if she was in another world.

"Hello Michelle, my name is Julie Watson. I'm the attorney —"

"Who sent you?"

Whoa...

From the moment she opened her mouth, I knew I would never forget that voice. Her words, while barely above a whisper, were confident and direct and she had the most exquisite southern accent. It had a disarming, almost seductive quality to it and I found myself thinking it was completely out of place coming out of the nervous, disheveled mess sitting across from me.

"Um," I stammered, trying to focus, "I met with your mother and —"

"Fucking Bitch!"

The sudden burst of anger at the mention of her mother was jolting, but not entirely unexpected. If what I suspected was true, she had every right.

"Michelle," I said calmly, "I would like to —"

"Who are you?"

She was looking at me now, for the first time. Her eyes were strikingly dark and even though there was an obvious sadness to them, it was easy to see that beneath that surface lied an intensity, a ferocity, that belied her tiny frame.

I found myself feeling a little uncomfortable.

That was just the beginning.

"Michelle," I smiled weakly, "my name is Julie Watson, I am the attorney handling your —"

"You have any children Ms. Watson?"

Her random interruptions were throwing me off but I needed her to trust me, so I went with it.

"Um," I replied, "yes I —"

"You probably do," she answered her own question, "just one I'd guess. A little girl perhaps? Do you beat her?"

WTF??!

"Michelle, I am here to —"

"My mother didn't beat me," she continued as if I wasn't in the room, "that was daddy's job. He would beat the shit out of me and my little brother Johnny. Johnny died when he was nine. I miss Johnny. You have any brothers Ms. Watson?"

"I'm an only child."

"Is that why you only have one little girl?" she smiled brightly, "you want her to be just like you?"

"Michelle, why don't we talk about you for a moment? Now, I've familiarized myself with the details of your —"

"Is your daddy still living?"

Stop fucking interrupting me!!!

"Yes Michelle," I smiled patiently, "my father is alive and lives in New Jersey."

"Do you fuck him?"

"Excuse me?!!"

Before I could say anything else, or slap her in the face, she looked back down to the floor and started crying.

"I loved my daddy," she said softly, "he said I was his special little girl. Mommy couldn't take care of him the way I —"

She looked back up at me as if she'd forgotten I was there. This time she had a panicked look in her eyes and was literally trembling.

"Please don't tell my mommy!" she pleaded, "mommy can never know! I will die and burn in hell if mommy ever finds out and then I will never see my daddy again. Daddy is in heaven waiting for me and I have to see him! I just have to! Please Miss Watson!!! Please don't make me burn in hell!!! Please!!!"

She threw her head down onto the table and started sobbing uncontrollably. I noticed the guard looking into the room and nodded in his direction, letting him know I was ok.

I wasn't.
Not even close.

"Michelle," I said calmly when I thought she might be ready to talk, "do you know why you're here?"

"I killed my baby," she cried softly.

"Well, actually you had an abortion and —"

"His name was Ryan and he was the most beautiful lil boy in the whole wide world."

"Michelle," I gently pressed, hoping to convince her to listen, "do you know what a post-viability abortion is?"

"An abortion," she observed innocently, "is when you kill your baby."

"An abortion, of any kind, means you terminate an unwanted pregnancy BEFORE any baby is born. A post- viability —"

"Who sent you?"

"I told you before, I met with your mother and —"

"Fucking Bitch!"

"I was trying to say I think your mother sent me here to help you."

"My mother sent you here to get me out of prison. How much is she paying you?"

The transition was smooth enough that I didn't catch it at first. I was no longer talking to a scared little girl, I was about to meet Michelle Smith.

"Sweetheart I'm sure your mother will be happy to discuss those details with you. I'm just here to get some information and see about getting you a bail hearing."

"Bail? Who said anything about bail?"

"The bail hearing is the part of the process where —"

"I know what bail is Ms. Watson, and for your information, if I had wanted to post bail I would have done so by now. I am staying right here."

"Um," I started stammering, "Michelle, I'm sorry but my instructions are —"

"Ms. Watson, regardless of what my mother may have told you, you work for me and me alone. I am sure you have been paid handsomely for your services and in return for said compensation, I will accept nothing less than your best efforts in support of me, your client. Please note my use of the term, 'in support of' as opposed to 'in defense of.' See, you are here as my advocate Ms. Watson, not as my defender. Now your acceptance of these terms is non-negotiable if we are to continue any further along this path. I trust I have made myself clear?"

I just nodded.

"Excellent," she smiled as the guard came to escort her back to her cell, "give mother my love for me will you?"

• • •

A part of me wanted to pick up my things and run, not walk, back to my office.

But a bigger part of me couldn't give up on her, even though she obviously needed a kind of professional help I wasn't qualified to give. She just seemed so lost and helpless, I found myself wanting to look out for her, wanting to protect her.

I would soon learn just how wrong I was about exactly who and what I was dealing with…

…Coming 2015

22722264R00248

Made in the USA
San Bernardino, CA
18 July 2015